The Man of My Dreams

ed on or before the last d
requested by

ALSO BY CURTIS SITTENFELD
FROM CLIPPER LARGE PRINT

American Wife

The Man of My Dreams

Curtis Sittenfeld

W F HOWES LTD

This large print edition published in 2011 by
W F Howes Ltd
Unit 4, Rearsby Business Park, Gaddesby Lane,
Rearsby, Leicester LE7 4YH

1 3 5 7 9 10 8 6 4 2

First published in the United Kingdom in 2006
by Random House

A CIP catalogue record for this book is available
from the British Library

ISBN 978 1 40747 317 8

Typeset by Palimpsest Book Production Limited,
Falkirk, Stirlingshire
Printed and bound in Great Britain
by MPG Books Ltd, Bodmin, Cornwall

FSC
www.fsc.org

MIX
Paper from
responsible sources
FSC® C018575

CONTENTS

PART I

CHAPTER 1

JUNE 1991

Julia Roberts is getting married. It's true: Her dress will be an eight-thousand-dollar custom-made two-piece gown from the Tyler Trafficante West Hollywood salon, and at the reception following the ceremony, she'll be able to pull off the train and the long part of the skirt to dance. The bridesmaids' dresses will be seafoam green, and their shoes (Manolo Blahnik, $425 a pair) will be dyed to match. The bridesmaids themselves will be Julia's agents (she has two), her makeup artist, and a friend who's also an actress, though no one has ever heard of her. The cake will be four-tiered, with violets and seafoam ribbons of icing.

'What I want to know is where's our invitation?' Elizabeth says. 'Did it get lost in the mail?' Elizabeth – Hannah's aunt – is standing by the bed folding laundry while Hannah sits on the floor, reading aloud from the magazine. 'And who's her fiancé again?'

'Kiefer Sutherland,' Hannah says. 'They met on the set of *Flatliners*.'

'Is he cute?'

'He's okay.' Actually, he *is* cute – he has blond stubble and, even better, one blue eye and one green eye – but Hannah is reluctant to reveal her taste; maybe it's bad.

'Let's see him,' Elizabeth says, and Hannah holds up the magazine. 'Ehh,' Elizabeth says. 'He's adequate.' This makes Hannah think of Darrach. Hannah arrived in Pittsburgh a week ago, while Darrach – he is Elizabeth's husband, Hannah's uncle – was on the road. The evening Darrach got home, after Hannah set the table for dinner and prepared the salad, Darrach said, 'You must stay with us forever, Hannah.' Also that night, Darrach yelled from the second-floor bathroom, 'Elizabeth, this place is a bloody disaster. Hannah will think we're barn animals.' He proceeded to get on his knees and start scrubbing. Yes, the tub was grimy, but Hannah couldn't believe it. She has never seen her own father wipe a counter, change a sheet, or take out trash. And here was Darrach on the floor after he'd just returned from seventeen hours of driving. But the thing about Darrach is – he's ugly. He's really ugly. His teeth are brownish and angled in all directions, and he has wild eyebrows, long and wiry and as wayward as his teeth, and he has a tiny ponytail. He's tall and lanky and his accent is nice – he's from Ireland – but still. If Elizabeth considers Kiefer Sutherland only adequate, what does she think of her own husband?

'You know what let's do?' Elizabeth says. She is holding up two socks, both white but clearly

4

different lengths. She shrugs, seemingly to herself, then rolls the socks into a ball and tosses them toward the folded pile. 'Let's have a party for Julia. Wedding cake, cucumber sandwiches with the crusts cut off. We'll toast to her happiness. Sparkling cider for all.'

Hannah watches Elizabeth.

'What?' Elizabeth says. 'You don't like the idea? I know Julia herself won't show up.'

'*Oh*,' Hannah says. 'Okay.'

When Elizabeth laughs, she opens her mouth so wide that the fillings in her molars are visible. 'Hannah,' she says, 'I'm not nuts. I realize a celebrity won't come to my house just because I invited her.'

'I didn't think that,' Hannah says. 'I knew what you meant.' But this is not entirely true; Hannah cannot completely read her aunt. Elizabeth has always been a presence in Hannah's life – Hannah has a memory of herself at age six, riding in the backseat of Elizabeth's car as Elizabeth sang 'You're So Vain' quite loudly and enthusiastically along with the radio – but for the most part, Elizabeth has been a distant presence. Though Hannah's father and Elizabeth are each other's only siblings, their two families have not gotten together in years. Staying now in Elizabeth's house, Hannah realizes how little she knows of her aunt. The primary information she has always associated with Elizabeth was acquired so long ago she cannot even remember learning it: that

5

once, soon after Elizabeth became a nurse, a patient left her a great deal of money and Elizabeth squandered it. She spent it on an enormous party, though there was no occasion, not even her birthday. And she's been struggling to make ends meet ever since. (Hannah has been surprised to find, however, that her aunt orders takeout, usually Chinese, on the nights Darrach is gone, which is at least half the time. They don't exactly *act* like they're struggling to make ends meet.) It didn't help, financially speaking, that Elizabeth married a truck driver: the Irish hippie, as Hannah's father calls him. When she was nine, Hannah asked her mother what *hippie* meant, and her mother said, 'It's someone fond of the counterculture.' When Hannah asked her sister – Allison is three years older – she said, 'It means Darrach doesn't take showers,' which Hannah has observed to be untrue.

'Would we have our party before or after the wedding?' Hannah asks. 'She gets married on June fourteenth.' Then, imagining it must appear on the invitations like this, all spelled out in swirly writing, she adds, 'Nineteen hundred and ninety-one.'

'Why not *on* the fourteenth? Darrach can be my date, if he's here, and Rory can be yours.'

Hannah feels a stab of disappointment. Of course her date will be her eight-year-old retarded cousin. (That's the final piece in the puzzle of Elizabeth's financial downfall, according to

Hannah's father: that Rory was born with Down's. The day of Rory's birth, her father said to her mother, as he stood in the kitchen after work flipping through mail, 'They'll be supporting that child all the way to their graves.') But what did Hannah think Elizabeth was going to say? *Your date will be the sixteen-year-old son of one of my coworkers. He is very handsome, and he'll like you immediately.* Sure, Hannah expected that. She always thinks a boy for her to love will fall from the sky.

'I wish I could find my wedding dress for you to wear at our party,' Elizabeth says. 'I wouldn't be able to fit my big toe in it at this point, but you'd look real cute. Lord only knows what I did with it, though.'

How can Elizabeth not know where her wedding dress is? That's not like losing a scarf. Back in Philadelphia, Hannah's mother's wedding dress is stored in the attic in a long padded box, like a coffin.

'I gotta put the other load in the dryer,' Elizabeth says. 'Coming?'

Hannah stands, still holding the magazine. 'Kiefer bought her a tattoo,' she says. 'It's a red heart with the Chinese symbol that means "strength of heart."'

'In other words,' Elizabeth says, 'he said to her, "As a sign of my love, you get to be poked repeatedly by a needle with ink in it." Do we really trust this guy?' They are on the first floor, cutting through the kitchen to the basement steps. 'And do I dare ask where the tattoo is located?'

'It's on her left shoulder. Darrach doesn't have any tattoos, does he? Even though that's, like, a stereotype of truck drivers?' Is this a rude question?

'None he's told me about,' Elizabeth says. She appears unoffended. 'Then again, most truck drivers probably aren't tofu eaters or yoga fanatics.'

Yesterday Darrach showed Hannah his rig, which he keeps in the driveway; the trailers he uses are owned by the companies he drives for. Darrach's current route is from here in Pittsburgh, where he picks up axles, to Crowley, - Louisiana, where he delivers the axles and picks up sugar, to Flagstaff, Arizona, where he delivers the sugar and picks up women's slips to bring back to Pittsburgh. The other night Darrach let Rory demonstrate how to turn the front seat around to get in the sleeper cab. Then Darrach pointed out the bunk where he meditates. During this tour, Rory was giddy. 'It's my dad's,' he told Hannah several times, gesturing widely. Apparently, the rig is one of Rory's obsessions; the other is his bus driver's new puppy. Rory has not actually seen the puppy, but discussion is under way about Elizabeth taking Rory this weekend to visit the bus driver's farm. Watching her cousin in the rig, Hannah wondered if his adoration of his parents would remain pure. Perhaps his Down's will freeze their love.

After Elizabeth has moved the wet clothes into

the dryer, they climb the basement steps. In the living room, Elizabeth flings herself onto the couch, sets her feet on the table, and sighs noisily. 'So what's our plan?' she says. 'Darrach and Rory shouldn't be back from errands for at least an hour. I'm taking suggestions.'

'We could go for a walk,' Hannah says. 'I don't know.' She glances out the living room window, which overlooks the front yard. The truth is that Hannah finds the neighborhood creepy. Where her family lives, outside Philadelphia, the houses are separated by wide lawns, the driveways are long and curved, and the front doors are flanked by Doric columns. Here, there are no front porches, only stoops flecked with mica, and when you sit outside – the last few nights, Hannah and Elizabeth have gone out there while Rory tried to catch fireflies – you can hear the televisions in other houses. The grass is dry, beagles bark into the night, and in the afternoon, pale ten-year-old boys in tank tops pedal their bikes in circles, the way they do on TV in the background when some well-coiffed reporter is standing in front of the crime scene where a seventy-six-year-old woman has been murdered.

'A walk's not a bad idea,' Elizabeth says, 'except it's so damn hot.'

Then the living room, the whole house actually, is quiet except for the laundry rolling around downstairs in the dryer. Hannah can hear the ping of metal buttons against the sides of the machine.

'Let's get ice cream,' Elizabeth says. 'But don't bring the magazine.' She grins at Hannah. 'I don't know how much more celebrity happiness I can take.'

Hannah was shipped to Pittsburgh. She was sent away, put on a Greyhound, though Allison got to stay in Philadelphia with their mother because of exams. Hannah thinks she should still be in Philadelphia for the same reason – because of exams. But Hannah is in eighth grade, whereas Allison is a high school junior, which apparently means that her exams matter more. Also, Hannah is viewed by their parents as not just younger but less even-keeled, and therefore potentially inconvenient. So Hannah's school year isn't even finished, but she is here with Elizabeth and Darrach indefinitely.

According to the letter signed by Dr William Tucker and hand-delivered by her mother to the principal's office, Hannah has mononucleosis and the family has requested that she be allowed to make up her coursework later in the summer. This is a lie. Dr William Tucker does not exist but was concocted by Hannah's mother and Hannah's aunt Polly, her mother's sister. It is with Polly's family that Hannah's mother and Allison have been staying for the last ten days. Hannah does not have mono (the other option her mother and Aunt Polly considered was chicken pox, but they decided Hannah seems too old not to have had

10

it yet, and besides, people might wonder later why she didn't have scars). Hannah is missing school because one night, her father exiled her and her mother and Allison from the house. This was, obviously, somewhat insane. But it wasn't more insane or cruel than other things he's done, which is not to say that he's insane or cruel all the time. He's himself; he can be perfectly pleasant; he's the weather system they live with, and all of their behavior, whenever he is around, hinges on his mood. Don't the three of them understand that living with him simply is what it is? To complain or resist would be as useless as complaining about or resisting a tornado. This is why her mother's current refusal to return home bewilders Hannah most, and why it's her mother as much as her father whom Hannah faults for the upheaval. Since when has her mother stood up for herself? She is no longer playing by the family rules.

Maybe it was the external aspect that made it worse, having to drive over and knock on Aunt Polly and Uncle Tom's door after midnight, when usually the effects of her father's rages are confined within the house, out of sight. Or maybe it was the escalated aspect, how his making them leave was, in its way, more dramatic than the usual shouting, the slammed door or occasional shattered plate. And it's true that it was embarrassing (Hannah was standing there in front of her cousins Fig and Nathan in her pink nightshirt with gumballs on it, which is from fifth grade), but the episode wasn't

11

shocking. For her mother to refuse to return home – she's acting like it's shocking. She's acting like they, any of them, can make normal demands of Hannah's father. But they all *know* they can't make normal demands of him. And Hannah's mother is the one who has accommodated him most all these years, the one who has taught Hannah and Allison, both by example and by instruction, exactly how accommodation works.

Hannah turns off the television – having it on in the daytime reminds her of being sick – and picks up the magazine from the day before. She is in the house alone: Elizabeth is at work, and Rory is at school, and Darrach, who is leaving for another run tomorrow, is at the hardware store.

It would be good to be famous, Hannah thinks as she turns the page. Not for the reasons people imagine – the money and glamour – but for the insulation. How could you ever be lonely or bored if you were a celebrity? There wouldn't be time, because you'd never even be by yourself. You'd be getting shuttled between people and appointments, reading scripts, being fitted for the beaded silver gown you'd wear to the next awards ceremony, doing stomach crunches while your trainer Enrique loomed over you and barked encouragement. You'd have an entourage, people would vie to talk to you. Reporters would want to know your New Year's resolution or your favorite snack; they'd care about this information.

Julia Roberts's parents divorced when she was four – her father, Walter, was a vacuum cleaner salesman, and her mother, Betty, a church secretary – and then her father died of cancer when she was nine, which must have been terrible unless it was a relief. Regardless, Julia's childhood was a long time ago, in Smyrna, Georgia. Now she's twenty-three, living in California, which is a place Hannah has never been but imagines as windy and bright, full of tall people and shiny cars and a sky of endless blue.

It is a little after one o'clock, and Hannah ate a peanut butter and jelly sandwich an hour ago, but she starts thinking of food she knows to be in the kitchen: Darrach's vegetarian enchiladas left over from last night, chocolate-chip ice cream. She is gaining weight, which is something she'd been doing prior to her arrival in Pittsburgh. Since the beginning of eighth grade, she has gained eleven pounds; she now has hips, and the bra she wears is a displeasing and once-unimaginable 36C. Also, abruptly, a stranger's nose has appeared on her face. She didn't realize it until she saw her most recent class picture: her light brown hair and pale skin, her blue eyes, and there it was, an extra knob of flesh at the end of her nose when before she'd always had her mother's small, upturned model. Hannah's mother is a petite woman, partial to headbands, who maintains blond highlights and plays doubles tennis every morning, summer or winter, with Aunt Polly and two other women.

She got braces at the age of thirty-eight, then had them removed at the age of forty – last year – but in fact she'd always possessed the personality of an attractive adult woman with braces: privileged yet apologetic, well meaning but hard to take that seriously. She has never remarked on Hannah's weight per se, but she'll sometimes make overly enthusiastic comments about, for instance, celery. In these moments she seems to Hannah less critical than protective, tentatively trying to prevent her daughter from taking the wrong path.

Is Hannah becoming ugly? If so, it seems like the worst thing that could happen; she is letting down her family and, possibly, boys and men everywhere. Hannah knows this both from TV and from boys' and men's eyes. You can *see* how what they want the most is beauty. Not in a chauvinistic way, not even as something they can act on. Just instinctively, to look at and enjoy. It's what they expect, and who they expect it from most of all is teenage girls. When you're older, like Elizabeth, it's all right to get heavy, but when you're a teenager, being beautiful or at least cute is your responsibility. Say the words *sixteen-year-old girl* to any group of males, eleven-year-olds, fifty-year-olds, and they will leer maybe a lot or maybe a little or maybe they'll try not to leer. But they will be envisioning the sixteen-year-old's smooth tan legs, her high breasts and long hair. Is expecting her beauty even their fault?

She should do jumping jacks, Hannah thinks,

right now – twenty-five of them, or fifty. But instead there's the block of cheddar cheese sitting in the refrigerator, the crisp and salty crackers in the cupboard. She eats them standing by the sink until she feels gross and leaves the house.

Her aunt's street dead-ends onto a park, on the far side of which is a public pool. Hannah gets within twenty yards of the pool's fence before turning around. She sits at a dilapidated picnic table and pages through the magazine again, though she has by now read every article several times. She was planning to work as a candy striper this summer in Philadelphia, and she could do it at the hospital where Elizabeth is a nurse if she knew how long she was staying. But she has no idea. She has talked on the phone to Allison and her mother, and nothing at home appears to have changed: They are still staying with Aunt Polly and Uncle Tom, her mother still will not return home. What's weirdest, in a way, is picturing her father in the house alone at night; it's hard to imagine him angry without them. It must be like watching a game show by yourself, how calling out the answers feels silly and pointless. What is fury without witnesses? Where's the tension minus an audience to wonder what you'll do next?

A guy wearing jeans and a white tank top is walking toward Hannah. She looks down, pretending to read.

Soon he's standing right there; he has walked all the way over to her. 'You got a light?' he says.

She looks up and shakes her head. The guy is maybe eighteen, a few inches taller than she is, with glinting blondish hair so short it's almost shaved, a wispy mustache, squinty blue eyes, puffy lips, and well-defined arm muscles. Where did he come from? He is holding an unlit cigarette between two fingers.

'You don't smoke, right?' he says. 'It causes cancer.'

'I don't smoke,' she says.

He looks at her – he seems to be removing something from his front teeth with his tongue – then he says, 'How old are you?'

She hesitates; she turned fourteen two months ago. 'Sixteen,' she says.

'You like motorcycles?'

'I don't know.' How did she enter into this conversation? Is she in danger? She must be, at least a little.

'I'm fixing up a motorcycle at my buddy's.' The guy gestures with his right shoulder, but it's hard to know what direction he means.

'I have to go,' Hannah says, and she stands, lifting one leg and then the other over the picnic bench. She begins to walk away, then glances back. The guy is still standing there.

'What's your name?' he asks.

'Hannah,' she says, and immediately wishes she had told him something better: Genevieve, perhaps, or Veronica.

★   ★   ★

16

At a slumber party when she was nine, Hannah learned a joke wherein whatever the joke teller said, the other person had to respond, 'Rubber balls and liquor.'

When her father picked her up from the party on Sunday morning, she decided to try it out on him. He seemed distracted – he was flipping between radio stations – but went along with it. It felt important to tell him in the car, when it was just the two of them, because Hannah doubted her mother would find it funny. But her father had a good sense of humor. When she couldn't fall asleep on the weekend, she sometimes got to stay up with him in the den and watch *Saturday Night Live*, and he brought her ginger ale while her mother and Allison slept. At these times she would watch the lights of the television flickering on his profile and feel proud that he laughed when the TV audience laughed – it made him seem part of a world beyond their family.

In the car, Hannah asked, 'What do you eat for breakfast?'

'Rubber balls and liquor,' her father said. He switched lanes.

'What do you eat for lunch?'

'Rubber balls and liquor.'

'What do you buy at the store?'

'Rubber balls and liquor.'

'What do you—' She paused. 'What do you keep in the trunk of your car?'

'Rubber balls and liquor.'

'What—' Hannah could hear her voice thickening in anticipation, how the urge to laugh – already! – nearly prevented her from finishing the question. 'What do you do to your wife at night?'

The car was silent. Slowly, her father turned his head to look at her. 'Do you have any idea what that means?' he asked.

Hannah was silent.

'Do you know what balls are?'

Hannah shook her head.

'They're testicles. They're next to a man's penis. Women don't have balls.'

Hannah looked out her window. *Boobs*. That's what she'd thought balls were.

'So the joke makes no sense. Rub *her* balls? Do you see why that doesn't make sense?'

Hannah nodded. She wanted to be out of the car, away from the site of this embarrassing error.

Her father reached out and turned up the radio. They did not speak for the rest of the ride home.

In the driveway, he said to her, 'Women who are ugly try to be funny. They think it compensates. But you'll be pretty, like Mom. You won't need to be funny.'

When Elizabeth gets home from work, as soon as Rory hears her key in the lock, he runs around to the far side of the couch and crouches, his hair poking up visibly. 'Hey there, Hannah,' Elizabeth says, and Hannah points behind the couch.

'You know what I feel like?' Elizabeth says loudly.

18

She's wearing pink scrubs and a macaroni neck-lace Rory made at school last week. 'I feel like a swim. But I wish I knew where Rory was, because I bet he'd like to go.'

Rory's hair twitches.

'We'll have to leave without him,' Elizabeth says. 'Unless I can find him before—'

Then Rory bursts out of hiding, flinging his arms skyward. 'Here's Rory,' he cries. 'Here's Rory!' He runs around the couch and throws himself against his mother. When she catches him, they both fall sideways on the cushions, Elizabeth pressing Rory down and repeatedly kissing his cheeks and nose. 'Here's my boy,' she says. 'Here's my big hand-some boy.' Rory squeals and writhes beneath her.

At the pool, Elizabeth and Hannah sit side by side on white plastic reclining chairs. Elizabeth's bathing suit turns out to be brown, and around the stomach, there is a loose bunching to the ma-terial that Hannah sneaks looks at several times before she understands. But it would be impolite to ask the question directly, so instead she says, 'Did you just get that suit?'

'Are you kidding?' Elizabeth says. 'I've had this since I was pregnant with Rory.'

So it *is* a maternity suit. Elizabeth cannot be pregnant, however; shortly after Rory's birth, she got her tubes tied (that was the expression Hannah heard her parents use, causing her to picture Elizabeth's reproductive organs as sausage links knotted up).

19

Rory is in the shallow end of the pool. Elizabeth watches him with one hand pressed to her forehead, shielding her eyes from the late-afternoon sun. He does not seem to be playing with the other children, Hannah notices, but stands against a wall wearing inflatable floating devices on his upper arms though the water comes only to his waist. He watches a group of four or five children, all smaller than he is, who splash at one another. Hannah feels an urge to get into the pool with Rory, but she is not wearing a bathing suit. In fact, she told Elizabeth that she doesn't own one, which is a lie. She has a brand-new bathing suit – her mother purchased it for her at Macy's just before Hannah left Philadelphia, as if she were going on vacation – but Hannah doesn't feel like wearing it in front of all these people.

And Elizabeth hasn't said, *Of course you have a bathing suit! Everyone has a bathing suit!* Nor has she said, *We'll go to the mall and buy one for you.*

'How are your movie stars?' Elizabeth asks. 'Not long till Julia's big day.'

She's right – the wedding is this Friday.

'We've got to get cracking on our party,' Elizabeth says. 'Remind me Thursday to pick up cake mix after work, or maybe we should splurge and buy petits fours at the bakery.'

'What are petits fours?'

'Are you kidding me? With your fancy parents, you don't know what petits fours are? They're little

20

cakes, which I probably haven't eaten since my deb party.'

'You were a debutante?'

'What, I don't exude fine breeding?'

'No, I meant—' Hannah starts, but Elizabeth cuts her off.

'I'm just teasing. Being a deb was horrible. We were *presented* at some museum, and our dads walked us up a long carpet so we could curtsy in front of this old aristocratic fart. And I was just sure I would trip. I wanted to throw up the whole time.'

'Did your parents make you do it?'

'Mom didn't really care, but my dad was very socially ambitious. He was the one who thought it mattered. And you know your grandpa had a temper, too, right?' Elizabeth is acting purposely casual, Hannah thinks; she's sniffing Hannah out. 'But I probably shouldn't blame my parents for all my misery,' Elizabeth continues. 'I made everything much harder by being so self-conscious. When I think back on how self-conscious I was, I think, *Jesus, I wasted a lot of time.*'

'What were you self-conscious about?'

'Oh, everything. The way I looked. How dumb I was. Here your dad goes to Penn and then to Yale Law, and meanwhile I'm muddling through Temple. But then I decided to do nursing, I got a job, I met Darrach, who's the cat's pajamas. Do you see Rory, by the way?'

'He's behind those two girls.' Hannah points

21

across the cement. There is cement everywhere around the pool, as if it's in the middle of a sidewalk. At her parents' country club, the pool is set in flagstone. Also, you have to pay three dollars just to get in here, at the snack bar you use cash instead of signing your family's name, and you must bring your own towels. The whole place seems slightly unclean, and though it is a humid evening, Hannah isn't sorry she lied about not having a bathing suit. 'How did you and Darrach meet?' she asks.

'You don't know this story? Oh, you'll love it. I'm living in a house with my wacky friends – one guy calls himself Panda and makes stained-glass ornaments that he drives around the country and sells in the parking lots at concerts. I've gotten my first job, and one of my patients is this funny old man who takes a shine to me. He has pancreatic cancer, and when he dies, it turns out he's left me a chunk of money. I think it was about five thousand dollars, which today would be maybe eight thousand. At first I'm sure I won't get to keep it. Some long-lost relative will crawl out of the woodwork. But the lawyers do their thing, and no relative comes forward. The money really is mine.'

'That's amazing,' Hannah says.

'If I were smart like your father, I'd have put it in the bank. But what I do instead is I give some to a cancer charity, 'cause I feel all guilty, and I take the rest and throw a party. I can't convey to

22

you how out of character this was for me. I'd always been so shy and insecure, but I just said to hell with it, and I told everyone I knew and my housemates told everyone they knew and we hired a band to play out in the backyard. It was August, and we had torches and tons of food and beer, and hundreds of people came. Everyone was dancing and sweating, and it was just a great party. And this tall, skinny Irish fellow who's absolutely the sexiest man I've ever seen shows up with his friend. The Irish fellow says to me, "You must be Rachel." I say, "Who the hell is Rachel?" He says, "Rachel, the girl giving the party." It turns out he and his friend – his friend was Mitch Haferey, who's now Rory's godfather – are at the wrong party. They were supposed to be one street over, but they heard the music and came to our house without checking the address. Three months later, Darrach and I were married.'

'And now you live happily ever after.'

'Well, I'm not saying what we did was smart. We probably rushed things, but we were lucky. Also, we weren't exactly babes in the woods. I was twenty-seven by then, and Darrach was thirty-two.'

'Julia Roberts is twenty-three.'

'Oh, good Lord. She's a child.'

'She's only four years younger than you were!' Hannah says. Twenty-three is certainly *not* a child: When you are twenty-three, you are finished with college (Julia Roberts actually didn't go – she left Smyrna for Hollywood at the age of seventeen,

23

the day after she graduated from high school). You have a job and probably a car, you can drink alcohol, you live somewhere without your parents.

'Oh!' says Elizabeth. 'Look who's paying us a visit.' Rory is standing by Elizabeth's chair, his teeth chattering behind bluish lips, his body shivering. His narrow shoulders fold in; his chest is very white, his nipples dime-sized and peach. Elizabeth wraps Rory in a towel and pulls him onto her reclining chair, and when Hannah can tell the smother-and-kiss routine is about to start, she stands. The routine is cute, but a little different here in public.

'I think I'll go back to the house,' she says. 'I need to call my sister.'

'You don't want to wait and get a ride?' Elizabeth says. 'We'll leave soon.'

Hannah shakes her head. 'I could use the exercise.'

This is what getting married means: Once, at least one man loved you; you were the person he loved most in the world. But what do you do to get a man to love you like that? Are you pursued, or do you pursue him? Julia Roberts's wedding will take place at Twentieth Century Fox's Soundstage 14. Already, it has been decorated to look like a garden.

When Hannah tries to call her sister in Philadelphia, it is her cousin Fig who answers the phone. Fig is exactly Hannah's age, and she is Hannah's class-mate in school; they have spent much of their lives together, which is not the same as actually liking each other. 'Allison isn't here,' Fig says. 'Call back in an hour.'

'Will you give her a message?'

'I'm leaving to meet Tina Cherchis at the mall. Would I look good with a double pierce?'

'Are you allowed to?'

'If I wear my hair down, they probably won't even notice.'

There's a silence.

'My mom thinks your dad is a maniac,' Fig says.

'That isn't true. I'm sure your mom is just trying to make my mom feel better. Are people at school asking about my mono?'

'No.' There's a clicking noise, and Fig says, 'Someone is on the other line. Just call back later tonight and Allison will be here.' She hangs up.

Hannah's worst memory – not the episode of her father's greatest anger but the episode that makes Hannah saddest to think of – is a time when she was ten and Allison was thirteen and they were going with their father to pick up a pizza. The pizza place was about three miles from their house, owned by two Iranian brothers whose wives and young children were often behind the counter.

It was a Sunday night, and Hannah's mother had stayed at home to set the table. Also, it had been planned in advance that for dessert Hannah and Allison would get to have vanilla ice cream with a strawberry sundae sauce, which Hannah's mother had been talked into buying that afternoon at the grocery store.

In the car, they came to an intersection, and Hannah's father braked for the red light. Just after the light changed to green, a guy who looked like a college student approached the crosswalk, and Allison reached out and touched their father's upper arm. 'You see him, right?' Allison said, then gestured to the pedestrian to go ahead.

Immediately – their father bit his lip in a particular way – Hannah could tell that he was furious. Also, even though Hannah could see only the back of her sister's head, she could feel that Allison was oblivious to this fury. But not for long. After the pedestrian crossed, their father roared through the intersection and jerked the car to the side of the road. He turned to face Allison. 'Don't you *ever* interfere with the driver like that again,' he said. 'What you did back there was stupid and dangerous.'

'I wanted to make sure you saw him,' Allison said quietly.

'It's not your business to make sure of anything!' their father thundered. 'You don't tell the pedestrian if he can walk or not. I want to hear an apology from you, and I want to hear it now.'

'I'm sorry.'

For several seconds, he glared at Allison. Lowering his voice, though it still simmered with anger, he said, 'We'll just go home tonight. You girls can have pizza some other time when you decide to behave yourselves.'

'Dad, she said she was sorry,' Hannah said from the backseat, and he whirled around.

'When I need your input, Hannah, I'll ask for it.'

After that, none of them talked.

At home they filed silently into the front hall, and their mother called from the kitchen, 'Do I smell pizza?' then came out to greet them. Their father brushed past her and stormed into the den. The really bad part was explaining to her what had happened, observing her face as she grasped that the evening had turned. Plenty of other evenings had turned – the why and how were only variations on a theme – but their mother had usually been present for the turning. To have to tell her about it – it was awful. She wouldn't let Allison and Hannah find something in the refrigerator to eat because she wanted them to wait while she tried to coax their father out of the den (which Hannah knew wouldn't happen) and made offers to go and pick up the pizza herself (which Hannah knew he wouldn't let her do). After about forty minutes, their mother told them to make sandwiches and carry them up to their rooms. She and their father were going to have dinner at a restaurant, and he didn't want to see Hannah or Allison downstairs.

Hannah did not cry at all that night, but

sometimes now, thinking of the table her mother had set, the blue plates, the striped napkins in their rings, and thinking of the brief segment of time after they weren't going to eat pizza together but before their mother knew they weren't, when she was still getting ready – that particular sadness of preparing for an ordinary, pleasant thing that doesn't happen is almost unbearable. Soon after her parents left the house, the phone rang, and when Hannah answered, a man's voice said, 'It is Kamal calling about your pizza. I think it is getting cold and you want to come get it.'

'Nobody here ordered a pizza,' Hannah told him.

While they were at the pool, Darrach made lasagna for dinner. There is fresh spinach in it, and lots of basil.

'My compliments to the chef,' Elizabeth says. 'Do you remember, Darrach, how Hannah's parents helped us get ready for our wedding? I was thinking about this earlier.'

'Of course I remember.'

'It was wild.' Elizabeth shakes her head. 'We got married at the house where I lived instead of in a church, and my parents refused to come.'

'That's awful,' Hannah says.

'Mom was kicking herself for years afterward. She felt worse about the whole thing than I did. Your dad wasn't exactly a fan of what he perceived as my flaky lifestyle, either, but he and your mom

28

drove here from Philly the day of the wedding. They arrived mid-afternoon, and they'd brought about a million pounds of shrimp, frozen in coolers in the backseat. The reception was supposed to be very casual, but your parents wanted it to seem nice. We were literally peeling shrimp when the justice of the peace arrived, and your mom was worried that Darrach and I would be smelly at our own wedding.'

'Can I be excused?' Rory asks.

'One more bite,' Darrach says. Rory forks a large piece of lasagna into his mouth and leaps up from the table, still chewing. 'Good enough,' Darrach says, and Rory darts into the living room and turns on the television.

'It was all very frenzied,' Elizabeth says, 'but fun.'

'And no one smelled like seafood,' Darrach says. 'The bride smelled, as she always does, like roses.'

'See?' Elizabeth says. 'A charmer, right? How could I resist?'

Darrach and Elizabeth look at each other, and Hannah is both embarrassed to be in the middle of all this gloppy affection and intrigued by it. Do people really live so peacefully and treat each other so kindly? It's impressive, and yet their lives must lack direction and purpose. At home, she knows her purpose. Whenever her father is in the house – in the morning before he goes to the office, after work, on the weekends – his mood dictates what they can talk about, or if they can talk at all, or which rooms they can enter. To live with a person who might at any moment spin out of control makes everything so clear: Your goal is to not instigate, and if you are successful, avoidance is its own reward. The things other people want, what they chase after and think they're entitled to – possessions or entertainment or, say, fairness – who cares? These are extraneous. All you are trying to do is prolong the periods between outbursts or, if this proves impossible, to conceal these outbursts from the rest of the world.

Hannah goes to the bathroom and is on her way back to the kitchen when she hears Darrach say, 'Off to Louisiana tomorrow, alas.'

'A trucker's work is never through,' Elizabeth says.

'But wouldn't it be so much better,' Darrach says as Hannah steps into the kitchen, 'if I stayed here and we could fuck like bunnies?' The way he pronounces *fuck*, it rhymes with *book*.

Simultaneously, they turn to look at Hannah.

'Well.' Elizabeth, still sitting at the table, smiles sheepishly. 'That was elegantly put.'

'Pardon me.' Darrach, who is standing at the sink, bows his head toward Hannah.

'I'll put Rory to bed,' Hannah announces.

'I'll help,' Elizabeth says. As she passes Darrach, she pats him lightly on the butt and shakes her head. In the living room, she says to Hannah, 'Have we traumatized you? Are you about to puke?'

Hannah laughs. 'It's okay. Whatever.'

30

In fact, the idea of Elizabeth and Darrach having sex *is* fairly disgusting. Hannah thinks of Darrach's brown teeth and unruly eyebrows and little pony-tail, and then she thinks of him naked, with an erection, standing tall and thin and pale in their bedroom. This is a turn-on to Elizabeth? She wants him to touch her? And Darrach, for that matter, doesn't mind Elizabeth's wide ass, or how her hair is threaded with gray, pushed back this evening by a red bandanna? Is it like they've struck a bargain – I'll be attracted to you if you'll be attracted to me – or are they *really* attracted to each other? How can they be?

Hannah's favorite image of her father is this one: After college, he joined the Peace Corps and was sent to work in a Honduran orphanage for two years. It was a difficult experience overall; he'd thought he would be teaching English, but more often they had him chopping potatoes for the cook, an older woman responsible for all three meals every day of the week for 150 boys. The poverty was unimaginable. The oldest boys were twelve and would plead with Hannah's father to take them back to the United States. In September 1972, shortly before her father was set to return home, he and a bunch of boys awakened in the middle of the night and gathered in the dining room to listen to the radio broadcast of Mark Spitz swimming the 100-meter butterfly in the Munich Summer Olympics. The radio was small, with poor reception.

Spitz had already broken world records and won gold medals for the 200-meter butterfly and the 200-meter freestyle, and when he broke another record – swimming the race in 54.27 seconds – all the boys turned toward Hannah's father and began clapping and cheering. 'Not because I was me,' he explained to her. 'But because I was American.' Yet she believed it was at least partly because he was him: because he was strong and competent, an adult man. That was her default assumption of men; her assumption of women was that they were a little wimpy.

So how exactly did her father go from a man cheered for by Honduran orphans to a man who would, nineteen years later, exile his own family from their house? Typically, when her mother has angered her father – she has prepared chicken when he said steak, she has neglected to pick up his shirts at the dry cleaner after promising in the morning – he has her sleep in the guest room; she sleeps in the twin bed on the left. This happens perhaps once a month, for perhaps three nights in a row, and it means an elevated level of tension. It doesn't always become an actual outbreak or toxic spill – sometimes it's just the threat. Her father ignores her mother during these periods, even though they all still eat dinner together, and he talks in an aggressively sociable way to Allison and Hannah. Her mother cries a lot. Before bed, her mother goes to the master bedroom to make a case for her return; she pleads and whimpers.

When Hannah was younger, she'd sometimes stand there, too, crying along with her mother. She'd shout, 'Please, Daddy! Let her sleep with you!' Her father would snap, 'Caitlin, get her away from the door. Get her out of here.' Or he'd say, 'I wouldn't try to turn the children against me, if you care about this family.' Her mother would whisper, 'Go away, Hannah. You're not helping.' During all of this, the TV in the bedroom would be turned up high, adding to the confusion. A few years ago, Hannah quit joining her mother outside the bedroom and started going to Allison's room, but after a time or two, she could see in her sister's face that she didn't like Hannah there because she was a reminder of what was happening. Now Hannah stays in her own room. She puts on headphones and reads magazines.

The night of the exile, around eleven-thirty, Hannah awoke to hear them fighting. Her mother hadn't been sleeping in the guest room on the prior nights, but now Hannah's father wanted her to move. She was refusing. Not firmly but by begging. 'But I'm already in bed,' Hannah could hear her saying. 'I'm so tired. Please, Douglas.'

Then it changed to he wanted her out of the house. He didn't care where she went – that was her problem. He said he was sick and tired of her lack of respect for him, given all he did for this family. She should take the girls, too, who appreciated him even less than she did. 'It's your choice,' he said. 'You tell them they need to get

33

out of here, or I'll wake them up myself.' Then her mother was calling out Allison's and Hannah's names, telling them to hurry, saying it didn't matter that they weren't dressed. That was on Thursday. The next morning Hannah didn't go to school – her mother took her shopping at Macy's so she'd have clothes – and on Saturday she boarded the Greyhound to Pittsburgh.

But this is the thing: Hannah suspects her mother and Allison are actually enjoying themselves. The last time she spoke to her sister, Allison said, 'But how are *you*? Are Elizabeth and Darrach being nice?' Before Hannah could respond, Allison said, 'Fig, turn the radio down! I can barely hear Hannah.' Maybe it's like when her father goes on business trips, how abruptly relaxed everything becomes. Dinner is at five P.M. or at nine o'clock; they eat cheese and crackers and nothing else, or a pan of Rice Krispie treats divided three ways, which they consume standing up by the stove; all three of them watch television together, instead of retreating to separate rooms. The lack of tension feels like a trick, and in a way, because it's temporary, it is. But maybe while staying with their cousins, Hannah's mother has realized their lives could be like this all the time. Which is not a wrong or unreasonable conclusion, and yet – if Hannah and Allison and their parents all live in the same house, they're still a family. They seem perfectly normal, possibly enviable: athletic father, kind and attractive mother, pretty older sister who's just been

34

elected vice president of the student council, and younger sister with not much to recommend her yet, it's true, but maybe, Hannah thinks, there'll turn out to be something special about her. Maybe in high school, she'll join debate and soon she'll be attending national championships in Washington, D.C., using words like *incontrovertible*. The life they live together in their house isn't *that* bad, and it doesn't look like it's bad at all, and even if their cousins on both sides are in on their secret now, well, those are only their cousins. It's not like regular people know.

Hannah is supposed to meet Rory when his bus comes home. Usually, the person who meets him is Mrs Janofsky, who's sixty-eight and lives across the street, but Elizabeth says Rory hates staying at Mrs Janofsky's house, and if Hannah doesn't mind, it's really a huge favor for everyone. This might be true, or Elizabeth might be trying to give Hannah something to do.

An hour before the bus is due – she has been watching the clock – she takes her second shower of the day, brushes her teeth, and applies deodorant not only below her arms but also at the V of her upper thighs, just to be safe. She ties a blue ribbon around her ponytail, decides it looks fussy, removes it, and takes out the rubber band as well. She can't be certain that the guy will be in the park, but this is approximately the time he was there before.

He is. He's sitting on a picnic table – not the one where she was last time, but in the same general area. Immediately, she wonders, what is it he does in the park? Is he a drug dealer? When they're twenty feet apart, they make eye contact, and she looks down and veers left. 'Hey,' he calls. 'Where you going?' He smiles. 'Come over here.'

When she gets to the picnic table, he gestures to the space beside him, but she remains standing. She crosses one leg in front of the other and folds her arms over her chest.

He says, 'You was swimming, right? Can I see your swimsuit?'

This was a bad idea.

'I bet it looks good,' he says. 'You ain't too skinny. A lot of girls is too skinny.'

It's because her hair is wet – that must be why he thinks she was swimming. She is simultaneously alarmed, insulted, and flattered; a warmth is spreading in her stomach. What if she *were* wearing a swimsuit, and what if she actually showed it to him? Not here, but if he followed her over to the grove of trees. Then what would he do to her? Surely he'd try something. But also – this knowledge gnaws at her – she probably doesn't look, underneath her clothes, like what he's expecting. Her soft belly, the stubble at the top of her thighs, just below her underwear (she's heard other girls say in the locker room after gym class that they shave there every day, but she

36

forgets a lot). He doesn't necessarily want to see what he thinks he wants to see.

'I can't show you right now,' she says.

'You think I'm being dirty? I ain't being dirty. I'll show you something,' he says, 'and you don't even have to show me nothing.'

If she is raped right now, or strangled, will her father understand that it's his fault? Her heart pounds.

The guy laughs. 'It ain't that,' he says. 'I can tell what you're thinking.' Then – they are five feet apart – he pulls his tank top over his head. His chest, like his arms, is muscular; his shoulders are burned, and his skin, where his shirt covered it, is paler. He stands, turns, and leans forward, his hands against the picnic table.

This is what it is: a tattoo. It's a huge tattoo that takes up most of his back, a bald eagle with wings spread wide, head in profile, a ferocious glaring eye, and an open beak with a purposefully protruding tongue. Its talons are poised to grip – what? A scampering mouse or possibly patriotism itself. It's the biggest tattoo she's ever seen, the only one she's seen this close. The rest of his back is hairless and broken out in places. Most visibly, it's broken out at the corners of his shoulders, after the tattoo stops.

'Does it hurt?' she asks.

'It hurt to get it, but it don't hurt now.'

'I think it's cool,' she says.

After a pause, almost shyly, he says, 'You want, you can touch it.'

37

Until the moment of contact, the tip of her index finger against the skin on his back, she's not sure she's really going to. Then she runs her finger over the eagle's yellow talons and black feathers and beady red eye. *The Chinese symbol that means strength of heart*, she thinks. She runs her finger back up, and the guy says, 'That feels soft.' Her hand is just below his neck when she notices that her watch reads ten past three.

'Oh my God,' she says. 'My cousin!'

Later, she doesn't remember lifting her hand from his back, she doesn't remember what else she tells him; she is already running across the park. Rory's bus should have gotten in at three, and she was with the guy for only a few minutes, but it took her so long to get dressed that it must have been almost three by the time she started talking to him. If something has happened to Rory, she will have to kill herself. That she could ruin Elizabeth's family – it's unthinkable. She has always been a bystander in family destruction, never realizing she herself possessed the capacity to inflict it.

Rory isn't at the bus stop. Less than a block up, he is standing in front of his house, in the middle of the yard. He's looking around, wearing the backpack that's wider than his back. A few nights ago, at Rory's request, Elizabeth sewed an owl patch on the outermost pocket.

'I'm so sorry,' Hannah says. She is breathless. 'Rory, I'm so glad to see you.'

'You were supposed to meet me at the bus.'

'I know. That's why I said I'm sorry. I just was running late, but now I'm here.'

'I don't like you,' Rory says, and Hannah feels first surprised and then humiliated. He is perfectly justified. Why *would* he like her?

She unlocks the front door, and they walk inside the house. 'How about if we get ice cream at Sackey's?' Hannah says. 'Would that taste good?'

'We have ice cream here,' Rory says.

'I just thought if you wanted a different kind.'

'I want Mom's ice cream.'

She fixes him a bowl of chocolate, then one for herself, though he eats in front of the television and she stays in the kitchen. She is getting increasingly upset, weirdly upset. Something horrible could have happened because of her. But also, what would the guy have done if she hadn't had to get Rory? Maybe something could have unfolded that felt good, maybe the beginning of her life. Yet she's selfish to be thinking this way. Elizabeth and Darrach have opened their home to Hannah, and Hannah has repaid them by neglecting their son. There are resolutions she needs to make, she thinks, steps that must be taken so that she becomes a very different sort of person. She's not positive what the steps are, but surely there are several.

She keeps walking into the living room, imagining she hears Elizabeth's car, but when she looks out the front window, it's nothing, a

39

phantom engine. Then, finally, Elizabeth is really there. Hannah can't even wait for her to get inside. She runs out as Elizabeth is unloading groceries from the trunk, and Elizabeth looks up and says, 'Hey there, Hannah, you want to give me a hand?' But Hannah has begun to cry; the tears are spilling down her face. 'Oh, no,' Elizabeth says. 'Oh, I'm so sorry. I saw on TV at the hospital, but I didn't know if you'd heard. Poor Julia Roberts, huh?'

Through her sobbing, Hannah says, 'What did you see?'

'Just the quick snippet on one of the networks. If it's true he cheated on her, I say she's right to call it off.'

'Kiefer *cheated* on her?' This is when Hannah's tears become a flood; she can't see, she almost can't breathe.

'Oh, sweetie, I don't know any more than you do.' Elizabeth's arm is around Hannah's shoulders. She has guided them both to the stoop to sit. 'Probably nobody knows for sure but the two of them.'

When Hannah can speak, she says, 'Why would Kiefer cheat on Julia?'

'Well, again, maybe it's not even true. But we have to remember celebrities are real people, with their own sets of problems. They live in the same world as the rest of us.'

'But they were a good couple,' Hannah says, and a new gush of tears surges forth. 'I could tell.'

Elizabeth pulls Hannah even closer, so one side

40

of Hannah's face is pressed to Elizabeth's breasts. 'They're no different from anyone else,' Elizabeth says. 'Julia Roberts goes to bed without brushing her teeth. I'm not saying every night, but some-times. She probably picks her nose. All celebrities do – they feel sad, they feel jealous, they fight with each other. And Hannah, marriage is so hard. I know there's this idea that it's glass slippers and wedding cake, but it's the hardest thing in the world.'

Hannah jerks up her head. 'Why are you always defending my dad? I know you know that he's an asshole.'

'Hannah, your dad has some demons. He just does. We all do the best we can.'

'I don't care about his demons!' Hannah cries. 'He's a bully! He's so mean that no one will stand up to him.'

At first Elizabeth is quiet. Then she says, 'Okay. He is a bully. How can I pretend he's not? But something you won't understand until you're older is how unhappy your dad is. No one acts like that unless they're unhappy. And he knows. He knows what he's like, and for him to know he's failing his family, to see himself acting just like our father did – it must tear your dad apart.'

'I *hope* it tears him apart.'

'You'll leave all of this behind, Hannah. I promise. And if your mom can stay away, it already won't be as bad when you get home. That's the mistake my mom made, that she just stayed with

41

Dad forever. But your mom is getting out while she can, which is the smartest, bravest thing she can do.'

So her parents are splitting up. They must be. Hannah is pretty sure Elizabeth doesn't realize what she's just revealed, and perhaps at this point it's not definite, but when Hannah's mother drives to Pittsburgh in early August to pick her up and tells her over fish sandwiches at Dairy Queen on the ride home that she has moved into a condo, Hannah will not be surprised. The condo will be in a nice neighborhood, and her mother already will have decorated Allison's and Hannah's bedrooms. Hannah's will have pink striped curtains and a matching pink bedspread over a double bed. Hannah will soon like the condo better than she ever liked the old house, which is where her father will live for several more years – the condo will not be so large that it makes her nervous to be there alone, and it will be within walking distance of a drugstore, a grocery store, and several restaurants where Hannah and her mother will go sometimes on Saturday nights. Hannah and Allison will have lunch with their father on Sundays and won't see or speak to him besides that. He'll tell them they're always welcome to come over for dinner or to spend the night, but they'll go only a few times, to gather the belongings their mother hasn't moved already. Their father will start dating someone from the country club, an attractive woman whose husband

42

died in a boating accident in Michigan. The woman, Amy, will have three young children, and Hannah will wonder whether her father purposely conceals what he's like from Amy, or whether Amy chooses not to see it. For a long time, Hannah's mother will not date.

These will be the details of the Julia Roberts rumors: that Kiefer was cheating with a dancer named Amanda Rice, though the name she goes by at the Crazy Girls Club where she works is Raven. The day the wedding was scheduled for, Julia will fly to Dublin with Jason Patric, another actor who's a friend of Kiefer's. At the Shelbourne Hotel, where suites cost $650 a night, hotel employees will report that Julia looks gaunt, her hair is orange, and she is not wearing her engagement ring.

Two years later, she will marry the country singer Lyle Lovett. They'll have known each other for three weeks, she'll be barefoot for the ceremony, and the marriage will last only twenty-one months. He will be ten years older than she is, with puffy hair and a lean, dour face. In 2002, Julia Roberts will marry a cameraman named Danny Moder. Their wedding will be at midnight on the Fourth of July, at her ranch in Taos, New Mexico, but before it occurs, Danny Moder will have to divorce his wife of four years, a makeup artist named Vera.

Insofar as Hannah will have an opinion on the subject anymore, the Vera part will make her a little queasy, but she'll believe overall that Danny and Julia are a good match. In photos, they'll look comfortable and happy, only slightly too beautiful for normal life. However, except while paging through magazines in the waiting room of the dentist's office, or in line at the grocery store, Hannah will no longer follow Julia Roberts's activities; she won't spend her own time attending to celebrities. Not because she'll have decided it's frivolous – it is, of course, but so are most things – but because she'll be preoccupied; she'll be a grown-up. On a daily basis, Hannah will not feel markedly different from the way she felt when she was fourteen, but this will be one of the signs that she must be: that she used to know many things about Julia Roberts, and now she knows very few.

Far in the future, Hannah will have a boyfriend named Mike with whom she'll talk about her father. She'll say she isn't sorry about her upbringing before the divorce, that she thinks in a lot of ways it was useful. Being raised in an unstable household makes you understand that the world doesn't exist to accommodate you, which, in Hannah's observation, is something a lot of people struggle to understand well into adulthood. It makes you realize how quickly a situation can shift, how danger really is everywhere. But crises, when they occur, do not catch you off guard; you have never believed you live under the shelter of some essential benevolence. And an unstable childhood makes you appreciate calmness and not crave excitement. To spend a Saturday afternoon mopping your kitchen floor while listening to opera on the radio, and to go that night to an Indian restaurant with a friend and be home by nine o'clock – these are enough. They are gifts.

Once, Hannah's boyfriend will cry as she tells him about her father, though she will not be crying. Another time he'll say he thinks she has Stockholm syndrome, but he'll be a psych major and, in Hannah's opinion, rather suggestible. During sex, Hannah will memorize a particular section of Mike's back, the view from over his left shoulder, and sometimes when she's trying to come, she'll imagine that just out of her line of vision is an enormous eagle tattoo; she'll run her fingers over the place where the tattoo should be. She'll never have seen the guy with the real tattoo after that day she left Rory waiting. Though she'll stay for two more months at her aunt's, she'll never return to the park.

In this moment on the front stoop, when Hannah is still fourteen, she is sitting so close to Elizabeth that she can smell the hospital soap on her aunt's hands. Elizabeth's grocery bags are in the yard where she dropped them. Rory is about to come outside and plead to be taken to the pool, and after they go, because Darrach is out of town, for dinner they will order wonton soup and cashew chicken and beef with broccoli. 'Are my parents getting a divorce?' Hannah asks. 'They are, aren't they?'

'You just have to realize how weak most men are,' Elizabeth says. 'It's the only way you can forgive them.'

PART II

CHAPTER 2

FEBRUARY 1996

The plan is that they'll pick up Hannah at nine o'clock, but at five to nine Jenny calls to say it will be more like nine thirty or quarter to ten. She says that Angie got off work late and still needs to shower. (Hannah has no idea what Angie's job is.) 'Sorry about this,' Jenny says.

Hannah is sitting at her desk. She turns in her chair and looks around her dorm room: the stack of newspapers that has grown so high, waiting to be recycled, that it's like an ottoman; her shoes lined up against one wall; the trunk she uses as a bedside table, with a plastic cup of water on it; and her bed, which she made a few minutes ago, even though it's nighttime, because she had finished getting dressed and wasn't sure what else to do with her nervous energy. It is the sight of the bed, its pillows plumped and flannel-sheathed duvet smoothed flat, that tempts Hannah to tell Jenny they don't need to swing by after all because she'll just stay here tonight. She could be asleep within ten minutes – all she'd have to do is go down the hall and wash her face, then change into

49

her pajamas, apply ChapStick, and turn out the light. She regularly goes to bed this early. It's kind of strange, not like other college students, but she does it.

'So we'll be there in half an hour or forty-five minutes,' Jenny says.

The words are formed already: *You know what, I'm kind of tired.* Here, Hannah could laugh apologetically. *I think I might stay in. I'm sorry, I know it's totally lame. But thank you so much for inviting me. And definitely tell me how it goes. I'm sure it'll be really fun.* If Hannah opens her mouth, the words will jump into the air and travel across campus through the telephone wires to Jenny, and Hannah won't have to go. Jenny will be nice – she *is* nice – and maybe try to persuade Hannah otherwise, but when Hannah is firm, Jenny will let it drop. She'll let it drop, and then they'll never become true friends because Hannah will be the weird girl who flaked at the last minute the time they were driving to western Massachusetts. And Hannah will have spent another night doing nothing, sleeping. She'll wake at six A.M., the campus dark and silent, the dining hall not open for five whole hours because it's the weekend. She'll shower, eat dry cereal from the box on her windowsill, start her homework. After a while, when she has finished Marxist Theory and gone on to Evolutionary Biology, she'll look at the clock and it will be seven forty-five – only seven forty-five! – and still no one else will be awake, not even

50

close to awake. She will be sitting there with her hair combed out straight and wet, squeaky clean, with page after page of her textbooks highlighted, and she will feel not industrious, not diligent, but panicked. The morning will be a rush of gray air she must fill alone. Who cares if her hair is clean or she's read about pathogen population structure? Who is her hair clean for, who does she have to talk to about pathogen population structure?

Go, Hannah thinks to herself. *You should go.*

'I'll wait by the main entrance,' she says to Jenny.

When she hangs up the phone, she is, as she was before Jenny called, unsure what to do. She shouldn't do homework – either she won't be able to concentrate or she'll become so absorbed that she'll entirely lose the mood she's losing now anyway, the mood that ascended as she stood under the hot water in the shower, raising her left leg and running the razor up her calf, then putting down her left leg and raising her right. Back in her room, she turned the radio way up and stood in front of the closet inspecting her clothes. She pulled out two black shirts, trying on one and then the other. She imagined which her cousin Fig would recommend (Hannah is a freshman at Tufts, and Fig is a freshman at Boston University). Fig would say to wear the tight one.

She wishes she owned nail polish so she could paint her nails right now, or that she wore makeup and could stand before the mirror with her lips puckered, smearing them some oily, sparkly shade

51

of pink. At the very least, she wishes she had a women's magazine so she could read about other people doing these things. She does have a finger-nail clipper – that's not festive, but it's something. She returns to her desk chair, pulls the trash can in front of her, and sticks the tip of a nail into the jaw of the clipper.

This doesn't take long. When she's finished, she stands and looks at herself sideways in the full-length mirror on the back of the door to her room. The shirt she chose isn't that flattering. It's tight in the arms but loose across the boobs – tight in the wrong way, and actually, it's not even that tight, not compared to what the other girls will probably be wearing. She changes into the second one.

The song on the radio ends, and the DJ says, 'Who's psyched that it's Friday night? We've got more of today's greatest dance hits coming up after this, so stay tuned.' An advertisement for a car dealership comes on, and Hannah turns the radio down. She listens to the radio a lot, including when she's studying, but she rarely listens to it on Friday or Saturday nights for this very reason: the DJs' delighted tone of anticipation. Every Friday afternoon at five, the station plays a song with the lyrics 'I don't want to work / I just want to bang on the drum all day,' and that's when Hannah switches off the radio. She imagines the working men and women of Boston leaving their offices, pulling out of parking garages or hopping on the T.

The people in their twenties call their friends and plan to meet at bars, and the families in the suburbs make spaghetti and rent movies (it is the families she's more jealous of), and the weekend opens up to them, the relief of empty hours. They will sleep late, wash their cars, pay bills, whatever the things are that people do. Sometimes on Fridays Hannah takes cough medicine so she can fall asleep even earlier than usual, once as early as five thirty in the afternoon. This is probably not the best idea, but it's only cough medicine, not real sleeping pills.

Tonight it is strange to be part of the DJ's universe, to be going out. She looks at her watch and thinks she might as well go downstairs. She pulls on her coat, feels in the pocket – ChapStick, gum, keys – and looks once more in the mirror before heading out the door.

They are late, which she expects. She reads the campus newspaper, first today's, then yesterday's, then the classifieds from today's. Other students cut through the entry hall of the dorm, several of them conspicuously drunk. One guy wears jeans so many sizes too large that six inches of his boxer shorts are visible in the back. 'What's up?' he says as he passes her. He is with another guy, who holds a bottle inside a paper bag. The other guy grins at her. Hannah says nothing. 'Yo, that's cool,' says the first guy.

She is sitting on a bench, and every few minutes she walks to the window next to the front door and presses her face against the glass, peering into the blackness. She is looking out the window when the car pulls up; she doesn't recognize it as the car she's waiting for, but then Jenny waves from the passenger seat. Hannah steps away from the window, zipping her coat. There is a moment when she's standing in front of the door, a massive door of dark wood, when they can't see her and she thinks that she could crouch down and back up on all fours and sneak upstairs, that by the time one of them came inside to look for her, she'd have vanished.

'Hey,' Jenny says when Hannah is outside. 'I'm sorry we're so late.'

Climbing inside the car, Hannah is bombarded with music and cigarette smoke and the creamy, perfumed smell of girls who take better care of themselves than she does.

Jenny turns around from the front seat. 'This is Kim.' Jenny gestures to the driver, a tiny girl with short dark hair and diamond earrings whom Hannah has never seen before. 'And this is Michelle, and you know Angie, right?' Angie is Jenny's roommate, whom Hannah has met while studying with Jenny. In Jenny's room, she has also met Michelle, though Michelle says, 'Nice to meet you.'

'It's Michelle's friend who goes to school at Tech,' Jenny says. 'So what have you been up to – still recovering from the stats test? If I just pass, I swear I'll celebrate.'

Hannah and Jenny know each other from statistics class, though they met during the freshman orientation camping trip, when they slept in the same tent. Hannah remembers most of this trip dimly, a blur of other freshmen who seemed to be trying embarrassingly hard; she did not understand that this was the part when you had to try. Her one distinct memory is of awakening around three in the morning, with girls whose names she didn't know in sleeping bags on either side of her, the air in the tent hot and unbreathable. She lay with her eyes open for a long time, then finally stood, hunching, stepping over arms and heads, whispering apologies when the other girls stirred, and pushed through the tent flap into the night. She could see the bathroom, a cement structure thirty yards away, on the other side of a dirt road. In bare feet, she walked toward it. On the women's side of the structure, greenish light illuminated three stalls whose doors were scratched with initials and swear words. When she looked at her face in the mirror above the sink, Hannah felt a desperate wish for this moment to pass, this segment of time not to exist anymore. Her misery seemed tangible, a thing she could grasp or throw.

The next morning they returned to campus, and Hannah didn't talk to anyone she'd met on the orientation. She saw the people sometimes; at first it seemed that they were pretending not to recognize her, then, after a few weeks, it seemed that they were no longer pretending. But one day in

January a girl fell into step beside Hannah as they were leaving the lecture hall after statistics class. 'Hey,' the girl said. 'You were on my orientation trip, weren't you?'

Hannah looked at the girl, her blond bangs and brown eyes. Something in her features made her seem friendly, Hannah thought, and realized it was her teeth: The incisors were disproportionately large. But she wasn't unattractive. She wore a white tailored shirt underneath a gray wool sweater, and jeans that looked pressed. It was the kind of outfit Hannah imagined on a coed from the 1950s.

'I'm Jenny.' The girl stuck out her hand, and Hannah shook it, surprised by the firmness of Jenny's grasp.

'So I have to confess something,' Jenny said. 'I have no idea what's going on in that class. I mean, not a thing.'

That Jenny's confession was so bland was both a relief and a disappointment. 'It's pretty confusing,' Hannah said.

'Have you heard of any study groups?' Jenny asked. 'Or would you be interested in studying together? I think it might be easier with someone else.'

'Oh,' Hannah said. 'Okay.'

'I'm starving,' Jenny said. 'Have you had lunch yet?'

Hannah hesitated. She ate only breakfast in the cafeteria because you could eat breakfast alone;

56

other people did it. 'Yeah, I have,' Hannah said, then regretted it immediately. In her room, she ate bagels and fruit for lunch and dinner. It had become disgusting. She wanted something hot or wet – a hamburger or pasta. 'But maybe after class on Wednesday,' Hannah said.

'Let me give you my number,' Jenny said. They had reached the path leading to the cafeteria. When Jenny passed a scrap of paper to Hannah, she said, 'So I'll see you in class, assuming I don't stab myself in the heart doing the reading before then.'

Walking back to her dorm, Hannah thought, *A friend*. It was miraculous. This was how she'd once imagined she'd meet people in college, just this effortlessly, but it had never happened. She'd seen it happen to other students, but it hadn't happened to her. The first problem was that, randomly, she'd been assigned to a single. The second problem was Hannah herself. She had had friends before this – not a lot, but some – and she'd believed college would be a vast improvement over high school. But upon her arrival at Tufts, she hadn't joined clubs. She hadn't initiated conversations. Early on, when her hall would go en masse to watch student improv troupes or a cappella groups, Hannah didn't go because she didn't want to, because she thought improv and a cappella were kind of stupid. (Later, that seemed like poor reasoning.) On Saturday afternoons, she'd take the T over to Fig's dorm at BU and hang out while Fig got dressed for frat parties, and then Hannah would return to Tufts around eight P.M. and her own dorm would be silent except for certain throbbing rooms, and these Hannah would hurry past. All her decisions alone were trivial, but they accumulated and she felt herself sliding backward. By October, when the kids who lived around her were going out, she couldn't go not because she didn't want to but because she just couldn't. Because what would she say to them? Really, she didn't have anything to say to anyone. Five months passed, the longest months of Hannah's life, and then she met Jenny.

As far as Hannah can see, there is nothing remarkable about Jenny except for her reaction to Hannah. Jenny does not seem to realize that she is Hannah's only friend. The last time they were studying, Jenny said, 'A bunch of us are going to Springfield on Friday. My friend Michelle went to high school with a guy who goes to this engineering school there, where it's like ninety percent men.' Jenny raised her eyebrows twice, and Hannah laughed, because she knew she was supposed to. 'You should come,' Jenny said. 'It might be a bust, but at least it'll be a change of scenery. And I'm so sick of the guys here.' Jenny had previously outlined to Hannah the saga of her relationship with a guy who lives two doors down, with whom Jenny has sex when they both end up drunk at the same party, even though she thinks he's a jerk and not that cute. The breezy way Jenny told this story implied that she assumed Hannah had found herself in similar entanglements, and Hannah did not correct her. In actuality, Hannah has never been involved with a boy, not at all. She has never even kissed anyone. That guy with the eagle tattoo – that's as close as she got. Her inexperience at the age of eighteen makes her feel by turns freakish and amazing, as if she should be placed under glass and observed by scientists. Also, in times of danger – turbulent plane flights home, say – it makes her feel immune. She thinks that it must be impossible, against the laws of nature, to make it through high school and then die before kissing another person.

In the car, as they pull onto the street leading away from campus, a song by a female rapper comes on the radio, and Angie, who is sitting between Michelle and Hannah, lunges into the front seat and turns up the volume. The gist of the song is that if a man won't perform oral sex on her, the rapper wants nothing to do with him. This is not the radio station Hannah listens to, but she's heard the song spilling from other students' rooms. Apparently, Angie and Michelle have memorized all the lyrics, and they belt them out, nodding their heads from side to side and laughing.

The backseat is tight, and Hannah's thigh is pressed against Angie's. She pulls the seat belt down from over her shoulder and gropes for the buckle between her and Angie. She can't find it. She gropes some more, then gives up, imagining some gruesome scene of smashed metal, shattered glass, and blood. This situation seems ripe for just such an accident – young women gearing up for a good time, a long dark drive in winter. In this case, the immunity that comes with being unkissed might not even protect Hannah. Among them, these four other girls must have had so much sex that it would cancel out her own inexperience.

Jenny lights a cigarette and passes it to Kim, then lights another for herself. Jenny's window is open a few inches at the top, and when she ashes out of it, Hannah observes Jenny's smooth, glossy nails; they are painted dark red, the color of wine. Jenny turns around and says something that is inaudible over the music.

'What?' Hannah says.

'The smoke,' Jenny says more loudly. 'Is it bothering you?'

Hannah shakes her head.

Jenny turns back around. The loud music is actually a relief, precluding real conversation.

It takes almost two hours to get to Springfield. As they turn off the highway, Hannah's eyelids keep falling. Her mouth is dry; she suspects that if she spoke, her voice would be raspy.

Michelle's friend lives in an apartment complex at the top of a hill. Michelle has been here before but says she can't remember which entrance is his, so they drive around looking at the addresses.

'It's in the middle somewhere,' Michelle says. 'I'm sure of that. Oh, here, turn here.'

'Thanks for the warning,' Kim says in a joking tone as she pulls into the driveway and parks behind an SUV.

As Hannah follows the girls to the door, Jenny and Angie are each carrying two six-packs they retrieved from the trunk. They enter a hallway of brown carpet and white stucco walls, a bank of mailboxes on the left. 'I feel the testosterone,' Kim says, and everyone laughs.

When they climb the stairs, there is the brushing sound of winter coats. At the landing, Angie turns around and says, 'Is my lipstick okay?'

Hannah does not realize right away that Angie is talking to her, even though she's directly behind Angie. Then Hannah says, 'Yeah, it's fine.'

Michelle knocks on the door. Hannah can hear music. 'Is my lipstick okay?' Angie says to Jenny, and Jenny says, 'It's perfect.' The door opens, revealing a stocky, dark-haired, red-faced guy with stubble, holding a beer can in one hand. 'Michelle, ma belle,' he says, and he envelops Michelle in a hug. 'You made it.' He gestures with the beer can. 'So who's the bevy of beauties?'

'Okay.' Michelle points with her finger. 'Angie, Jenny, Kim, Hannah. Guys, this is Jeff.'

Jeff nods several times. 'Welcome, welcome,' he says. 'Anything I can do to make you girls feel comfortable this evening, you just say the word.'

'You can start by giving us something to drink,'

61

Michelle says. She is already walking past him into the apartment.

'Right this way.' Jeff extends one arm, palm open, and they file past him. Hannah notices Kim and Jeff look at each other. Hannah cannot even see Kim's face, but she thinks suddenly that Jeff and Kim will hook up tonight. Probably they will have sex. She realizes with a jolting clarity that this is what the entire night is about: hooking up. At some level, she already suspected as much, but now it is palpable.

Ten or twelve guys are in the living room, and two girls. One girl is a pretty blonde wearing tight jeans and black leather boots. The other is wearing a hooded sweatshirt and a baseball cap. In the swirl of introductions, Hannah comes to understand that the pretty girl is a girlfriend visiting from out of town, and the other girl is a student at the college. Hannah does not absorb the names of either girl or any of the guys. The stereo and the TV are both on – the TV is set to a basketball game – and the room is mostly dark. People are standing in clusters or sitting on the floor or on one of the two couches, smoking. One guy talks on a cordless phone, walking between the living room and the back of the apartment. Hannah enters the brightly lit kitchen. Angie passes her a beer, then Hannah returns to the living room and stands beside the couch. Her eyes are drawn to the television, and she pretends to watch.

'Don't tell me you're a Sonics fan.'

She looks over. A guy is on the couch, his feet propped on the coffee table in front of him.

'No,' she says.

It appears this was too brief an answer; if she wants him to keep talking to her, she has to say something more.

'What's the score?' she asks.

'Seventy-five to fifty-eight. The Knicks have it in the bag.'

'Oh, good,' Hannah says. Then she's afraid he'll unmask her, so she hastily adds, 'Not that I really follow basketball.'

This confession seems to please the guy. In a playful voice, he says, 'Girls just don't understand the spiritness of sports.'

'The spiritness?'

'It's what brings people together. Church is like – who goes to church anymore? But check this out: There are ten seconds left on the clock. The Bulls are down by one. Pippen inbounds the ball to Jordan, and Jordan brings it up the court. He watches the clock tick down. The crowd is going wild. With two seconds left, Jordan pulls up for the jumper and wins the game. And the fans go crazy – total strangers hugging each other. Tell me that's not spirit.'

While he talked, Hannah was thinking, *Enlighten me some more, Einstein*. But during the last part about total strangers hugging each other – how could that not make her imagine being hugged by him? Did he say it on purpose? He is wearing a plaid flannel shirt, and she thinks of his arms around her.

'Overall, I see sports as a positive force,' Hannah says.

'What else is there?' the guy says. 'Name one other thing that brings people together like that.'

'No, I know,' Hannah says. 'I'm agreeing with you.'

'And when I hear parents say that garbage about how athletes are bad role models, I'm just like, *You're the ones raising your kids. Or you should be.* You know? Fuckin', like, Dennis Rodman is not putting little Johnny to bed every night. If athletes snort coke or beat their wives, that has nothing to do with their performance.'

'I wouldn't say snorting coke and beating your wife are the same thing,' Hannah says.

'No shit.' The guy grins. 'Beating your wife is a lot cheaper.'

So, Hannah thinks, *domestic violence as springboard for flirtation.* But she half smiles; she doesn't want to be a wet blanket.

'By the way,' the guy says, 'I'm Todd.'

'Hannah.'

He motions beside him. 'Care to sit?'

Hannah hesitates, then says, 'Okay.'

On the couch, she immediately likes him better than she did standing up. She likes his presence next to her, the side of his arm touching the side of hers. Maybe he will be the first person she ever kisses. She will think back on him as *Todd, wearing a plaid shirt, that night in Springfield.*

'So what do you study over there at Tufts?' Todd asks.

'I haven't declared a major yet. I like my art history class, though.'

'That's where you look at paintings and use big words to describe how they make you feel – is that about right?'

'Exactly. And we wear black turtlenecks and black berets.'

He laughs. 'I don't even remember the last time I was in a museum. I bet it was grade school.'

'Well, I'm not definitely majoring in art history. I have a while to decide.'

He looks at her. 'You know I'm joking about the big words, don't you? I was just giving you a hard time.'

Hannah glances at him, then glances away. 'I wasn't offended,' she says.

Neither of them speaks.

'So what about you?' she says. 'You guys all study engineering, right?'

He leans back. 'I'm a gearhead,' he says. 'Mechanical engineer.'

'Wow.' But he doesn't elaborate, and she can't think of anything else to ask besides, what *is* mechanical engineering? She finishes her beer in a long swallow and holds up the empty bottle. 'I think I'll get another. Do you want anything?'

'Nope, I'm cool.'

In the kitchen, Jenny and Angie are talking to two guys. Jenny squeezes Hannah's shoulder. 'Having fun?'

'Yeah, of course.'

'That didn't sound very enthusiastic.'

'Hell, yeah!' Hannah exclaims, and this is when she knows she's drunk. It has taken one beer.

Jenny laughs. 'Who's that guy you're talking to?'

'Todd. But I don't know.'

'You don't know what?' Jenny elbows Hannah. 'He's totally cute.' Jenny lowers her voice. 'Now, what do you think of—' She rolls her eyes to the left.

'With the glasses?' Hannah whispers.

'No, the other one. His name is Dave.'

'Thumbs-up,' Hannah says. 'You should go for him.' She is not sure which is more unlikely: the fact that they are having this conversation three feet away from the guy in question, or the fact that she is part of the conversation in the first place. It turns out she does know which words and inflections to use. She should draw on the ability more often; perhaps she has only fabricated the difficulty of making friends.

But when she returns to the living room, Hannah sees that Michelle is sitting next to Todd. It's okay, though. There is room on his other side. She steps over their legs and murmurs, 'Hey,' as she sits down.

Neither of them responds. 'My dad bought a BMW M5,' Michelle is saying. 'It was his fiftieth-birthday present to himself.'

'Are you guys talking about when men have a midlife crisis?' Hannah asks.

Michelle looks at Hannah and says, 'We're talking about cars.' She turns back to Todd. She says, 'I'm always like, "Dad, if you want me to run *any* errands, all you have to do is say the word."'

'The current Beemers compared to the older models—' Todd begins, and Hannah turns away. On the other couch, which is shoved against this couch with no space between the armrests, the girl who's an engineering student is doing shots with three guys. On television, the basketball game appears to have ended. Two commentators hold microphones and say things Hannah cannot hear. Her energy is plummeting. She tips her bottle and gulps down the beer. She could go back into the kitchen and stand with Jenny, but she doesn't want to be clingy.

'Hey.' Todd kicks her lightly in the calf. 'You hanging in there?'

'I kind of had a long day.'

'What, studying paintings?' He smiles, and she thinks that maybe he has not yet chosen Michelle over her.

'It's more tiring than you'd think,' Hannah says.

'I don't have Friday classes this semester,' Michelle says. 'It's so sweet.'

Hannah also doesn't have Friday classes, which might be the reason for the cough medicine problem – by the time Friday afternoon rolls

67

around, she's already been untethered for over twenty-four hours.

'You liberal arts people,' Todd says. 'You don't know how good you have it.'

'I'm premed, man,' Michelle says. 'I'm working my ass off.'

'Okay, but she' – he jabs his thumb at Hannah – 'is studying art history. Any questions you have about the *Mona Lisa*, Hannah's on it.' He's making an effort, Hannah thinks. It might be small, but he's making an effort. And he's not bad-looking, and she suspects he's drunk, which is good, because maybe if he's drunk, he won't be able to tell when he kisses her that she has no idea what she's doing.

'Hannah and I don't really know each other,' Michelle says. To Hannah, she says, 'Before we picked you up, I thought you were going to be someone else. But I think that girl's name is Anna.'

'Here I was thinking you're all best friends,' Todd says. 'I'm seeing images of you doing Hannah's hair while she's borrowing your pantyhose.'

'Sorry, but no one under the age of seventy wears pantyhose,' Michelle says.

'What's she wearing?' Todd points at Kim, who is standing by the stereo with Jeff.

'Those are tights,' Michelle says. 'Pantyhose are see-through. They're, like, nude.'

'Nude, huh? I like the sound of that.'

No, Todd probably will not be the first guy Hannah kisses. She wishes she knew for sure, though, so she could stop trying. The dynamic between her and Michelle – Michelle with her tight pink V-neck shirt and department-store necklace of flat, thick gold – is ridiculous and unreal, something from a movie: bitchy girls fighting over a guy. Maybe at this point, Todd is hoping for both of them.

Now they are talking about the internship Todd will have this summer with Lockheed Martin. Hannah glances again toward the other couch. She could rest on the arms between them, she thinks, just lean over and shut her eyes. This would seem odd, but she can't imagine that anyone would really care, and besides, they'd probably assume she'd passed out. She angles herself against the cushions and closes her eyes. Immediately, she is falling through darkness. The darkness is an overlay, as if there is all sorts of activity occurring on its other side, people bumping a black stage curtain from behind.

'Check that out,' she hears Todd say. 'You think she's okay?'

'It looks like she's just sleeping,' Michelle says. 'She didn't seem like she was having a very good time.' Hannah waits for a more vehement expression of contempt – *And she's a loser anyway!* – but instead Michelle says, 'Are we going to this bar or not?'

'Let me ask around,' Todd says.

Go, Hannah thinks. *Hook up. Give each other chlamydia.*

More movement occurs around Hannah. From the other couch, a guy says, 'Is that girl asleep?' She is afraid her face will twitch or, worse, she will smile and give herself away.

'Hannah.' Someone is tapping her arm, and she opens her eyes. Then, feigning disorientation, she shuts them, swallows, opens them again. Jenny is kneeling in front of her. 'You fell asleep,' Jenny says. 'Do you feel okay?'

'Yeah, I'm fine.'

'Everyone's going to a bar, just for an hour or so. Do you want to stay here or do you want to come?'

'I think I'll stay here.'

'Do you need water or anything?' There is a certain brightness to Jenny's eyes, a sloppy emphaticness to her words, that makes Hannah pretty sure Jenny is quite drunk.

Hannah shakes her head.

'All right, then. Sweet dreams.' Jenny smiles at Hannah, and a wish flickers through Hannah for genuine friendship with her. She almost believes that if she revealed to Jenny what she is really like, Jenny would still accept her.

They shut off the television and the stereo and cut the lights, except in the kitchen. When they've all left, the quiet is astonishing. Hannah thinks that she might be able to fall asleep for real. She realizes she has no idea how or when anyone is planning to return to campus. Maybe they are staying here all night. The thought dismays her – having to look at these same guys in the unforgiving light of morning, waiting in line for the bathroom. She wishes she had brought a toothbrush.

Less than five minutes have passed when Hannah hears the front door open again. There are two people, a guy and a girl, both of them laughing and whispering. Soon they are not even whispering, just speaking in low voices. The girl, Hannah realizes, is Jenny, and she assumes the guy is Dave, the one from the kitchen.

'I left it inside the sleeve of my coat, so if it fell out, it should be on the closet floor,' Jenny says. 'But don't turn on the light. Hannah's sleeping.'

They are quiet for a while, and when Dave speaks, his voice is different – it is thicker. 'Do you even have a hat?' he says.

Jenny laughs. 'What's that supposed to mean?'

'What do you think it's supposed to mean?' This must be when he touches Jenny's forehead or her neck. 'It's okay if you don't,' he says. 'I like being alone with you.'

'I swear it's here somewhere,' Jenny says. Her voice is different, too, softer and slower. The apartment is silent – Hannah feels as if she's holding her breath – and then there is the slight smack of their lips meeting, the rub of their clothes.

To Hannah's horror, they move from near the closet onto the other couch. They don't talk much, and soon they're both breathing more quickly. Hannah can hear snaps being pulled apart. After

71

several minutes, Jenny says, 'No, it fastens in the front.' Their feet point toward Hannah's head, separated from her by only a few inches of cushions and the armrests of the two couches. 'You're sure she's asleep, right?' Dave says, and Jenny says, 'She went out like a light.' Hannah wonders if Jenny really believes this.

There is more rubbing around. It seems to last for a long time, fifteen minutes maybe, though Hannah has not opened her eyes since Jenny and Dave entered the apartment and has no idea what time it is. A zipper comes undone, and after a few seconds, Dave says quietly, 'You like this, don't you?'

Actually, Jenny's moans sound like weeping, except that clearly they aren't. But there is something soft and mournful, something infantile, in the noises she makes. *Please just don't have an orgasm*, Hannah thinks. *Please*. She finds that she herself is crying. One at a time, the tears fall from between her squeezed eyelids in long drops, tip off her chin, and settle around her collarbone.

Dave murmurs, 'You're so hot.'

Jenny says nothing, and even through her tears, Hannah is surprised by this. It seems like Jenny should acknowledge the compliment. Not by saying thank you, necessarily, but by saying something.

'Hold on a second,' Jenny says suddenly, and her voice is almost normal. They shift, and Jenny rises from the couch.

After a minute, the sound of vomiting is clearly

audible from the bathroom. 'Holy shit,' Dave says. He stands and walks toward the noise.

Hannah opens her eyes and exhales. She wishes she could move into one of the bedrooms, even the outside hall – she doesn't care. But if she moves in their absence, they will know she was awake all along and maybe it will seem like she wanted to overhear them.

At the approach of footsteps, she snaps her eyes shut. She assumes the footsteps are Dave's, but it is Jenny who hisses, 'Hannah. Hannah!'

Hannah makes a grumbling noise.

'Wake up,' Jenny says. 'I just got sick. And I'm hooking up with this guy. He's in the bathroom cleaning it up. Oh God, I want to get out of here. Can we leave? Let's leave.'

'And go where?'

'Back to school. I have Kim's keys. And you can drive, right? You didn't have that much to drink?'

'If we leave, how will Kim and everyone get back?'

'We can go by the bar and pick them up. And if they don't want to come, which I'm sure they won't, we can get them tomorrow.'

'But what about this guy?'

'Oh God. I don't know what I'm doing with him. He just tried to kiss me in the bathroom, *after* I threw up. I was like, are you out of your mind? So let's go. Can we go?'

Hannah props herself up on her elbows. 'The car's not stick, right? Because I can't drive—'

Jenny pushes her down. 'He's coming. Go back to sleep.'

'Hey,' Hannah hears Jenny say. 'Talk about a party foul.'

'Not a problem,' Dave says. 'It happens to all of us.'

'You know what?' Jenny says. 'I'm going to call it a night and head back.'

'Are you serious?'

'I just feel like it would be better.'

'Don't worry about this,' he says. 'You should stay.'

'I really think I want to go. Hannah, wake up.' How can Jenny refuse Dave? He will accept her, vomit and all, and she is refusing him. It doesn't seem gross to Hannah that he tried to kiss Jenny after she threw up; it seems kind.

'We don't have to do anything,' Dave is saying. 'We could just sleep.' He's saying it in a light way, as if acting casual will be more likely to convince Jenny.

'Another time,' Jenny says. 'Hey, sleepyhead Hannah.'

For the third time tonight, Hannah pretends to awaken. Now that Jenny knows she is faking, Hannah wonders if Jenny realizes she is acting exactly the way she did the other times.

'We're taking off,' Jenny says. 'You get to sleep in your own bed.'

'Okay.' Hannah sits up and glances at Dave. 'Hi,' she says.

'Hi.' He is watching Jenny as she pulls on her coat.

Jenny tosses the keys to Hannah. As Hannah retrieves her coat from the closet, Jenny hugs Dave. 'Great to meet you,' she says.

'When you guys come back, you should stay for longer,' Dave says.

'Definitely.' Jenny nods. 'That'd be fun.'

Then they are out in the hallway, the door to the apartment shut, Dave left inside. Jenny grips Hannah's wrist and whispers, 'That guy was *so* cheesy.'

'I thought he seemed pretty nice.'

'He was creepy. If we'd woken up together, he would have said he loved me.'

Hannah says nothing.

'You were smart to go to sleep,' Jenny says. 'Good decision.'

Decision? Hannah thinks incredulously. *I didn't decide anything.* Then she thinks, *Did I?*

They reach the car. It is freezing outside, the air icy. The bar is at the bottom of the hill, and Hannah keeps the motor running while Jenny hurries in to tell the other girls that they're leaving. Hannah suspects the girls will be angry, but Kim appears in the window of the bar, smiling and waving. Hannah waves back.

'We're supposed to call them tomorrow afternoon,' Jenny says as she climbs in again. 'But probably we don't need to come get them until Sunday morning. You'll drive back with me, won't you?'

The request surprises Hannah – it seems she has not behaved so oddly tonight that Jenny plans to drop her altogether. This fact should probably make Hannah grateful.

They take only one wrong turn before finding the highway. Few other cars are out – it is after three, Hannah sees when she looks at the digital clock on the dashboard – and shadowy clumps of trees line either side of the road. Michelle's car drives smoothly, so smoothly that when Hannah looks at the speedometer, she sees that she is going almost twenty miles over the limit. She knows she should slow down, but there is something heartening in the movement of the car. She realizes that she was disappointed to leave. Underneath it all, she must have harbored some secret belief that the others would return from the bar, that Todd would have tired of Michelle, and that she, Hannah, would end up making out with him – that, by the end of the night, she would have kissed someone. But now she is glad to be gone. If she and Todd ran into each other tomorrow on the street, he probably wouldn't recognize her.

As her disappointment fades, so does her resentment toward Jenny. It *would* be unnerving for a guy to say he loved you a few hours after meeting. Only in theory does it sound appealing. Either way, it is difficult for Hannah to imagine such an event in her own life. She wonders how long it will be before she kisses someone, before she has

76

sex, before a guy tells her he loves her. She wonders if these delays are due to something she does that other girls don't do, or something they do that she doesn't. Maybe she will never kiss anyone. By the time she is old, she will be as rare as a coelacanth: a fish, according to her Evolutionary Biology textbook, that was thought to have gone extinct seventy million years ago until one was found off Madagascar in the 1930s, and then again in a marketplace in Indonesia. She will be lobe-finned and blue-scaled and soundless, gliding alone through dark water.

Half an hour elapses in silence. Just after they pass a sign advertising a truck stop at the next exit, Jenny says, 'Want some coffee? My treat.'

'Do you want some?' Hannah says. She doesn't drink coffee.

'If you don't mind.'

Hannah puts on the turn signal and pulls off the highway. From the end of the exit, she can see a blazing hundred-foot sign featuring the name of the truck stop, and a mostly empty parking lot aglow with light. She waits for the stoplight to change.

'Weird,' Jenny says. 'I'm having déjà vu.'

'About the truck stop?'

'About everything. This car, you driving.'

'Déjà vu is when your eyes absorb a situation faster than your brain,' Hannah says. 'That's what I read somewhere.' Jenny doesn't respond, and then – Hannah can feel herself blurting this out, talking quickly and breathlessly – she says, 'But that's such a boring explanation. It's so clinical. Sometimes I think about, like, ten years from now, I think, what if I get married and have kids and I live in a house and what if some night my husband and I are making dinner and I'm chopping vegetables or something and I have déjà vu? What if I'm like, oh, wait, this is all familiar? I just think that would be really weird, because it would be like I always knew that things were going to end up okay. I knew that I would turn out happy.' Hannah's heart is pounding. 'That probably sounds strange,' she says.

'No.' Jenny seems very serious in this moment, almost sad. 'It doesn't sound strange at all.'

They turn in to the parking lot. Advertisements for a sale on two-liters of soda hang in the window, and behind the counter, Hannah can see two women in red smocks. The whole complex seems to buzz with electricity.

'I haven't hooked up with that many guys,' Hannah says.

Jenny laughs softly. 'You're lucky,' she says.

CHAPTER 3

APRIL 1997

Riding the T back to school after her appointment with Dr Lewin, Hannah takes notes on their conversation. *Jared probably flattered*, she writes. *Why freakish gesture? Why not thoughtful?* She is using her Islamic Art notebook, and in the dorm, she'll rip out the paper and stick the notes in the manila file she keeps in the top drawer of her desk. When enough pieces of paper have accumulated, Hannah will, she hopes, understand the secret of happiness. It is not clear how long this will take, but so far Hannah has been seeing Dr Lewin for a year, every Friday afternoon since her freshman spring. Dr Lewin charges Hannah ninety dollars an hour, a seemingly outrageous amount that actually reflects a sliding-fee scale. To cover this cost without asking either of her parents for money – that is, without telling her parents she is seeing a psychiatrist – Hannah has gotten a job shelving books in the veterinary library. 'What are you worried it will make them think?' Dr Lewin once asked, and Hannah said, 'I just don't want to talk about it with them. I don't see the point.'

Dr Lewin is in her late thirties, trim and fit; Hannah guesses she is a runner. She has dark curly hair that she keeps short, fair skin, and intense blue eyes. She favors white or striped button-down shirts and black pants. They meet in the finished basement of Dr Lewin's large gray stucco house in Brookline. According to the diplomas on the wall in Dr Lewin's office, she attended Wellesley College, graduating summa cum laude, and went on to medical school at Johns Hopkins University. Hannah has a hunch Dr Lewin is Jewish, though *Lewin* does not sound to Hannah like a Jewish name. Dr Lewin has two elementary-school-age sons who appear to be adopted, perhaps from Central or South America – in the framed photo on Dr Lewin's desk, they have caramel-colored skin. Hannah knows nothing of Dr Lewin's husband. At times she imagines him as a fellow psychiatrist, a man Dr Lewin met at Hopkins who admired her intelligence and seriousness, but at other times (Hannah has a preference for this version) Hannah imagines him as a sexy carpenter, a smoldering guy with a tool belt who also, though in a different way, admires Dr Lewin's intelligence and seriousness.

The subject they talked about in today's session was how Hannah gave a bottle of cough syrup to a guy in her sociology class named Jared. It's a small class, only twelve students, and the professor is an earnest bearded guy who wears jeans. The students all sit around a large table, and Hannah and Jared usually sit next to each other and never talk, though a benign energy sometimes passes between them; she suspects he is noticing the same things she is, finding the same other students amusing or annoying. Jared dresses in a very particular style that is possibly punk or possibly gay: large red or navy or olive denim shorts that are much longer than normal shorts, hanging well past his knees; white tube socks that he pulls up over his thin ankles and calves; suede sneakers; and nylon warm-up jackets that zip in the front and have vertical white stripes on the arms. If you leave the classroom behind him, you can see a silver chain running between a back pocket and a front pocket, conspicuously connecting something Hannah isn't sure of (a wallet?) to something else she isn't sure of (keys? a pocket watch?). He has dyed black hair and she sees him around campus on a skateboard, with other guys who dress about like he does, and with a girl who has her right eyebrow pierced.

What made Hannah give Jared the cough syrup was, logically enough, that he was coughing a lot for several classes in a row. Sitting next to him one day, Hannah had a sudden memory of a bottle of cough syrup in a box in her dorm closet, left over from when she would take it to get to sleep. (She stopped last year around the time she became friends with Jenny, which is also the time she found a therapist.) The bottle still had a clear seal over the cap; the syrup was cherry flavored. When Hannah placed it in her backpack before the next class, she noticed that the expiration date on it had passed, but whatever, right? It wasn't like it was milk. She gave it to him as they were leaving the classroom – when she said, a few steps behind him, 'Jared?' it was the first time she had used his name – and he seemed first mildly confused and then, after she explained, mildly pleased. He thanked her and turned again and kept walking. They did not begin walking together, not even just out of the building. The next time the class met, which was today, he said nothing to her, in fact they never made eye contact, which Hannah thinks might be unprecedented for them. As the minutes of the class ticked away, Hannah felt a building, billowing regret, practically a nausea. Why is she so fucking weird? Why did she give this punky boy she's never talked to expired cough syrup? Did she think she was flirting? Also, what if the expiration date on cough syrup actually does matter and there was gross cherry mold floating inside when he opened the bottle, *if* he opened the bottle, although he probably wouldn't have and his cough is merely from using some kind of new club drug Hannah has never heard of.

Listening to all of this, Dr Lewin remained, as always, unfazed: less concerned with discussing whether Jared now sees Hannah as strange than why Hannah herself thinks she wanted to give him the cough syrup, why Jared would have interpreted the syrup as anything other than a gesture of kindness, and what non-syrup-related reasons might have caused him not to make eye contact with Hannah during today's class.

'You want me to name actual reasons?' Hannah asked.

Dr Lewin nodded calmly. (*Oh, Dr Lewin*, Hannah sometimes thinks, *let it be true that you're as decent and well adjusted as you appear! Let the life you have put together be genuinely gratifying, make you exempt from all the nuisances and sorrows of everyone else.*)

'I don't know – maybe if he was tired because he stayed up all night writing a paper,' Hannah said. 'Or if he had a disagreement with his roommate.'

Both perfectly plausible, Dr Lewin said. Also, she did not see a reason for Hannah to announce to Jared in class this coming Monday, in case he hadn't noticed it, the fact of the cough syrup's expiration. Dr Lewin considered there to be no major health risk, and she is, after all, a doctor.

The way Hannah ended up seeing Dr Lewin was by calling the Tufts student health services center and getting a referral. What prompted her to call the student health services center – who prompted her – was Elizabeth. They talk on the phone every few months, and once Elizabeth called on a Friday at seven P.M. and awakened Hannah. 'You're taking a nap?' Elizabeth asked, and Hannah said, 'Sort of.' That Sunday, Elizabeth called again and said, 'I want to tell you something, and you have to understand this isn't a comment on your personality, which is spectacular. I think you're depressed and you should find a therapist.' Hannah did not reply immediately, and Elizabeth said, 'Are you offended?' 'No,' Hannah said. She wasn't. The possibility that she was depressed had occurred to her; what hadn't occurred to her was to do anything about it. 'Some therapists are real weenies,' Elizabeth said. 'But the right one can make a difference.' Dr Lewin was the first person Hannah called from the list she received, and she liked her right away. In fact, Dr Lewin initially reminded Hannah of Elizabeth, but as time passed, Hannah saw that this was a false association, no doubt sprung from the circumstances of her seeking therapy, and the two women were not particularly similar at all.

By the time Hannah is back in her room, it is nearly six o'clock. She opens the top desk drawer, inserts the new piece of notebook paper into the manila file, slides the drawer shut, and sits there a minute at the desk, motionless. She is scheduled to work in the veterinary library tonight, a prospect that makes her think, *Thank God.* Friday-night intimidation, the impulse to hide in her room, doesn't overtake her as easily if she knows there's a place she's supposed to be later on. She can sometimes swing by the cafeteria, not to eat a real meal, but she'll pick up an apple or a granola bar. And then, in the library, sliding the books in their clear plastic sheaths onto the metal shelves, tidying the gray or pale blue periodicals, the table of contents on their covers listing the articles – 'Equine Arthroscopic Surgery of the Musculoskeletal System' – in the quiet stacks, in the unstrenuously preoccupying and repetitive activity of those moments, Hannah is almost peaceful.

It is three o'clock on Saturday when the phone rings. Hannah is reading about sixteenth-century Iznik tiles, has talked to no one since Friday night, and is expecting Jenny's voice on the other end when she picks up the receiver. Now that it's warm, she and Jenny have been getting frozen yogurt together on Saturday afternoons. Instead, it is Hannah's cousin Fig who says, 'So I'm calling to check on Granny.'

'What are you talking about?'

'Oh, God,' Fig says. 'Oh, no. Oh, that's horrible. Yes, of course.' In a whisper, Fig adds, 'Play along.' Resuming her loud voice – her abnormally, theatrically loud voice, Hannah realizes – Fig adds, 'Yeah, I guess I should. I don't know, maybe if you can come get me. Really, you don't mind?'

'Fig?'

'The house where I'm staying is in Hyannis. You basically have to follow Three South and then you pick up Six, and then once you get into town, you take Barnstable Road – are you writing this down?'

Hannah is silent before asking, 'Is that a pretend question or are you actually talking to me?'

Again in a whisper, practically hissing, Fig says, 'I'm with this professor, but he's being really lame and I want to leave. I need you to find Henry and get him to drive here. He's not answering his phone, but if you go over to SAE, he's probably outside playing Frisbee, or just ask someone where he is. Oh,' she adds, now loudly and forlornly, 'I can't believe it, either. It happens fast sometimes.'

'You're acting bizarre,' Hannah says. 'Is something dangerous going on?'

'I'm pretending Granny just died,' Fig whispers. 'Can you leave right now?'

'You mean Granny who's been dead for four years?'

'Hannah, what did I just tell you? Play along. Were you writing down the directions before?' Fig gives them again, and this time Hannah does write them down, though Fig is going fast in her strange voice. 'You've been to the Cape, right?' Fig asks.

'Cape Cod?'

'No, the Cape of Good Hope. For Christ's sake, Hannah, what do you think?'

'Sorry,' Hannah says. 'I've never been. Does Henry know how to get there?'

'Oh, please don't be upset,' Fig says. 'Hannah, it was her time.'

'You're kind of creeping me out.'

Whispering again, Fig says, 'I'll explain it in the car.' Then, louder, 'Drive safely, okay? Bye, Han.'

'Give me the number there,' Hannah says, but Fig has already hung up the phone.

In the middle of switching T lines to get from Davis Square to the BU West stop, it occurs to Hannah that perhaps she should have taken a cab. Is time of the essence? *Is* Fig in danger? Sigma Alpha Epsilon turns out to be a redbrick townhouse with a semicircular front stoop and, over the stoop, a roof, also semicircular, supported by skinny Ionic columns; two guys, one shirtless, sit on the roof on lawn chairs, the chairs taking up almost all the space behind a black wrought-iron railing. Holding her hand above her eyes, Hannah squints up at them. 'Excuse me,' she says. 'I'm looking for Henry.' She realizes she has no idea what Henry's last name is. She has met him just once, a few months ago, when she was visiting Fig's dorm room. He is a senior, two years older than Fig and Hannah. He was handsome, which was not surprising, and nice, which was; unlike any of Fig's previous boyfriends, he asked Hannah questions about herself.

'You gotta tell us what Henry did before we tell you where he is,' one of the guys says. 'That's the rule.'

Hannah hesitates, then says, 'I'm his girlfriend's cousin – Fig's cousin.'

'You're *Fig's* cousin,' the shirtless guy repeats, and both of them laugh. Hannah is tempted to say, *It's an emergency*, but she doesn't know if it really is, and also it feels awkward to change the tenor of the exchange so drastically. The guys are friendly, and it's her own fault for not conveying urgency sooner.

Trying to sound cheerful, she says, 'I'm so sorry, but I'm sort of in a hurry. I heard he might be playing Frisbee?'

The shirtless guy stands, leans over the railing, and points inside the house. 'He's watching the game.'

'Thanks.' Hannah quickly climbs the steps. The door is painted red, propped open with a tan plastic wastebasket, and as she pushes the heavy wood, she hears one of them say, 'Bye, Fig's cousin.' She is glad, because it must mean she didn't seem completely humorless.

It is darker inside than out, and the television is enormous. She stands in the threshold of the living room – one guy looks over at her, then looks away – and observes the backs of perhaps seven guys' heads. The guys are arranged on various chairs and sofas. She's pretty sure the one who's Henry is a few feet in front of her, and she walks around the side of the sofa. 'Henry?' she says – it's definitely him – and when he turns, she sets her hand against her collarbone. 'It's Hannah,' she says. 'I don't know if you remember me – we met before – with Fig—?'

Whatever she imagined he'd do – jump to attention, maybe – he doesn't. 'Hi,' he says, and he looks quizzical.

'Can I talk to you for a second?' Hannah gestures to the entry hall. 'Out there?'

When they've retreated from the television, Henry stands before her with his arms crossed, though not unpleasantly. He's about six feet tall, wearing a plain white T-shirt and blue athletic shorts and flip-flops. His hair is dark brown, almost black, and his eyes are also brown. He is so cute, so exactly the image of what you think a boyfriend should be when you are nine or ten years old – what you think your own boyfriend will be, your birthright – that he breaks Hannah's heart a little. She hardly knows him (maybe he isn't that great), but it's still unfair that only some girls grow up to get boys like this.

Hannah takes a breath. 'Fig needs us to go get her. She's with her professor.'

'What are you talking about?'

She'd assumed he would know everything, and then be able to explain it to her. That he is reacting exactly the way Hannah herself did is unnerving and intriguing.

'She called me' – Hannah glances at her watch – 'about an hour ago. She wants us to go pick her up. She's in Hyannis.'

'Is she with Mark Harris?'

'Is that her professor?'

'Her professor – yeah, right.'

'He's not?'

Henry regards Hannah for a few seconds. 'Fig and I aren't really together anymore,' he says. 'I get the feeling she hasn't told you that.'

So therefore what? Does Hannah go back to Tufts now? She's not expected to rent a car and get Fig on her own, is she? It's conceivable that this is the errand's abrupt termination. Yet she also can feel that Henry is not completely averse. He's not saying no; it's more like he wants to be on the record as reluctant.

'I don't think Fig is in *danger*,' Hannah says, and is half disgusted with herself for being so accommodating. *Here, my self-centered cousin, and here, her wishy-washy quasi-boyfriend, allow me to simultaneously push the situation toward the outcome you both desire while alleviating any discomfort you might feel.* 'But,' Hannah adds, 'she didn't sound quite like herself.'

'Hyannis is like seventy miles from here,' Henry says.

Hannah says nothing. She holds his gaze. Whatever convincing Henry is an exercise in, and however compromising to Hannah herself, she's surprisingly good at it.

Finally, Henry sighs and looks away. 'You have directions?'

Hannah nods.

'My keys are upstairs,' Henry says. 'I'll meet you out front.'

★   ★   ★

90

She wishes she had sunglasses, but otherwise it's so nice to be headed down the highway on a perfect late-April afternoon, so nice just to be going somewhere. She hasn't ridden in a car since she was home for spring break over a month ago. And she was prepared for Henry to listen to some terrible kind of male music – heavy metal or maybe pretentious white-men rappers – but the CD that's playing is Bruce Springsteen. Quite possibly, this is the happiest Hannah has ever been in her entire life.

Henry does have sunglasses, with a faded purple strap, a sporty strap, around the back. He keeps an atlas in the car, already folded open to a two-page spread, also faded, of Massachusetts. 'You're navigating,' he said when they got in the car, and when Hannah saw how far away Hyannis was, a flash of excitement went off inside her.

They don't talk at first, except Hannah saying, 'Do you need to take Ninety-three to get on Three?' and Henry shaking his head. Almost half an hour has passed by the time he turns down the volume on the car stereo.

'So she just called you out of the blue and said "Come get me"?' he asks.

'More or less.'

'You're a good cousin, Hannah.'

'Fig can be pretty persuasive.'

'That's one way to put it,' Henry says. Hannah does not point out that he, too, is in the car.

They don't speak – 'I got laid off down at the

lumberyard,' sings Bruce Springsteen – and then Hannah says, 'I think I got frustrated with her more when we were younger. In the beginning of high school, especially, because that's when Fig would get invited to parties by juniors and seniors. Or I'd hear people talking about something that had happened, like she'd been doing Jell-O shots in the parking lot at the basketball game, and I'd think, wait, my cousin Fig? *That* Fig?' The fact that Henry seems vaguely annoyed, and the fact that he's Fig's – even if he and Fig are broken up, he's still Fig's, and off-limits to Hannah – are both liberating, and Hannah feels uncharacteristically chatty. It's not like she's trying to appear attractive to him, or to impress him; she can just relax. 'Of course, I'm not sure I even wanted to go to junior and senior parties,' she continues. 'Probably I wanted to be invited more than I wanted to go. I'm kind of a dork, though.'

'Or maybe Jell-O shots aren't your thing,' Henry says.

'I've actually never tried one.' She wonders if this seems to him like a confession. If so – ha! Given that she still hasn't even kissed anyone, Jell-O shots are the least of what she's never tried. 'But my main point about Fig is that you don't expect her to meet you fifty-fifty,' Hannah says. 'You sort of appreciate her good qualities and don't take it too personally when she blows you off.'

'Which good qualities are you referring to?'

Hannah glances at him. 'You've spent time with her,' Hannah says. 'You know what she's like.'

'True,' Henry says. 'But I'm curious about what you mean specifically.'

'Why don't you go first?'

'You want me to say what I like about Fig?'

'That's what you're asking me to do.'

'The two of you didn't just break up,' he says. 'But I'll play.' He switches into the left lane, passes a Volvo, switches back. He is a good and also a confident driver. 'First of all, she's gorgeous.'

Blah, blah, blah, Hannah thinks.

Henry looks over. 'That's not offensive, right? I'm allowed to say that a good-looking girl is good-looking?'

'Of course you're allowed to,' Hannah says. The only thing that could be more boring than talking about Fig's prettiness is talking about how Henry's entitled to talk about it.

'It's not only looks,' Henry says. 'But I'd be lying if I claimed that's not a factor. Also, she's a wild card.'

This, Hannah suspects, is a euphemism for good in bed.

'She keeps you guessing,' Henry continues. 'She has so much energy, and she's up for anything. If it was three in the morning and you said, "I want to go skinny-dipping in the Charles right now," she'd be like, "Great!"'

Okay, Hannah thinks. *I've gotten the idea.*

Then Henry says, 'All of which I guess makes it not that surprising that she sees me as a big fuddy-duddy.'

'Yeah, but Fig likes fuddy-duddies.'

'You think so?'

'She needs an audience. It's like she's defined in contrast to whoever's around her.' Hannah has never discussed this, but she's pretty sure she believes what she's saying. 'When we were in sixth grade, there was a girl named Amanda on our softball team who was always goofing off – she could play "Yankee Doodle" on her armpit, or she'd be doing cartwheels while the coach was trying to explain stuff to us, but it was obvious he still liked her. When we drove in the van, Amanda sat in the front seat and chose the radio station. She'd say, "Drive straight, Coach Halvorsen," and then he'd swerve. It was like Amanda was out-Figging Fig. And Fig hated her.'

'Wait a second,' Henry says. 'This girl played "Yankee Doodle" on her *armpit*?'

'It was sort of her special trick.'

'Well, no wonder Fig was threatened.'

Hannah smiles. 'I guess you're right that it was unusual, but I never thought about it,' she says. 'Amanda would pull up her shirt and flap her arm, like she was pretending to be a chicken, and her armpit would squeak.'

'Geez, and I thought I was cool because I could turn my eyelids inside out.'

'I remember that,' Hannah says. 'That's what

94

the boys I rode the bus with would do, and all the girls would scream.'

'So what was your elementary-school talent? You can't say you didn't have one.'

The only thing Hannah can remember right now is not what you say to a cute guy. But again: He's Fig's. She isn't trying to lure him. 'In fourth grade,' she says, 'in the middle of social studies, I once sneezed and farted at the same time.'

Henry laughs.

'I denied that it was me. I was sitting near the back of the room, and all the kids around me had heard and were like, "Who was that?" and I said, "*Obviously* it wasn't me, because I'm the one who sneezed."'

'That was very clever of you.'

'They probably thought it was Sheila Waliwal, who was this scapegoat for everything gross or weird in our class. She was the first one to get her period, when we were in fifth grade, and all hell broke loose. Sheila was hiding in a stall while the rest of the girls were freaking out, running in and out of the bathroom. And Fig was at the helm – she was like the director and producer of Sheila's period.'

'That actually sounds sort of sweet.'

'I guess all the girls did rise to the occasion. I think we were just so happy it wasn't one of us who'd gotten it first, although looking back, for all I know, there were girls who had gotten theirs already but just didn't tell everyone. But Sheila told Fig, which was the same as making a public announcement.'

'When my twin sister got her period,' Henry says, 'my dad congratulated her at the dinner table. I almost couldn't finish eating. We were thirteen, meaning I looked and acted about nine and Julie looked and acted about twenty-five.'

'I didn't know you're a twin,' Hannah says. 'I always thought that would be fun.'

'You and Fig are almost like twins. You're just a couple months apart, right?'

'She's three months older,' Hannah says. 'But it's not the same. We grew up in different houses, with different parents. Besides, the cool part of being a twin—'

'Are you going to say the ESP? Because Julie and I can't do that at all.'

'Actually, I was going to say the slumber parties. I used to think if I had a boy twin, he'd invite his friends over and I could eavesdrop and find out who they had crushes on.'

'More like when Julie had slumber parties, I'd be banished from the house. One time that I was supposed to stay over at my friend's, he got sick at the last minute and I couldn't go. My mom just wigged out, like, "Don't make Julie's friends uncomfortable. Don't play any tricks on them." Not that I was planning to – I was probably more uncomfortable than they were. But my mom made me sleep in her and my dad's room, in a sleeping bag on the floor by their bed. All night long, every few hours, she'd sit straight up and say, "Henry, are you still there?"'

'Where did you grow up?' Hannah asks.

'New Hampshire. Live free or die.'

'I grew up outside Philly. Well, duh – the same as Fig. I have no idea of the state motto, though.'

Without hesitating, Henry says, '"Virtue, liberty, and independence."'

'Really?'

'Massachusetts: "By the sword we seek peace, but peace only under liberty." That's a tricky one.'

'Are you making these up?'

'We had to memorize them in social studies,' Henry says. 'That's what some of us did while others were busy farting.'

Hannah hits his arm with the back of her hand. It's light, more of a tap, but right away she has the highly unpleasant memory of her father's warning never to touch the driver. 'Sorry,' she says.

'For what?' Henry asks.

Still thinking of her father, Hannah wonders, are there situations, long-term situations, where conflict does not wait around every bend, where time does not unspool only in anticipation of your errors? It's like imagining an enchanted mountain village in Switzerland. Aloud, she says, 'I'm sorry for doubting you. What about Alaska – do you know that one?'

'"North to the future."'

'Missouri?'

'"The welfare of the people shall be the supreme law." Some of these are translated from Latin.'

'Maryland?'

'"Manly deeds, womanly words."'

'That is *not* the state motto of Maryland,' Hannah says.

'What is it, then?'

'What would "Manly deeds, womanly words" even mean? What's a manly deed or a womanly word?'

'I think a manly deed is something like splitting wood. And a womanly word is . . . *mascara*, maybe? *Doily*? By the way, am I right in assuming I just stay on Three until the Sagamore Bridge?'

Hannah picks up the atlas by her feet. 'It looks like after that, Three turns into Six, which is the same as the Mid-Cape Highway. You have about ten miles.' They both are quiet, and then she asks, 'So why are you a fuddy-duddy?'

'I mostly meant compared to Fig. I'm just not that into partying. When you're single, you go out a lot, but being in a relationship – sometimes I just wanted to stay in and chill out. But your cousin likes to have fun. She likes her rum and Cokes, right?'

'Her partying isn't why you broke up, is it?'

'We're overall headed in different directions. I'm graduating in a couple weeks, and I'll be working as a consultant, which means crazy hours. And the fact that Fig still has two more years of school – it's cleaner this way than constantly wondering what she's up to.' So Fig cheated on him. That must be what he means. 'But it's like you said,' he continues. 'Accept Fig for her good qualities, and don't expect too much of her.'

Did Hannah say that? She can barely remember now.

'Mark Harris isn't a real professor, by the way,' Henry adds. 'He's some jackass T.A. grad student studying, like, Chaucer – he's Mr *Sensitive*. And he's been after Fig since the fall.'

'Is he her T.A.?'

'Not this semester. But the guy's just a total sleazeball. I seriously wouldn't be surprised if he wears a velvet cape.' Hannah laughs, but Henry doesn't. He says, 'What kind of T.A. has a house on Cape Cod? It has to be his parents', doesn't it?' He shakes his head. 'I've gotta say that a part of me really wants to turn the car around.'

At first Hannah says nothing. There was the suddenness of Fig's call, and immediately, the situation had its own momentum. But really, who knows what's going on? She thinks of when she and Fig were little, how Fig would come over to play and they'd be drawing or baking cookies and then, without warning, Fig would want to leave when Hannah had thought they were having a perfectly good time. It even happened in the middle of the night, and Hannah's father, who considered Fig a brat, eventually barred her from staying over.

The likelihood that Fig is presently in harm's way is slim. It's probably just that she got sick of the T.A., whom Hannah now pictures, because of the velvet cape, as Sir Walter Raleigh. But if Hannah and Henry turn around, their time together will be over sooner. The reasons she wants to continue have little to do with Fig.

'I think we should keep going,' Hannah says. 'I just do. So, want to hear a weird story?'

'If you're trying to distract me, you're not being very subtle.'

'No, I really want to tell you this. The other day' – she was planning, actually, to bring this up with Dr Lewin yesterday, but then there wasn't time – 'I was in poli sci, which is a lecture. And I was sitting kind of close to the front, and I thought, *The next person who walks through the auditorium door, I'm going to marry.* It was just this idea that popped into my head. And then the door started to open, but it shut again without anyone coming through. So do you think that means my destiny is to be alone?'

'Did anyone come in after that?'

'Yeah, but no one had come through that time, which had been when I had the thought.'

'You're not serious, are you?'

'It's not like I definitely believe it, but it was a pretty weird coincidence.'

'Hannah, you're insane. That's the most ludicrous

thing I've ever heard. What if a girl had walked in the door – would you have thought you were supposed to marry her?'

'Well, maybe I meant the next *guy* who walks through.'

'But more guys *did* come through, right?'

'I guess so, although not—'

'If you don't want to get married, fine. But you can't think some weird mind game you're playing with yourself is the determinant.'

'You never do that? Like, "If I wake up right on the hour, I'll get an A on my paper"?'

'"If I find a penny, I'll have good luck"?'

'Not generic superstitions,' Hannah says. 'Ones you invented but you feel like they're true. You barely remember inventing them.'

'"If a snowflake falls into my left ear, I'll win the lottery."'

'Never mind,' she says. For his benefit, she pretends to sulk.

'"If I pass a giraffe on the sidewalk, I'll grow a third nipple,"' he says.

'Very funny.'

'"If I sneeze and fart at the same time—"'

'I'm seriously never telling you anything again.'

'What?' Henry grins. 'Did I hurt your feelings?' With the middle finger and thumb of his right hand, he flicks the side of Hannah's head. It is thrilling – first, that he's touching her for no reason. Also it makes it okay that she hit his arm before. In the math of their knowing each other, she'd been at a deficit, but now they're even. Then he says, 'I bet you believe in love at first sight, too,' and her heart feels like it's warm and liquidy. Isn't he *definitely* flirting with her?

But her voice sounds surprisingly normal when she says, 'Why – do you not believe in it?'

'I believe in attraction at first sight,' Henry says, and his voice sounds normal, too, no longer teasing. 'And then maybe you fall in love as you get to know each other. I guess I believe in chemistry at first sight.'

She is on a balance beam, and if she says anything too corny or too clinical, she'll tip to one side. But possibly, if she says the exact right thing, Henry will fall in love with her. (No, of course he won't! He's Fig's ex-boyfriend! And any guy who would go out with a girl like Fig in the first place . . . Also, he can't be flirting with Hannah, because doesn't having a conversation about romantic topics automatically mean they don't apply to the people discussing them? If Henry felt remotely attracted to Hannah, wouldn't this all seem way too obvious?) 'I'm not sure what I think,' she says.

Henry shakes his head. 'Cop-out. Try again.'

'Then I guess I'd say I don't believe in love at first sight. Does that disappoint you?'

'What about the guy who was going to walk through the auditorium door?'

'We wouldn't have fallen in love that day. That would have just been a preview. Maybe we wouldn't even have talked in that class, or for the rest of this year, but then next year we'd have another class together and that's when we'd meet.'

'That's a pretty elaborate plan.'

'Well, it's not like I'd thought it all out. I'm just saying because you're asking me.'

'It's interesting,' Henry says, 'because Fig is kind of crazy, and you're kind of crazy, but you're crazy in really different ways.'

'And what way are you crazy?'

'I already told you, I'm your typical all-American bore. I played baseball in high school. We had a golden retriever. My parents are still married.'

'And now you're going to be a consultant – that seems like a good job for a boring person.'

'Touché,' Henry says, but – she checks – he's smiling.

'You did just call me crazy.'

'Maybe I should have said eccentric. You definitely seem a lot more down-to-earth than Fig,' he says.

'Actually – well, first, I don't think I'm crazy. But second, I sort of think guys like a certain amount of craziness in girls. All the time, I see guys going out with girls who are just so whiny and moody. They're so *irrationally* whiny and moody.'

'What about girls who go out with jerks?'

'It's not the same. The kind of girl I'm talking about, she's always complaining or crying or making a scene. I just think if I were her boyfriend,

103

I wouldn't stay with her five more minutes. But the fact that he does stay must mean he likes the drama.'

'You never know from the outside what two people are giving each other.' The way Henry says it, evenly, makes Hannah pretty sure he's had several serious girlfriends; he seems mature and knowledgeable, as though he is speaking, unlike Hannah, from experience. 'What's visible to everyone else is only half the story,' he says. 'Plus, don't we act the way we're expected to? If your girlfriend is freaking out, of course you try to talk her down in the moment, even if she's not being completely logical. It's sort of a squeaky-wheel thing.'

'That makes it seem like if you want a boyfriend, you should just be a big pain in the ass.'

'I'd say your chances are better if you're wearing a low-cut shirt at the time.'

'So you don't agree with me?'

'I'm sure you're right in some cases, but you're making an awfully broad generalization.'

Hannah is quiet; her giddiness has passed. Obviously, she is pushing away Henry with her theory of high-maintenance girls – he's being diplomatic but isn't particularly interested. Yet the distance that's arising between them is almost a relief; the fever pitch of her own hope before was too much.

A few minutes pass, and Henry says, 'How you doing over there?'

'I'm okay.' But the air is also turning: She can feel out the open window that it's becoming evening. When they cross the Sagamore Bridge, she tells herself not to pretend that she is thirty-one and Henry is thirty-three and their two kids (a six-year-old and a four-year-old) are in the back; tells herself not to pretend they are going for the weekend to a cottage on the beach. It's just that college dating, all the rituals and weird outfits and coded things you're supposed to say — they seem so removed from her particular desired outcome. It would be better if she were ten years older, past the time when she's supposed to be fun and kicky. All she really wants is someone to order takeout with, someone to ride beside in the car, exactly like this except she'd be playing the female lead instead of the supporting actress; she'd convince Henry to drive somewhere not for Fig but for *her*.

The Cape is tackier than she expected. She pictured it preppy, but there are lots of strip malls. They are nearing Hyannis, and then they are in Hyannis. Their conversation tapered off about twenty minutes ago, and Henry's voice is practically a surprise when he says, 'You see that Mexican place? Are you hungry at all?'

'I guess so,' Hannah says. 'Sure.'

Inside, the restaurant has a fast-food feel, though Hannah doesn't think it's a chain. They both get burritos — in some gesture toward being ladylike, she declines guacamole and sour cream — then carry them outside to a picnic table near the road. Henry sits on top of the table, so Hannah does, too. They are facing the cars, which is almost like watching television; it takes the pressure off talking.

Hannah is nearly finished with her burrito when Henry says, 'It's not that you're wrong about guys liking needy girls – I'd basically say you're right. But I think what you're under-estimating is how much it means to a guy to be needed. It sounds really silly, but if a girl's relying on you and you come through for her, you feel like a superhero.'

Why, exactly, is this so depressing for Hannah to hear?

'In the long term, the girl who can't take care of herself isn't who you want to end up with,' Henry says. 'But for a while – I don't know. It's pretty fun. The lows are lower, but the highs are really fucking high.'

Hannah keeps watching the cars. She sort of detests him.

He is talking more slowly when he says, 'I know I only met you once before today, but you seem like you have your act together. You don't seem like you need rescuing.'

Is the depressing part that he's only half right – it's not that she doesn't need rescuing but that nobody else will be able to do it? She has always somehow known that she is the one who will have to rescue herself. Or maybe what's depressing is that this knowledge seems like it should make life easier, and instead it makes it harder.

'You realize that's a good thing, don't you?' Henry says. He pauses and then says, 'You shouldn't think you won't get married, because you're exactly the kind of girl a guy marries.'

She is afraid to look at him, afraid to react. She is bewildered because he has given her one of two types of compliments, but the types are opposites. He's speaking either from pity or else from attraction. He's comforting her, or else he's revealing something about himself. And she should be slightly insulted by his brotherly friendliness, or else she should be embarrassed – a good and happy embarrassed – by his declaration. Pleadingly, she thinks, *Just say a little bit more. Go one step further. Make it definitely not pity.* She looks at him sideways, and when their eyes meet, his expression is serious. If he were speaking out of pity, wouldn't he be smiling encouragingly? She looks back at the traffic and says softly, 'Yeah, maybe.' It seems not impossible that he could kiss her or take her hand in this moment, and that perhaps whether he will hinges on if she meets his gaze again. She is delaying looking at him rather than avoiding it altogether, or at least she feels like that for the minute before he stands, crumples his burrito foil into a ball, and throws it into a metal trash bin. Abruptly, it no longer seems like he ever might have kissed her.

Back in the car, nearing the supposed street for

the house where Fig is, they make several wrong turns. Hannah suggests returning to the main road and finding someone to ask for directions. But then Henry sees the street they're looking for. It's called Tagger Point, which is not altogether different from, as Hannah had written it, *Dagger Point*; in her defense, Dagger Point seems like a much better street name for Sir Walter Raleigh.

'At least it exists,' Hannah says. 'We weren't on a wild-goose chase.' She can feel that Henry is grumpy from being lost. His grumpiness is not entirely unwelcome, though. It's a distraction, it restores normality.

'How much do you want to bet Fig is sitting on the beach having a cocktail right now?' Henry says. 'And that asshole is probably reading her a sonnet.' As he speaks, he is driving slowly, looking at addresses. It is disappointing when he turns in to a driveway of broken white shells beyond which sits a medium-sized blue shingle house – it's disappointing that their time alone together is over.

More lightheartedly than she feels, Hannah says, 'You think they're doing Jell-O shots?' and this is when Fig comes tearing out of the house. Literally, she is running. She's wearing jeans and a black V-neck cotton sweater, and over her right shoulder is a white canvas weekend bag with pale pink trim (is Hannah imagining that her mother gave this bag to Fig a few years ago for Christmas? She's kind of surprised to see Fig actually using it). Fig's long straight brown hair is flying behind her, and Hannah does not see this part at first, as Fig sprints across the yard, but after Fig opens the back door of Henry's car and tosses her bag onto the seat and climbs in and slams the door shut and says, 'Go. Start driving. Henry, *drive*' – at this moment Hannah, turning around from the front seat, notices that Fig has a split lip. It's on the lower left: a vertical cut with glistening lines of blood padding the two sides, and dryer blood in an irregular cloud going away from the cut. Also, there is an extra redness edging over the corner of her mouth onto the skin around it, and within this redness a few tiny dots, like minuscule freckles of an even deeper red hue. The car still isn't moving: Henry, too, is turned around. Fig is not crying, nor does she look like she's been crying, and she does not seem afraid. What she gives off most is an air of impatience.

'What the hell is going on?' Henry says.

'Don't even think of going in there,' Fig says. 'Start driving, or else give me the keys and I will.'

'That asshole punched you or something – is that what happened?' Henry seems both horrified and disbelieving; he seems confused.

'Can we go?' Fig says. Then, with a disdainful expression on her face, she lifts her hands and makes air quotes. '"I fell,"' she says.

Hannah can't tell if she's mocking their concern, or just the idea of bothering to pretend her split lip occurred by accident. 'Fig, are you okay?' she

109

says. 'Really – do you want us to take you to the hospital?'

Fig rolls her eyes skyward. (Does Henry also feel in this moment like Fig is the daughter and they are the parents? And not a cute six-year-old daughter in pigtails but a belligerent teenager.) 'You both need to get over yourselves,' Fig says. 'For the tenth time, can we just leave?'

At last Henry turns back to the steering wheel, and Hannah can see him intently watching Fig in the rearview mirror. As he reverses the car, pulling out of the driveway and onto the road, Hannah physically relaxes: Mark Harris won't come outside now, Henry won't try to go into the house.

'Oh, yeah,' Fig says from the back. 'Thanks for coming to get me.' Fig's ability to talk is almost normal. If Hannah couldn't see her, she might just think her cousin was speaking with food in her mouth.

'Fig, you should have told me,' Hannah says. 'I had no idea.'

Henry shakes his head. 'That guy's a caveman.'

'Guess what?' Fig says. 'Mark looks a lot worse than I do, and I'm not making that up.'

Henry glances over his shoulder. 'Are you proud of that?'

It's true that Fig sounds weirdly like she's gloating.

'Well, you don't need to avenge my honor or whatever you're thinking,' Fig says. 'I know how to take care of myself.'

110

'Clearly,' Henry says.

'You know what, Henry?' Fig says. 'Sometimes I fucking hate you.'

In the ensuing silence, Hannah realizes that the Bruce Springsteen CD has been playing continuously since she and Henry left Boston; they must have listened to the entire thing several times over by now. After a few minutes, when they are back on Main Street, Henry makes a right into a gas station.

'Oh, good idea,' Hannah says. 'Fig, we can get you a Band-Aid or something.' Later, this comment in particular makes Hannah think how foolish she is. Part of it is that she takes situations at face value. Fig and Henry are sniping at each other, which she thinks means they're angry. She really does kind of believe that if they all have a soda, they'll calm down and the ride back to Boston will be more pleasant and Henry will drop off Fig in her dorm, and Hannah will step out of the front seat to hug Fig goodbye, and then Hannah will climb back into the car and she and Henry will go out for dinner and on to the part of their lives where they become a couple. Really, she has to be the most naïve twenty-year-old in the world.

When he has turned off the ignition, Henry says to Fig, 'I want to talk to you.'

'I'll pump,' Hannah says.

They walk away, and Hannah inserts the nozzle into the gas tank. It is a pretty night, a cool spring

111

breeze rising, the edges of the sky turning pale purple. Obviously, the professor is some kind of creep, but Fig seems more or less okay, so maybe it's all right that it's been such a good day; it's sort of been a great day.

But then they don't return – wherever they went, they don't come back. Paying for the gas inside, Hannah doesn't see them among the aisles of chips and antifreeze. Just before Henry pulled into the lot, the idea Hannah had of their activities here were her standing by the sink in the women's bathroom with Fig, dabbing a wet paper towel on her cousin's face – sort of Florence Nightingale-ish – while Henry hovered outside. (Pumping air into the tires, maybe? Some background manly deed.) But there is no one in the women's bathroom, no one going in and out of the men's bathroom. Probably she knows then, but not yet consciously. She buys a bottled water and goes outside. In the parking lot, she calls, 'Fig?' then feels ridiculous. She walks around the side of the small building, and it turns out they are not so hard to find: Fig's back is against the back of the store, and Henry is kneeling before her, his arms around her waist, his face against her bare abdomen. She is rubbing his head. Though Fig's sweater is pushed up, they are both completely clothed; thank God for this. It is devastating to see – in a way, the tenderness is worse than if they were having wild sex – but it isn't shocking. In this moment, Hannah isn't shocked, and later, after she has a boyfriend, she

112

will understand how the situation called for it. Their recent breakup, Fig's injury, the painfully lovely spring night – how could they possibly stay out of each other's arms? Also, if you're part of a couple, even an estranged couple, your reunion is incomplete and unofficial until you've embraced. Even when you're just meeting in a restaurant for dinner – if you don't hug or kiss, Hannah thinks, there must be something wrong in the relation- ship. All of which is to say, they're playing their parts. They're not trying to be mean to her. Or at least that's not Henry's motivation, and it's possible to believe it's not Fig's, either, until she turns her head in Hannah's direction and smiles a small, closed-mouth smile. Immediately, Hannah retreats.

She leans against the outside of the car with her arms folded; she formulates a plan. She will kiss a boy. Or, ideally, several. She will kiss other boys and then someday – not tonight, obviously, and maybe not for a while – when Henry wants to kiss her, she'll be ready. He has given her a reason to prepare. She doesn't feel sad. She thinks of Jared from sociology, how distraught about the cough syrup stuff she was, and how there is very little she really knows about him. She doesn't even know if he's heterosexual. The truth is that she can't imagine anything more than being nervous around him – at best, enjoyably nervous, at worst, just nervous. But she can't picture kissing him. She's pretty sure she's not attracted to him. He's like a game she's been playing. He gives her something to think about, and something to talk about with Dr Lewin besides her parents.

With Henry, however, Hannah could sleep in a bed at night. She could eat cereal with him in the morning, or drink beer with him in a bar. Boring things, too – she could go with him to a department store to buy an umbrella, or wait in the car while he went into the post office. She could introduce him to her mother and sister. It's not that she envisions glittering romance; it's that there is no situation she cannot imagine experiencing with him, nothing she cannot imagine telling him. It seems like there would always be something to say, or if there wasn't, that would be fine, too, and not uncomfortable.

When Fig and Henry return to the car, they carry with them an exclusionary glow that Henry tries to dispel and Fig seems just fine with (once when they were fifteen, Fig got Hannah to walk four or five miles with her to some guy's house, then vanished with the guy into the attic, while Hannah sat in the kitchen waiting; embarrassingly, when the guy's mom got home, Hannah was eating a pear from the bowl on the table). Hannah does not protest when Fig slips into the front seat. Henry asks Hannah clumsily solicitous questions, as if they haven't been in the car together for two hours: When do her classes end? What are her plans for the summer?

A few days later, he e-mails her. *Hey there*

Hannah, the e-mail says. *Hope things are good with you. I found your address on the Tufts website.* (That's her favorite part, the idea of him typing in her name.) *Saturday was pretty crazy, huh? Fig and I have been hanging out, and she's doing okay. Thought you'd want to know. Take care, Henry. P.S. I'm sure I seem like a big hypocrite to you. I can just imagine if we had a conversation about it you would call me on my self-delusions.*

Hannah prints out the e-mail, and even after she has memorized all the words – the last sentence is her second-favorite part – she still sometimes looks at the hard copy. Because Hannah is not upset that Fig and Henry have gotten back together, Dr Lewin does not seem to grasp (it is highly unusual for Dr Lewin not to grasp something) that Hannah doesn't see Henry as emblematic of the type of guy she could like or be involved with; it is Henry himself, Henry specifically, with whom Hannah wants to be involved.

But again: not yet. Later, when she is more ready. This is why, driving back from the Cape, she almost doesn't mind when she is the one who gets dropped off by the two of them, she is the one hugged goodbye. As Fig climbs back into the car, Hannah leans over and waves at Henry, who remains in the driver's seat. 'Bye, Henry,' she says. 'Nice to see you again.' Is it possible he'll understand that she's using this pleasantly bland voice only as concealment?

He hesitates and then says, 'You, too, Hannah.'

It is entirely dark out as she watches the car pull away. For the first time in years, Hannah does not feel jealous of Fig, and the split lip is only part of it. It just seems like Fig is walking down a wrong road. To treat Henry the way she has – he won't allow it indefinitely, or karma won't, Hannah is certain. Before the car's taillights disappear from view, Hannah concentrates very hard, as if doing so means Fig really will receive the message, as if Hannah is capable of charging Fig with this responsibility. She thinks, *Take good care of the love of my life*.

CHAPTER 4

JULY 1998

When Hannah is home in May, before the start of her summer internship, she meets her father for lunch near his office. (Lunch is better than dinner because he is less menacing in daylight.) They go to a restaurant where they sit at a table on the sidewalk. She orders spinach ravioli, which comes in a cream sauce rather than a tomato sauce; the menu probably specified this, and she just wasn't paying attention. She takes a few bites, but it is one in the afternoon on a sunny day, and the idea of eating the whole hot, creamy bowl turns her stomach. Her father has finished his own meal, a Caesar salad with grilled chicken, when he says, 'Yours isn't any good?'

'It's all right,' Hannah says. 'Do you want some? I'm not that hungry.'

'If it's bad, send it back.'

'It's not that it's bad. I'm just not in a very pasta-ish mood.'

She knows as soon as she's said it. One of the signs with her father, the surest sign, is his nostrils. They flare now, like a bull's. 'I don't know that

I've ever heard of a pasta-ish mood,' he says. 'But I'll tell you what I do know. I know that ravioli cost sixteen dollars, and I know I'm going to watch you eat every bite.'

She can feel in herself, in equal measures, the impulse to burst into laughter and the impulse to burst into tears. 'I'm twenty-one years old,' she says. 'You can't make me finish my food.'

'Well, Hannah' – he's talking in his fake-casual voice, his tone of big-enough-to-humor-you, which actually means he won't be humoring you for long – 'here's the problem. When I see you being cavalier with money, I have to ask myself, is it really wise for me to pay your rent this summer so you can flit about at an ad agency? Maybe I'm not doing you any favors by spoiling you.' This, also, is one of her father's trademarks – the escalation. Every fight is about not just itself but all of your massive personal inadequacies, your fundamental disrespect for him.

'You're the one who encouraged me to take an unpaid internship,' Hannah says. 'You said it would look better on my résumé than nannying.'

They regard each other across the table. A waitress in black pants, a white button-down shirt, and a black apron tied around her waist passes by, carrying a tray. Wordlessly, Hannah's father points to the bowl of ravioli.

Beneath the table, Hannah is bundling her napkin, and she is telling herself not to forget her purse when she stands to leave. She swallows. 'I'm not eating it,' she says. 'And you don't need to pay my rent this summer. That probably wasn't a very good idea to begin with. You don't need to pay my tuition this year, either.'

The expression on her father's face is both shocked and delighted, as if she's told him an off-color but very funny joke. 'Hell,' he says. 'Here I was hoping to save sixteen bucks, and instead I've saved thirty thousand. I'm just curious about where you plan to find that kind of money. You think your mother can cough it up?'

Since the divorce, her mother's finances have been murky to Hannah. Years ago, her mother took a job four days a week at a store selling fancy kinds of linen and soap, but she seems to spend a good bit of her presumably modest salary on the merchandise there: The bathrooms in her condo are outfitted with the store's scalloped hand towels, its miniature bottles of English lotion. There has been alimony, obviously, and an inheritance when Hannah's maternal grandparents both died a few years back, but the sense Hannah has is more of surface genteelness than of any real security. However, she also has the sense that this surface genteelness plays a crucial role in maintaining her mother's spirits, that possibly it's a wise investment.

Regardless: Hannah stands. She hooks her purse over her shoulder. 'I guess I'll have to figure out a way,' she says. 'I don't want anything more to do with you.'

★　　★　　★

119

By ten thirty, there's still barely anyone in the office – it's the Friday before the Fourth of July – and someone from down the hall turns on the radio, tuned to a seventies station, as Hannah realizes after the fifth or sixth song. Around eleven, Sarie, who's the other intern and who's going into her senior year at Northeastern, arrives, appearing in the space where a doorway would be if the intern cubicle had a door.

'So he's completely late coming to get me,' Sarie says. 'As soon as I get in the car, he's like, 'I'm not that hungry. Want to just get coffee?' I'm like, no way, I don't want to just get coffee. Here I'd—' She mouths the words *gotten my legs waxed*. Resuming her normal voice, she says, 'I mean, I'd gone to some trouble. But I say sure. And we go to this freaking diner, not even Starbucks. I'm thinking there must be rats in the kitchen. We stay less than an hour, and then he drives me back. We're outside and he asks – this'll blow your mind, Han – he asks if he can come up.' Sarie shakes her head.

'I don't get it,' Hannah says. 'Why is that so weird?'

'He asks if he can come up for *coffee*. We'd just had coffee. How retarded is that? I didn't even answer him. I slammed the door in his face.'

'Oh,' Hannah says. 'Well, that's too bad.'

'No shit it's too bad,' Sarie says. 'If he would have taken me out for dinner, it would be a different story. But after that, forget it.' She scowls and mutters, 'Guys.'

120

'It's not all guys,' Hannah says immediately. 'It's one. Patrick, right?'

Sarie nods.

'No offense, but he sounded kind of like a dud from the beginning.'

'Yeah, you did think that, huh? I gotta listen to you more often, Han. They're all pigs.'

'They're not all pigs!' Hannah practically yells.

'I'm just yanking your chain.' Sarie grins. 'I need to run to the ladies' room.' As she turns, Hannah notices the length of Sarie's skirt, which is not very long at all: three inches below her ass, maximum; maroon; and made of a clingy material Hannah cannot identify because she owns no similar clothing. Before this summer, Hannah had not known people were allowed to come to the office wearing the sort of clothes Sarie wears. But apparently, there are many things you're allowed to do out in the wide world.

Sarie is short and curvy, and as she disappears from view, Hannah observes how nicely shaped Sarie's calves are. Sarie has what Hannah has come to believe is the type of body most preferred by most guys: not too tall, small but still voluptuous, topped off by a pleasingly bland face, and blond hair that's fakish but not definitively fake. Sarie wears skirts every day, while Hannah always wears pants. Also, Sarie wears thongs. Every time they're in the bathroom together, Sarie expounds on their virtues (they're so comfortable, they prevent panty lines) and

121

says that if only Hannah would try a thong, she'd never go back.

At moments – on the two evenings Sarie has actually persuaded Hannah to go to a bar with her and Hannah has sat there feeling huge and dull while, across the table, the men wind toward Sarie like she's some source of energy or light – Hannah has felt impressed by her. But then Hannah has thought of the afternoon Sarie said, 'Wait, is Shanghai a city or a country?' The worst part was that, possibly reacting to Hannah's shocked expression, Sarie then laughed self-consciously and said, 'That was a really stupid question, right? Don't tell anyone I said that.'

By quarter to twelve, the music coming from down the hall is so distracting that Hannah clicks off the meeting report she's been working on and pulls out a piece of company stationery. *Do laundry*, she writes at the top. Then *B-day present for Mom*. Then she can't think of anything else. She glances out at the hallway. Ted Daley, who was just promoted from cubicle to windowless office, is passing by. Their eyes meet, and he gives a little wave. 'Turn that frown upside down.' he says, and involuntarily Hannah actually does smile. 'Nice glasses,' Ted says. 'Are they new?'

'I think all this staring at the computer has affected my vision,' Hannah says. 'They're kind of nerdy.'

'No, they look really good. That's a bummer they're making you guys come in today, huh? Not being paid should have a few privileges.'

'I don't mind.' Originally, Hannah was supposed to work here five days a week, but she's ended up doing just three so she can babysit on the other days for a professor's children. Hannah tried to tell Lois, the intern supervisor, just enough about her new financial situation to make the scheduling change not seem flaky. As it's turned out, there's really not enough work to fill even three days. What there is consists primarily of sending faxes, making copies, and sitting in on meetings where senior-level employees take an hour to convey what seems to Hannah roughly three minutes' worth of information. Her main goal at this point is just to get a good recommendation she can use to apply for jobs, not in advertising, when she graduates.

'I wouldn't be here myself,' Ted says, 'but I'm going to Baja in October, and there's no way I'm wasting my vacation days.' He raises his arms as if keeping invisible walls from closing in on him and then wiggles his hips, or what he has of them. '"All I need are some tasty waves, a cool buzz, and I'm fine."'

'Huh?'

'*Fast Times at Ridgemont High*,' Ted says. 'The movie? Mid-eighties? Never mind – you were probably in kindergarten. I'm hoping to do some surfing in Baja.'

'Oh,' Hannah says. 'Cool.'

There is a lull during which Ted looks down at his watch and Hannah looks up at Ted's hearing

123

aid. *When someone with a hearing aid goes in the water*, she wonders, *does he take it out first, or are hearing aids waterproof?* Ted is only twenty-eight or twenty-nine – he's an assistant account executive – and when she arrived, she had a slight crush on him, if this is possible, *because* of his hearing aid. It made him seem sensitive, as if he had known difficulty but not difficulty so great that he'd be strange or bitter. His voice warbled endearingly, and besides that, he was tall and had green eyes. The crush passed, though, after less than a month. At a recent office happy hour she attended for sixteen minutes, she heard him having an animated conversation about what a bitch Lois is, which seemed first of all untrue to Hannah – Lois is perfectly nice – and also seemed both unwise and unbearably common. Hearing aid or not, Ted is no one special.

'We're ordering pizza for lunch,' Ted is saying. 'You want to go in on it?'

'Sure,' Hannah says. 'How much should I give?'

Ted enters the cubicle to collect the money, and Hannah instinctively flips over her list of errands, although it seems like Ted's not getting much work done right now, either. 'Writing love letters?' he asks as she reaches for her purse on the floor beneath her desk.

'Yeah, to you,' Hannah says.

'Huh?'

When she realizes he didn't hear her, she considers not repeating the joke, but then she thinks,

124

Oh, who cares? 'I was writing love letters to you,' she says more loudly.

He smiles. 'All the girls are.'

'The competition.' Hannah waves a hand in the air. 'Forget about them.'

'Is that right?' Ted says, and he's still grinning, but his expression has become a mix of curiosity and surprise. He is, Hannah realizes, appraising her, and abruptly, she can't think of anything to say.

She glances down, then looks back up at him. 'So is ten dollars okay?'

'That depends if you want to treat half the office.'

Hannah always offers to pay more than she knows she should, mainly out of a fear of appearing stingy. Most other people don't object.

'Five bucks should cover it,' Ted says. 'You'll be eating, what, two slices?' Then he adds, 'You keep writing me poetry until then,' and Hannah realizes that the mood before – the weird light energy passing between them – has been replaced with awkwardness only for her, not for him.

When the pizzas arrive, nine or ten people crowd into the kitchen. It turns out that only younger members of the staff are in today. Someone has ordered beer, and a bottle is passed to Hannah. 'I didn't pay for any,' she murmurs, but no one is listening, and then Lois, who is five months pregnant, hands Hannah the bottle opener. 'None for me,' Lois says, patting her stomach. She is eating a slice of mushroom pizza.

'So what are your plans for the Fourth?' Hannah asks.

Lois has just taken a bite, and she waves her hand in front of her mouth.

'Oh, sorry,' Hannah says.

Lois swallows. 'No major plans. Jim and I are having dinner with a few other couples.'

'Like a potluck?' Hannah asks brightly. Inside her head, she sneers at herself. Usually, she eats lunch alone, heading to a food court in the Prudential Building for Cobb salad in a clear plastic box and a waxy cup of Sprite.

'I suppose it's a potluck,' Lois says. 'But fancy, you know? I'm making dessert.'

'Oh, really? What are you making?'

'I made it last night. It's a chocolate torte Jim's mother gave me the recipe for.'

'That sounds tasty,' Hannah says. She has polished off her first slice of pizza. About thirty seconds pass, during which neither she nor Lois speaks, and Hannah begins chugging her beer. It's dark and heavy, like bitter soup.

'Hi, girls,' Sarie says, approaching them. 'How deserted is the office today?'

'You're telling me,' Lois says.

'Han, you want to come over and get dressed at my place tomorrow?'

'That's okay,' Hannah says. 'I won't be getting too decked out.'

126

'You two are hanging out for the Fourth?' Lois asks.

'Indeed we are,' Sarie says. 'My brother-in-law's apartment has a roof deck with an awesome view of the fireworks.'

Hannah tries not to cringe. But she hates herself for cringing – why does it matter what Lois thinks anyway? – and she just wishes to be away from both women. 'I'll be back in a second,' she says, and squeezes out of the kitchen.

In the hall are a cluster of men Hannah hardly knows: Ted, an AV guy named Rick, a copywriter named Stefan, and a guy whose name she can't remember. When Ted sees her, he lifts the beer out of her hand and squints at it. 'Looks like you need a replacement,' he says.

'I think one is plenty for the middle of the day,' Hannah says, but Ted has already gone into the kitchen.

'Any day when Nailand is out is definitely not a workday,' says Stefan.

'Didn't Nailand come to the office the day his wife was in labor?' Rick says, and everyone laughs.

'Actually, that's impossible, since the Nailands adopted their child,' Hannah says.

Ted is back by now, and at this comment, he leans over, puts an arm around her, and brings his mouth up to her ear as if to whisper. 'Drink your beer,' he says in a normal voice, and the guys all crack up again.

For lack of anything better to do, Hannah does

127

drink the beer. The men start talking about weekend plans, where people are traveling.

'I talked my girlfriend out of Nantucket, thank God,' Rick says. 'I fuckin' hate that scene.' Rick is the person at the agency whom Ted seems closest to, and also – this is the primary way Hannah thinks of him – someone Sarie had a fling with right when she started interning, unbeknownst to his Nantucket-loving girlfriend.

'So who's playing the crappy music so loud today?' asks Stefan.

'Watch it, dude,' says Ted.

'Does that mean it's you?' Stefan asks.

'Actually, no,' Ted says. 'But I'm not embarrassed to say that the seventies were a beautiful time musically. Show me the man who doesn't love "I Will Survive."'

'You're kidding, right?' Hannah says. 'You know that's, like, a feminist anthem, don't you?'

At this, the men positively roar with laughter, although Hannah wasn't trying to be funny.

Ted sets his beer on the floor, walks a few steps away, turns around, and takes a breath: '"First I was afraid, I was petrified / Kept thinking I could never live without you by my side . . ."'

'Goodness,' Hannah says. She re-enters the kitchen, picks up another beer, and says to Sarie and Lois, 'You guys should come see this.'

Out in the hall, Ted is prancing around singing the chorus, and the women join in, except Hannah. She's buzzed already, she's even kind

128

of smiley, but she's not drunk. She does feel pretty good, though. She rarely drinks, and then when she does, she wishes she could be tipsy all the time.

Ted's performance prompts the others to start singing songs they know all the words to: 'Stayin' Alive,' then 'Uptown Girl.' In the excitement, Lois kicks over Ted's half-full beer, but no one besides Hannah seems to notice as the liquid gets absorbed into the carpet. The atmosphere feels cheesily surreal: a scene from a sitcom about office life instead of a real office where, supposedly, people accomplish things during the day.

Then Ted grabs Hannah's shoulders from behind, whirls her around, and pulls out her arms. She laughs. But when he releases her, she stumbles backward and says, 'I've got to get back to work.'

'Work, huh?' Ted says. 'Fat chance.' Back in the intern cubicle, the walls look like they're shifting. She sits at her desk and grasps the mouse to the right of her computer monitor, checking her e-mail. No new messages, she sees, and shuts the account again quickly, before she mass-mails some incriminating message to the entire office – *I have never in my life seen so much mediocrity amassed under one roof*, or perhaps *Working with all of you is like dying a very slow death* – or, even worse, before she dashes off a declaration of love to Henry. Since the drive to Cape Cod over a year ago, they have exchanged sporadic and not particularly flirtatious e-mails (he once wrote to tell her there was an article in that day's *Globe* about state mottoes), but the e-mails are increasing in number now that Henry lives in Korea. He was transferred in March to the Seoul office of the same consultancy he worked for in Boston.

Less than twenty minutes have passed before Ted appears again. 'Hey there,' he says, and she says 'Hey' back. She feels extremely shy. It's not that she doesn't like the people here, she thinks. How could she not like them as individuals, standing before her with their own private tics and appetites, their intermittent gestures of friendliness? No, like this, like Ted is now, they're fine. She'd have to be cruel not to think they were fine. She just hadn't expected that offices – adulthood – would seem so ordinary.

'So the day is pretty much shot,' Ted says. 'We're heading over to Rick's if you want to come.'

'Where does Rick live?' Hannah asks, which feels like a pleasant way to turn down the invitation without turning it down.

'In the North End. And you're in Somerville, right? You can catch the T again at Haymarket to get home.'

Hannah is astonished that he knows where she's living this summer. 'Just give me a minute,' she says.

It is three thirty by the time they're all out on the street: Hannah, Ted, Rick, Stefan, and Sarie. The T is weirdly crowded for midday, and they

130

joke that the rest of Boston has been playing hooky while they've worked. They are talking loudly, but everyone else seems to be talking loudly, too. An electricity is in the air, the anticipation of the holiday weekend.

Rick's girlfriend isn't home when they get there. The apartment has a black leather sofa and upside-down milk crates for tables. *What an awful combination*, Hannah thinks. Then, based on the sofa, she finds herself wondering how much Rick makes.

Stefan and Ted are discussing what to get from the liquor store down the street, and Rick gives them directions. When they've left, he goes into the bedroom to change, and Hannah and Sarie sit on the sofa. 'Did I tell you about the Puerto Rican dude who called today?' Sarie says.

'I think I heard you on the phone,' Hannah says.

'It was so annoying. He was looking for some girl named Margaret, and I kept being like, "There's no intern here by that name." And he'd be like, "Please to give me Miss Margaret?"'

Hannah reaches forward and picks up an issue of *Sports Illustrated* from the milk crate in front of her. She starts paging through it, looking at the ads.

Sarie keeps talking. As the story progresses, the caller changes from Puerto Rican to Mexican. After four minutes, Hannah glances at her watch and wonders if they all would think she was really strange for the rest of the summer if she got up

131

right now and left. Then Stefan and Ted return, and what they proceed to do is get hugely, sloppily drunk – all of them and, in fact, Hannah especially. Rick brings a Trivial Pursuit set out of the bedroom, and they play for a while, but they're doing shots, and within an hour no one is getting any answers right. They abandon the game, and someone turns on the TV. Another forty-five minutes pass, and when Hannah rises from the sofa to use the bathroom, she finds she must grab Sarie's shoulder to steady herself. In the mirror above the bathroom sink, she peers at her flushed cheeks and, inexplicably, beams. The hand towels are red – the fact that Rick even owns hand towels makes her like him more – and she dries her fingers one by one, pretending she's a hand model.

When she gets back to the living room, Sarie and Ted have switched places, and the next hour is filled with intricate maneuvering and Hannah's hyperconsciousness of, and only of, any moments when she and Ted have physical contact. These moments occur increasingly frequently until they have resulted in his arm resting across her shoulders, just lightly but definitely there.

At this juncture – more and more signs indicate something will happen – Hannah returns to the bathroom, pulls a toothbrush from a cup on the sink, and brushes her teeth. In her current state, this act of borrowing feels jaunty and rather adorable.

At some point, Rick's girlfriend gets home,

carrying several shopping bags and seeming miffed, and she and Rick go down the hall and proceed to bicker loudly. It's the kind of thing that, sober, Hannah would find shamefully enthralling, but right now she is far too distracted to appreciate the drama. She closes her eyes – everything is reeling – and when she opens them, she sees Ted go into the kitchen. She can't help herself; she follows him. She has nothing to say, she has no excuse to be in there. She just wants to stay near him.

The volume of the TV has been growing progressively louder over the course of the afternoon and evening – it is past seven o'clock – and now it's blaring, lending the gathering a feel of chaos far greater than it really possesses. 'Are you having fun?' Ted calls to her when she's entered the kitchen. He is standing by the sink, filling a glass with ice. 'I'm glad you came,' he adds.

And even as he says this, she and Ted are both smirking, he is setting down the ice tray, they're tilting toward each other and leaning in until they're touching. His lips graze her jaw, that is the first instance of contact. Then comes a tiny, exquisite moment of facial negotiating – so this is kissing – and then they are making out in earnest. She never imagined that her first kiss would take place in the kitchen of a person she barely knows, with a guy who's almost thirty, while she's wearing glasses; she didn't even know you *could* kiss while wearing glasses. Also, there's a decent chance everyone in the living room can see them. But she's so drunk that who cares about any of it!

He grasps her face with both hands, his fingers gripping the back of her neck where her hairline ends, his thumbs pressed up beside her earlobes. He steps forward – into her – so their bodies meet at all points. This is not a tentative, goofy kiss; it's a pre-sex kiss. How does she recognize it? She just does. Sure enough, he pulls away but runs his palm over her hair and says, 'You want to get out of here?'

She nods.

In the living room, they bid farewell to the others. Ted makes some excuse that she barely listens to while she goes around hugging everyone except Sarie, who apparently has passed out in the bathtub. Then they stumble down the steps and out into the humid evening. They debate where to go, her apartment or his, and decide on hers because her roommates, Jenny and Kim, have already left town for the weekend. The absence of Hannah's inhibition is so pronounced it feels as if she and Ted have escaped from the company of some judgmental third party – a pursed-lipped great-aunt, perhaps.

The T is packed – she's not sure why, at this in between hour – and riding to her stop, she and Ted are standing very close and, on top of that, keep heaving into each other. Even Hannah can't tell how much of this is the jerking of the T and how much is willful on her part or Ted's. When they step out of the station at Porter Square, the sun is setting and she realizes that she's starting to sober up. It's okay, though. Surely the widest gulf is between not touching and touching, not between touching and whatever comes afterward. They head up the sidewalk and around the corner to the apartment she and Jenny and Kim are subletting. She opens the first door, then turns the lock on the second one with her key. Climbing the stairs to the second floor, she feels like all the blood in her body is surging, propelling her forward.

Inside, he says, 'Are you gonna give me the grand tour?'

Besides the unremarkable kitchen and un-remarkable living room, there are only the bedrooms. She and Jenny share a room with twin beds; Kim pays more and has a double bed in her own room. Hannah sees that she left her bed unmade this morning, and she and Ted are standing beside her tangled beige sheets when he kisses her again. This goes on for several minutes and at some point he removes her glasses. They don't talk at all, and it's so quiet in the apart-ment, especially after the raucousness of Rick's, that Hannah is conscious of the noises they're making, that slight slurping. She wishes she'd thought to put on a CD. But soon – somehow – they are lying down and she stops thinking about it. She's on her back, her feet dangling off the end of the bed, and he is leaning over her, and then they've scooted up toward the pillow. He unbuttons her blouse, then reaches around and unfastens her bra. 'Will you turn out the light?' Hannah says, but he doesn't respond. 'Can you turn out the light?' she says more loudly. 'The switch is by the door.'

'But I want to be able to see you,' he says.

There's not a chance. She says, 'No, really,' and nudges him from the side. He's kissing her neck, and he pauses and looks at her before rising to flick the switch. 'By the way,' he says when he's standing, 'do you have something for, ah, protection?' He lies down again, more next to her than on top of her.

'Actually, I thought the man always took care of that.' Hannah giggles and immediately is mortified, although Ted doesn't seem like the kind of guy who would realize that what she just said, or the way she giggled, was mortifying.

'Maybe I do have one,' he says. 'Hold on.' He rolls onto his side and reaches into his back pocket.

A window of time opens up and just as quickly starts to close again. If she is going to say anything, she has to say it now. 'Incidentally,' she begins, and already her voice is the one she uses when she's presenting meeting reports to Lois, 'I should probably tell you. This isn't a big deal, but I've never had sex before.'

There is such a long pause that Hannah starts to think Ted didn't hear her, and she decides maybe it's not such a great idea to tell him after all.

'You mean,' he says, and before he's said anything else, she can tell he heard her perfectly, 'you're, you're a virgin? That's what you're saying?'

'Well, I hate that word. I don't even like when people say virgin daiquiri or virgin wool. But yes, that's correct.'

'Are you religious?'

'No,' Hannah says.

'And you're, what, a sophomore or a junior?'

'I'll be a senior.'

'Did you – not to get personal, but was there a guy who treated you bad?'

'What, like molested me?' Hannah says. Her voice was getting a little quivery before, but now it comes back strong. 'That's what you mean, right?'

He says nothing.

'No,' she says. She's not going to explain anymore. Everything is finished. This moment has passed.

'I can't say I'm not flattered,' Ted says, 'but I think you should do this with someone you love.'

'Well, aren't you old-fashioned?'

'Hannah, you're cool.' Ted's voice is so earnest; it's warbling even more than usual. 'I like you. It's just, under the circumstances—'

'Why don't you leave?' she says.

'Come on. We can still have fun.'

'Really?' she says. 'Can we?' Then – she doesn't want to be this kind of person, doesn't want to give in to her own nastiness – she says, 'You should

137

have done your homework. It's Sarie who's the slutty intern.'

He looks directly at her for the first time in several minutes. Even in the dark, the eye contact is excruciating. She looks away. His body rising from the bed a few seconds later is peripheral, more like a shadow than an actual person.

He is standing, tucking in his shirt, putting his shoes on. 'I'll see you around,' he says. 'Thanks, Hannah.' Mentally, she adds *for nothing*. To be fair, his voice isn't sarcastic. It's just distant. He leaves the bedroom, and then the front door opens and clicks shut. The first thing that occurs to Hannah is that today is Friday, and she'll at least have the weekend before returning to the office.

She lies there exactly as he left her, her blouse half off, her bra unfastened, her legs parted. An indeterminable amount of time elapses, and then she hears the burst of firecrackers – they are very nearby, possibly in the courtyard below her window – and a whiteness flickers in the room like during a lightning storm. Who are the boneheads who always insist on setting off firecrackers on the third of July?

Before the summer started, she'd had a feeling that it would be different, that her life was beginning to change. She was staying in Boston instead of going home, subletting this place with Jenny and Kim, and she had the internship. She had been hopeful. She thinks of that day in May, after lunch with her father. The restaurant was on

Spruce Street, and when she got up from the table, she walked north on Twentieth – she was shaking – and took a right into Rittenhouse Square. The park was crowded with office workers eating outside, homeless men sitting on the benches surrounded by their bags of possessions, little kids running among the sculptures. On the far side of the park, she came out on Walnut, stopping to buy bottled water from a vendor. The temperature was eighty-five degrees, the first truly hot day of the year.

She'd parked her mother's car at Seventeenth and Walnut, and as she headed toward it, she passed a new clothing store that seemed to be holding some sort of grand-opening festivities. The employees were wearing jeans and brightly colored T-shirts, and they'd set up speakers outside the entrance that were playing the song that would become the catchy, inescapable hit of the summer; it was the first time Hannah had ever heard it. Just past Eighteenth Street, between a gourmet-food emporium and a fancy boutique with satin dresses in the window, Hannah fell into step behind three people who at first she thought were traveling separately but who, after a moment, she realized were together: a girl around Hannah's age, a man a few years older, a woman who looked like one of their mothers. Hannah watched their profiles when they spoke to one another. The couple – and they must have been a couple, Hannah thought when the man linked his arm through the girl's in a way too tender to make them siblings – were both quite good-looking, the man with broad shoulders and a strong nose. The girl wore a green sundress, and she had long white-blond hair; the lightness of it made her seem somehow vulnerable. She held her chin in the air, in almost a parody of fine breeding. The older woman was bulky and slower-moving, wearing a handkerchief wrapped around her head. Hannah wondered where they were going. The man said something to the girl, and the girl shook her head. Hannah could not hear their conversation, and she began to walk more quickly. But they didn't speak again for nearly a block.

Then, abruptly, the woman turned to the girl and said, 'Are you happy?' She had an accent of some sort, so the emphasis came out on both syllables: Are you *happy*? She was Eastern European, Hannah decided, maybe Hungarian.

The girl didn't respond, and it was ridiculous, but Hannah felt as if the question had been directed at her. How could the girl not answer? Had her entire life been like this, one long inquiry into whether things were going the way she wanted?

Across the street, a police car had on its flashing lights, and Hannah glanced at the swirl of blue, then looked at the police officer himself. He was writing a ticket to a man who sat in the driver's seat of a minivan, waving his hands emphatically.

They both seemed far away. The music from the store was still audible above the traffic, and, as she always did when she heard music while outside in an urban area, Hannah felt like she was in a movie. She had taken a drastic and possibly foolish step with her father. But she did not regret it. In a strange way, the ugliness with him contained its opposite, and everywhere around her lay the possibility that things would improve in the months to come. She drew closer to the Hungarian woman, so close she could have rested her palm on the woman's back. 'Are you *happy*?' the woman asked again, this time more insistently, and at that moment, heading up Walnut Street, Hannah was on the verge of saying yes.

CHAPTER 5

AUGUST 1998

In room 128 of the Anchorage Holiday Inn, Hannah's sister, Allison, has just finished brushing her teeth, and Hannah is washing her face. When Hannah sets her towel on the edge of the sink, Allison says, 'Hannah, I'm engaged! Sam and I are getting married.'

'Sam?' Hannah says his name as if she isn't certain who he is, though Sam is, right now, on the other side of the door, in this very hotel room. But she's been caught off guard. She and Allison were talking about nothing, about brands of sunscreen. 'Since when?' Hannah asks.

'He proposed last week. Look.' Allison holds out her left hand, on which she's wearing a silver band of curling waves. Hannah noticed the ring already, though it did not occur to her that it could represent an engagement. 'I almost let it slip over the phone, but I thought it would be more fun to tell you in person,' Allison says.

'Does Mom know?'

'She and Dad both do. Are you not happy for me or something? You might want to say

142

congratulations.' Allison laughs a little helplessly. 'I thought you liked Sam.'

'I don't *dislike* him. I just – I didn't have any idea you guys were that serious.'

'Hannah, we've lived together for a year.'

'Well, it didn't occur to me. You're only twenty-four – that's kind of young. Sam's fine, though. I mean, yeah, congratulations. I guess I just don't see him as very special.'

'My God, Hannah.'

'Sorry,' Hannah says. 'Is that rude? I was trying to be honest. Should I not have said that?'

'Yes,' Allison says, 'you shouldn't have said that.'

But it *didn't* occur to Hannah that her sister would marry Sam. Allison never accepts when someone asks her to marry him. She doesn't have to, because there will always be another man to fall in love with her. She has large green eyes and long, wavy light brown hair, and two guys before Sam have proposed. One was her college boyfriend, whom she turned down because, as she told Hannah, she wasn't ready for that level of commitment, and one was a guy outside a bar in San Francisco on Valentine's Day. Allison was waiting for her friend on the sidewalk, and when she turned, there was this tall, skinny guy with black hair and a black leather jacket and lots of silver hoop earrings, not Allison's type at all, but he and Allison looked at each other and the next thing she knew, their mouths were smashed together, his hands were in her hair. She imagined she really might swoon. The guy said, 'Marry me, gorgeous.' Hannah can picture this part, her sister looking at the guy with her big, surprised eyes; some people's eyes say no before the person speaks a word, but Allison's never do, not even to bums or ex-boyfriends or letches at bars. Then Allison's friend materialized and pulled Allison away, and she didn't resist. She and the guy lost each other and she never saw him again. But she said the reason she didn't say anything was that she was afraid she was going to tell him yes.

In the Holiday Inn bathroom, Hannah says, 'Don't be mad. I'm getting used to the idea already. Here—' She holds out her arms, and Allison, only slightly grudgingly, steps into them. 'It's exciting,' Hannah says as they hug. 'Hooray.'

When they leave the bathroom, Sam is lying in bed looking at a map of Prince William Sound, and Elliot, Sam's brother, is digging through his backpack, which is propped against one wall. 'I hear congratulations are in order,' Hannah says, and she swoops in to embrace Sam, feeling like a large and clumsy bird. This is her second time today clumsily hugging Sam; the previous time was in the airport.

Hannah was the first to arrive in Anchorage, and she wasn't sure what to do with herself, so she bought a turkey sandwich full of clammy, pale meat, most of which she pulled out, set on the plastic tray while continuing to eat the lettuce and bread,

144

then threw in the trash. She wandered over to a grizzly bear: a real though dead grizzly, nine feet tall with dark brown silver-tipped fur, paused midgrowl behind glass. According to the sign, an adult grizzly could weigh over eight hundred pounds and could smell carrion from eighteen miles away. *I'm in Alaska,* Hannah told herself. *Alaska. Alaska!* A wish flickered through her to be back in the sublet in Boston, watching television dramas about police precincts with Jenny and eating scrambled eggs for dinner. She entered a gift shop, examined the key chains and magnets, and considered buying postcards, but she felt like maybe she hadn't yet earned the right.

Four hours later – finally, she gave up and bought magazines to read while waiting – there was the flurry of the others' arrival. Allison and Sam and Elliot had flown in together from San Francisco, and when they came off the plane, Hannah was standing at their gate. When she first spotted her sister, Hannah felt that rising in her chest that always occurs when she sees Allison after several months apart. Allison is so familiar, every feature of her face, every gesture she makes, and she is so extraordinarily pretty, and she is Hannah's. In all this crowd of people, Hannah was the one Allison was looking for. Hannah actually had to blink back tears.

She and Allison embraced, and Allison said, 'I like your glasses. You look very intellectual,' and Hannah said, 'I saved you some cookies from the plane because they taste like cheddar cheese.' When Sam approached, Hannah was unsure whether they were about to hug or kiss, and she decided hug. But Sam zoomed in in such a way that she could tell he'd decided kiss, so at the last second she turned her cheek toward his approaching mouth and rested her hands abortively on his shoulders. By then, of course, he'd realized that she had anticipated he'd hug her, and he merely skimmed her forehead with his lips and threw his arms around her waist.

'This is my older brother, Elliot,' Sam said when he and Hannah had disentangled themselves.

'And this is my younger sister, Hannah,' Allison said.

'And today on *Family Feud* . . .' Elliot said. Elliot was alarmingly handsome, Hannah thought as they shook hands, definitely more handsome than Sam, though their looks were similar. Elliot was blue-eyed, with a straight nose, blond hair, and a reddish-blond beard. It wasn't the icky academic kind of beard, either, even though Elliot was in grad school; it was a sporty beard. Hugging Sam for the second time in the hotel room, Hannah thinks that maybe for cuteness alone, Elliot is the one Allison should marry.

'You'll be our flower girl, right?' Sam says.

'She'll be the maid of honor, you doofus,' Allison says. 'Won't you, Hannah?' Allison is climbing into bed alongside Sam.

'Of course,' Hannah says. 'This is so great.'

Observing her sister and Sam next to each other, it strikes her that they actually are compatible: Allison is a social worker, and Sam is a sixth-grade teacher. They make thoughtful dinners that involve cilantro, they do the *Times* crossword puzzle together on Sundays, and in the colder months, they favor hats and mittens knit by Paraguayan peasants. Also, Sam's father is CEO of a national chain of drugstores, so despite their own modest incomes, Sam and Allison still have the opportunity to vacation in Alaska. (It is probably Sam's father who, indirectly, paid for Hannah's plane ticket.) And Hannah wasn't lying when she said she doesn't dislike Sam. He's always perfectly nice to her, and when she calls their apartment in San Francisco, he'll ask her, before passing the phone to Allison, how she's enjoying the land of the bean and the cod.

Elliot goes into the bathroom, and Hannah sits on the edge of the empty double bed. A thought has just occurred to her, a concern she wants assuaged before she lies down. 'Allison, you're sleeping over here, right?' she says. 'It's brothers and sisters?'

Sam folds down a corner of the map so they can see each other. 'You think my brother smells?' She takes this to mean no, she's not expected to sleep next to Elliot, but as Sam is looking at the map again, he adds, 'Allison and I are used to sharing a bed. Is it that big a deal to you, Hannah?'

'I just assumed you and Elliot would stay in

one bed, and Allison and I would stay in the other,' Hannah says. Is her preference really so weird? She'd think that most everyone would agree it's nerve-racking to sleep in a bed with a very attractive man you hardly know, and it's easy to sleep in a bed with your sister; you feel no compunction about fighting over sheets.

'You guys—' Allison begins, but she's interrupted by Sam saying, 'If you're sleeping, why does it matter, anyway? I don't know about you, but I'm beat.'

You asshole, Hannah thinks.

Elliot emerges from the bathroom, and Hannah is momentarily too embarrassed to continue the discussion in front of him. Then Sam says, 'Elliot, Hannah doesn't want to share a bed with you. I told her the assault charges were dropped, but she doesn't believe me.'

Elliot grins. 'It wasn't even a real woman. It was a shemale!'

Allison says, 'Hannah, what about if you and Elliot share a bed tonight and a tent when we're in the back-country, but you and I share a kayak?'

This is typical of Allison; she's such a *compromiser*.

'If you want to spend time with your sister, that time is better spent awake than asleep,' Elliot says. His tone of voice is impatient yet eminently logical, and there is a silence during which it occurs to Hannah that she has the unpleasant power to ruin this vacation for everyone just by being herself.

'Fine,' she says. 'Allison and I will share the kayak.'

When they turn out the lights, everyone is immediately quiet. Hannah becomes conscious of how foamy her pillow feels, then she becomes conscious of how stuffy the room is. She looks for a while at Elliot's back in a gray T-shirt and wonders if he has a girlfriend and, if so, what she's like. An hour passes. Hannah begins to feel desperate. She gropes her way through the darkness to the bathroom. When she sits on the toilet, all that comes out is a tablespoon of bright yellow pee. She goes back to bed.

At midnight – four A.M. Hannah's time, an hour and forty-five minutes after they turned out the light, and roughly twenty hours since she left Boston – she considers nudging Allison awake, but Sam and Elliot would probably wake up, too. She also considers sneaking out, calling a cab back to the airport, and going home, though that would set off a chain of excitement that wouldn't be worth the trouble.

It is 12:25. Hannah has squirmed around so much that the fitted sheet has come loose from the mattress on her side of the bed and twisted around her ankles. *Just shut your eyes and don't open them no matter what*, she tells herself. This works for four minutes, as she notes on the digital alarm clock when she opens her eyes. *Okay, try again*. Somewhere outside, at a distance that's hard to gauge, an odd wailing rises. She can't tell if the wailing is human or animal. She lies listening to it, her body tensed, wondering what, if anything, she should do. She falls asleep while wondering.

In the morning, she takes her last shower for the next five days. They walk to a sporting-goods store because Sam needs more wool socks. The store fills two floors and is brimming with canoes and tents and sleeping bags and bright-eyed, fit-looking salespeople who seem to Hannah, in their khaki shorts and hiking boots, effortlessly competent in a way she will never be. Already, she sees that she's not the kind of person who goes camping in Alaska and that actually camping in Alaska, being able to say she's been camping in Alaska, will not make her into this kind of person.

Allison and Sam planned the trip months ago, and then in June they called to invite Hannah to come along and Allison said they were inviting Elliot, too, so there'd be no reason for Hannah to feel like a third wheel. She is pretty sure that Allison invited her because of the fight with their father – Allison probably has the idea that she'll talk Hannah into calming down. When Hannah declined the invitation, saying she couldn't afford it, Allison said, 'We'll pay your plane fare. You just get the gear.' This gear, which includes a so-called thermally efficient sleeping bag and an assortment of pants, jackets, and long underwear of varying degrees of water resistance, somehow added up to eight hundred dollars. Standing at the cash register in Cambridge, Hannah felt a queasy misgiving. She'll probably never use any of it again.

She is next to a row of raincoats when a sales-person approaches.

'Can I help you with anything?' he asks. He has curly hair and a goatee – he's cute – and he looks about her age.

'I'm just waiting for some other people.'

'You in Alaska on vacation?'

'We're kayaking in Prince William Sound.'

'Oh, yeah? You're in for a treat. You might even have a bear sighting. They're pretty awesome in their natural habitat – none of that zoo stuff.'

'But isn't it dangerous to see a bear?'

He laughs a little, a nice laugh. 'Believe me, they're more afraid of you than you are of them.' (In all her life, Hannah has never believed anyone who has said this to her about anything.) 'Usually, you only see their scat,' the guy continues. 'If you do see a bear, you're lucky. The grizzlies you want to avoid, but the black bears can be playful little guys.'

'But is it *likely* that we'll see one?'

'If you're worried, what you do is, when you're walking along, especially in an area with a lot of growth, you call out, like, "Hey, bear. Hey, dude." Or you can sing. The important thing is that you don't want to surprise them, especially a mama with cubs. If they hear you coming, they'll get out of the way. You're camping, what, on little islands?'

Hannah nods.

'It depends on the size of the islands. Clean up after yourselves. You know that, right? Don't wear perfume, hang up your food at night, that whole routine.'

Everything he's saying sounds familiar, like something Hannah read in the guidebook without paying attention to it – something she skimmed, maybe, that seemed irrelevant at the time. Now she thinks, *Bears? Real, actual bears?* She doesn't even like dogs.

'If you're worried, we sell these bells,' the guy says. 'Let me show you.' He starts walking toward the back of the store, and Hannah follows him. 'The other thing,' he says, turning, 'is pepper spray. I'll show you that, too.'

The bells are like Christmas bells. They come individually, painted in bright colors, on a strap with Velcro.

The guy holds up a red one. 'You fasten it to you,' he says. 'We'll try it on your belt loop.' When he squats, his head is near her waist, and she wonders if she looks fat from this angle. He stands and says, 'Now try walking.'

The bell jingles. 'How much is it?' she asks.

'It's three bucks. I'll show you the pepper spray. So how long are you here for?'

'A week, with travel and everything, but just five days kayaking.'

'Where you from?'

'Massachusetts.'

'No kidding? You came all the way from Massachusetts for five days?'

She should have said two weeks, she thinks.

The pepper spray is thirty-five dollars. 'Honestly, though,' the guy says, 'your money is better spent on the bell.'

She decides to get both. When she pays at the cash register, Allison, Sam, and Elliot are waiting. The guy starts talking to them about bears, too, and when she rejoins them, the guy puts a hand on one of her shoulders. 'Everything will go great,' he says. 'You're golden.'

'Are you scared?' Elliot asks.

'No,' Hannah says, and at the same time, the guy says, 'I was up in Denali with my girlfriend last weekend, *hoping* to see a bear, and we still didn't.' At the mention of a girlfriend, Hannah feels foolish for having imagined this guy might have noticed the size of her waist.

Elliot gestures toward Hannah's pepper spray. 'Did it occur to you that if the bear is close enough for you to hit his eyes with that, you're pretty much toast? Or maybe you have superhuman aim.'

'Fuck off,' Sam says lightly. 'Let her carry it if she wants to.'

Allison takes the bell from Hannah, holds it in the air, and rings it. 'Ho ho ho,' she says. 'Merry Christmas.' She turns to Sam. 'Have *you* been a good boy this year?'

*   *   *

153

They stop by a grocery store to stock up, then ride the train to Ander, which is where they'll pick up their kayaks and take a charter boat into Prince William Sound in the late afternoon. Ander is roughly a half mile of irregularly spaced small buildings – a grocery store, a couple of restaurants, several kayak-rental places – along with abandoned or stalled railroad cars and a giant building of pink stucco, a former army bunker where, apparently, two thirds of the three hundred locals now live. Rising behind the buildings are jagged mountains, green in some places and snowy in others; in front of the buildings is the blue stretch of the beginning of Prince William Sound, with more snowcapped mountains across the water. Though it's sunny out, there are puddles everywhere in the muddy gravel that makes up the town's roads.

It's three thirty, and for lunch they get salmon burgers, except Allison, who's a vegetarian and orders spaghetti. Their waitress seems drunk; she's about forty, has stringy hair and a dead front tooth, and cheerfully tells them how she's from Corvallis, Oregon, she came up here four years ago for the hell of it, and just two months ago, she married the cook, wearing the very jeans she has on at this moment, in this very restaurant. Now she and her husband live in the bunker on the fourth floor. She forgets what Allison ordered and has to come back, and Hannah feels an odd though not unfamiliar desire to *be* this waitress,

154

to be forty and calmly unattractive, to live in a strange and tiny town in Alaska with a short-order cook who loves you. Also, to not be headed out onto the water, toward the bears.

After lunch, they walk to the end of a dock and board a boat that slaps over rolling waves as it heads north toward Harriman Fjord. The captain is a big, older, bearded guy, and the others talk to him, but Hannah sits on one side of the boat, the air rushing at her face, numbing her skin. After an hour, the captain slows the motor, and they drift toward a rocky beach. Beyond the rocks are ferns and berry patches and big, bushy devil's clubs, then spruce and alder trees and, beyond the trees, a glacier. It is the first they have seen, melded to a mountain, covering an expanse of perhaps three square miles. Hannah imagined glaciers as clear and glittery and neatly edged, like an oversize ice cube from a tray, but this is more like a field of ruffled, dirty snow. It has a blue tint, as if squirted with Windex.

The kayaks are strapped to the top of the boat, and the captain climbs up with surprising agility to pass them down. They gently lay the kayaks against the rocks, then slosh back through the shallow water in their black rubber boots to retrieve their backpacks. The captain leaves. Everything feels enormous, the sea and the sky and the mountains and the vast, rocky un-peopled expanse of beach. Hannah cannot believe that this, all of this, exists. It exists while she babysits the professor's children, while she eats frozen yogurt with Jenny in the student center on campus. Now that seems distant and irrelevant. This is the world: the clearness of the air, the wind stirring the tall grasses, the way the late-afternoon sunlight glints off the tiny waves hitting the rocks. And yet she feels silly; thoughts about how small you are always feel small themselves. Besides, amazement does not preclude anxiety.

About fifty yards back from the water, they set up the tents. 'Just, if you can tell me what to do,' Hannah says to Elliot. He passes her the poles, which are folded up, with a rubbery cord running inside. The way you slide the metal pieces onto each other, something bent becoming something straight, reminds her of the wand in a children's magic show. The ground is soft, easy to push the stakes into. The tent is turquoise, and when Hannah climbs in, on her knees so as not to track in dirt, she notices that the nylon casts a shadowy blue on her forearms. At the back of the tent, Elliot has unzipped a flap of fabric to reveal a triangular screen – a window – that strikes Hannah as quaintly domestic. It's as if he's hung up wind chimes, or set out a mailbox with their names on it, should Allison or Sam wish to deliver a letter. Hannah sticks the sleeping bags inside the tent, still in their stuff sacks; the backpacks they lean against trees.

They won't kayak until morning. For dinner, the brothers make macaroni and cheese mixed with chopped veggie dogs. 'Don't put any veggie dog in Hannah's,' Allison says. 'She doesn't like the texture.' When they have cleaned up, Sam hangs their food in a tree. The brothers play chess on a tiny magnetic board while Allison sits on the beach, writing in her journal. Unsure what to do, Hannah goes into the tent, changes into long underwear and a different T-shirt, and gets inside her sleeping bag. In the fading light, she is reading a mystery Allison finished on the plane, except that she keeps spacing out and having to turn back a page. Forty minutes have passed by the time Elliot enters the tent. He greets her with a one-syllable noise of acknowledgment. He pulls off his T-shirt and fleece jacket, and with his back to her, his skin is golden, his arms lean but muscular. He takes off his jeans as well and climbs into his sleeping bag wearing gray boxer-briefs.

'You're getting your Ph.D. in neuroscience, right?' Hannah says. 'Which isn't the same as being a doctor?'

'I'll do research and possibly teach, but I'll never perform surgery, if that's what you're asking.'

'Do you have a special focus?'

'I'm on a team that's studying how different parts of the brain respond to stress. Right now we're looking at the amygdala, which I assume means nothing to you.'

'It sounds familiar.'

There's a long silence.

Fine, Hannah thinks. *Never mind.*

157

But at last Elliot says, 'You go to Tufts, right?'

'Yeah, I'm about to start my senior year. I was interning this summer at an ad agency. I like Boston pretty much. It's true what people say about drivers there, but I don't have a car, so I don't really mind.'

'I know what Boston is like. I went to law school at Harvard.'

'Wow – you've been busy.'

He doesn't respond. But they both have been lying on their backs, and it is impossible for Hannah not to feel a little like he's her husband. It's the blend of intimate and mundane, as opposed to intimate and sexy; her sophomore year, she once randomly helped the R.A. on her hall, a guy named Vikram, buy groceries for a study break, and it was like this, too. She wasn't attracted to Vikram, but they walked up and down the aisles together with the cart, conferring about prospective purchases: *Why are grapes so expensive? We want the salted pretzels, right?*

Elliot rolls onto his side, away from Hannah. She should just stay quiet – obviously, he's trying to go to sleep – but she hears herself ask, 'So what do you think of Sam and Allison getting married? Pretty wild, huh?'

'It's great,' Elliot says. 'I hope they're happy.'

'Did you know they were so serious?'

'He'd have been a fool if he wasn't. Your sister's awesome.'

Allison's awesomeness, usually a source of pride

to Hannah, feels like a tired subject. She says nothing more, and neither does Elliot. It is very dark, and she can hear the lapping water. Forty-five minutes pass, and – her stomach feels bloated and hard – she vacillates between worrying that she will never fall asleep or that she will fall asleep and then fart loudly. She imagines the bear's shaggy cinnamon fur and alert wet nose, its long claws, brown and slightly curved. It's an illusion, of course, but she's glad to be inside a tent, hidden away. How lucky the bear is, being the one everything else is afraid of; how free it must feel, roaming across the beaches and among the trees.

After breakfast, when they're putting on the spray skirts and life jackets, Elliot says, 'You're not wearing that in the kayak, are you? There aren't bears on the water.'

Earlier, Hannah attached the bear bell to the sleeve of her jacket, and it rings whenever she moves. She looks at Elliot, then looks away. She is sick of trying to make him like her. 'I want to,' she says just as Sam says, 'Hey, Hannah, what size life jacket do you have?'

'I don't know.' She unclips the plastic hooks in front and shrugs it off so she can look at the tag. 'It says large.'

'Switch with me, will you?' Sam tosses her a different one. 'The two mediums are for you and Allison, and the two larges are for me and Elliot.'

'But—' Hannah pauses. 'I know you're taller

159

than I am, but Sam, I have boobs. My chest is actually bigger than yours.'

Allison giggles. 'Hannah's pretty stacked,' she says. 'It's been my torment since high school.' This isn't true. By eighth grade, Hannah was wearing a larger bra than either her older sister or her mother, but it was her own torment. Still, for years, she and Allison have acted like there's at least one thing Allison envies about Hannah.

'It's a fact that I'm bigger,' Sam says. 'I'm not being sexist. Stand next to me, Hannah.'

First they stand side by side, then back to back.

'This is ridiculous,' Elliot says, but Hannah cannot tell what he's referring to. The situation? Her?

'It's hard to tell without a tape measure,' Allison says. She's still speaking with – pretending to feel, Hannah thinks – an air of amusement.

'Can you fasten the medium one?' Sam asks Hannah.

Hannah sticks her arms through the holes. She's sure it won't fasten, but then it does. But that probably means it would fasten for Sam, too, except that while she has been fiddling with the hooks, he has somehow eased the large life jacket out of her hands. There's nothing to do but launch the kayaks.

It's tippy at first, then smooth, almost as if they're gliding on the water itself, unseparated by fiberglass. Elliot and Sam paddle faster than she and Allison, and after they are a few hundred yards apart, Hannah turns her head and says over her shoulder – Allison is in the stern, steering – 'So what do you think of that dick move by your boyfriend or fiancé or whatever he is?'

'Hannah, calm down.'

'Thanks for defending me. Were you afraid he'd feel emasculated if you admitted that his chest isn't as big as he wants to think?'

Allison says nothing.

'But I do enjoy spending quality time with his brother,' Hannah says. 'What a warm guy.'

'Elliot's cute,' Allison says, and it enrages Hannah that Allison won't stick up for herself, she won't even say anything connected to what the conversation is about. When they were young, they had real fights – hair-pulling declarations of hatred – and though the physical aspect petered out, they still bickered until Allison was in seventh grade. And then – it was awful – she turned nice. The way that in junior high some girls turn popular, or anorexic, or Goth, Allison turned resolutely, personality-definingly nice. She turned pretty, too, which made her niceness seem even more generous and less necessary.

'You know what they both remind me of?' Possibly, Hannah thinks, this is going too far. '"Beware the man who's read one book." They're acting like I'm all paranoid about the bears, but it's not as if they have a ton of camping experience.'

'Sam's camped before,' Allison says. 'I promise.

161

Both of them grew up going on pack trips in Wyoming.'

'Well, lah-dee-dah,' Hannah says. 'Authentic cowboys.'

Again Allison says nothing.

'I do have one question,' Hannah says. 'Don't you feel shortchanged that his family is loaded, yet he only gave you a silver engagement ring?'

'Right now,' Allison says, 'I'm having a pretty hard time imagining you as the maid of honor at our wedding.'

'Is that a threat?'

'Hannah, why would I threaten you? But you're making it clear you don't like either Sam or Elliot. I wouldn't want to put you in a situation where you felt uncomfortable.'

'Like this one, you mean? It's obvious everyone would prefer that I hadn't come.' She waits for Allison to contradict her, and when Allison doesn't, Hannah adds, 'Including me.'

For more than twenty minutes, neither of them speaks. At first the life jacket felt to Hannah like a corset, but she's gotten used to it. And it's a relief to be in the kayak. Now she only has to get through the trip itself, not preparation for the trip *and* the trip.

Finally, Allison says, 'See the glacier up ahead? We can't get too close, because chunks can break off at any second. It's called calving.' Yes, Allison is more mature than Hannah, Allison is a better person, but there's also less at stake for her. Allison

162

can afford to capitulate conversation-wise because Hannah isn't where her attention lies; to Allison, Hannah isn't the primary person on the trip. 'You're doing well,' Allison adds. 'The first time I ever went kayaking, I got seasick.'

Grudgingly, Hannah says, 'Is that possible?'

'I vomited into the water. Ask Sam. He thought I was the biggest dork.'

Later in the afternoon, they see a bald eagle, and then a seal surfaces close to their kayak. There is something sorrowful in its wet brown head, Hannah thinks, as it ducks under again and disappears.

Before dinner, when Sam is boiling the water for couscous and Allison and Elliot are in the tents, Sam says to Hannah, 'No hard feelings about the life jacket, right?'

Hannah pauses, then says, 'Yeah, it's fine.'

Sam lowers his voice. 'Allison is really worried about your issues with your dad.'

'I didn't realize my issues with my dad were public information,' Hannah says, and Sam drops it.

After dinner, they play hearts in Sam and Allison's tent. It is so cold that they all put on jackets and wool hats. Around nine, when it starts getting dark – Alaska is not the land of the midnight sun this late in August – they pull out their flashlights and set them at angles pointing up, four moons inside the tent. But then it gets totally dark, and it's impossible to see the cards even with the flashlights.

Before following Elliot into their tent, Hannah walks over to a tree twenty feet away. As she pulls down her underwear, long underwear, and fleece pants, she imagines a bear coming up behind her and pawing her ass. She shakes her bear bell, and Allison calls out, 'I hear you, Hannah,' in a singsong. Hannah must squat there for an entire minute before she can relax enough to urinate. She's pretty sure she gets a little on her feet – she's wearing wool socks and flip-flops – but it is too dark, and she is too tired, to care.

The days develop a rhythm. They eat oatmeal or Pop-Tarts for breakfast and sometimes hot cocoa; for lunch they have carrots and apples and bagels with peanut butter; and for dinner Elliot or Sam makes pasta or refried beans over Elliot's stove. They each carry two water bottles, one bowl, one cup, and one set of utensils.

They move to a different island, and in the soil just above the beach, Hannah sees several piles of what must be bear shit: big mashed-looking clumps that are sometimes dark brown and sometimes almost pink, dotted by whole unchewed berries. She thinks of the guy in the store in Anchorage, the way he said, 'You're golden,' and she tries to hold his words close, like a talisman.

On the water, cruise ships appear in the distance. Sam and Elliot make sneering comments about their passengers, the inauthenticity of their Alaskan experience. 'Tourists,' they say scornfully,

164

and Hannah thinks, *But what are we?* She would rather be a cruiseship passenger: a gray-haired woman from Milwaukee carrying a camera in a gold lamé shoulder bag and eating halibut off a white plate every night. The faraway ships make Hannah feel that they are less alone, and she is always sorry when they disappear from view. She also is comforted when, one evening at their campsite, she finds a Band-Aid half buried in dirt. The Band-Aid has a Flintstones motif, and Hannah picks it up – she would never do this in normal life – and looks at it in her palm.

At night Hannah sleeps in a sports bra and, as Allison has instructed, lays wet articles of clothing – socks, mostly – against her stomach so they'll dry. At least once a day, it drizzles. When this happens, Hannah thinks that if she just suspends thought, time will pass and she will find herself back at Tufts, starting the new school year, kicking herself for not having appreciated her exotic and expensive vacation.

On the fourth afternoon, during a sunny interlude, the brothers – they are usually far in front – wait for Allison and Hannah, then begin to splash them with the paddles. More exactly, the brothers splash at Allison. Elliot, like Hannah, is sitting in the bow, but he angles his body so he is turned back toward Allison. As Allison shrieks and laughs, the expression on Elliot's face becomes one of such undiluted pleasure that he looks demented. His momentary, soaring

165

happiness is what makes Hannah suspicious. And then, that night at the campsite, Elliot goes with Allison to gather firewood, and Hannah sees them coming back along the beach. The giveaway is his relaxed but attentive posture; clearly, of anywhere in the world, here is where Elliot most wants to be.

It is in this moment, in his worship of Allison, that Hannah almost identifies with Elliot. Watching them, she can feel in her own hand the desire to touch this girl's wavy hair, this girl whose kindness and beauty could make your life right if you could get her to be yours. Hannah wonders if Elliot imagined that she would be another version of Allison.

When they are finished cleaning up after dinner, Elliot and Sam announce that they're going to explore. After they leave, Hannah walks with her bell and pepper spray to sit on a large rock that juts down to the water. The sky has a low-hanging, cottony whiteness, tinged slightly with pink, and the edges of everything are starting to darken. The Sound is flat and glassy. Allison joins her. They are silent for a long time. 'It's so beautiful I feel guilty going to sleep,' Allison says at last.

'I bet it'll still be here in the morning,' Hannah says.

'You know what I mean.' Allison pauses. 'Hannah, I really think you should talk to Dad. If you apologize to him, I'm sure he'll still pay your tuition this year.'

Ah, yes – Hannah knew it was coming. She says, 'There's no way I'm apologizing to him.'

'Where are you going to come up with the money?'

'I've already met with a guy in the financial aid office. This isn't your problem.'

'It kind of is. You're stressing out Mom, too. She can't afford to pay all your tuition herself.'

'I didn't ask her to. I'm taking out student loans.'

'You think that's appropriate? I'm sure someone from a less well-off family needs the money more than you do.'

'A loan, Allison, not a scholarship. I'll have to pay it back, so yes, I do think I'm entitled.'

'Dad paid for me to get my master's,' Allison says. 'I'm sure he'd pay for you to go to grad school, too, if you let him. He's actually an incredibly generous person.'

'Dad's a prick,' Hannah says. 'On a different subject, does Sam know his brother has the hots for you?'

Allison laughs. 'What are you talking about?'

Of course Allison *would* laugh it off. But at what point is her optimistic denial the same as shallowness? Surely it's not just that she's dumb. Hannah tells people (she has told Dr Lewin) that she and her sister are close, but is this really true? Do she and Allison enjoy each other's company, do they know even the most basic things about each other anymore?

'Has he ever come on to you?' Hannah asks.

167

'Why are you asking me this?' Allison says, which is certainly less than a denial.

'What a slimeball,' Hannah says.

'It was once. He tried to kiss me at a party when he was really drunk, and the next day he was mortified.'

'Did you tell Sam?'

'Why do you care if I did?' Allison's voice wavers between defiance and self-pity. 'Either way, you'll just sit there and judge us.'

Oh, how Hannah has missed the elementary-school Allison, the Allison capable of taking digs when adequately provoked!

'You know, I used to almost feel bad for you that men hit on you all the time,' Hannah says. 'I knew I should envy you, but all those guys seemed like a burden. You barely ever liked them back, but you still had to return their phone calls or let them kiss your cheek or just, like, *manage* their interest in this way that seemed tedious. But now I think I was wrong. You thrive on managing their interest. Why else would you have invited Elliot on this trip, knowing he likes you?'

'That's so unfair.'

'Was it so Elliot could watch you and Sam frolic in nature?'

'You can't ever give it a rest, can you?' Allison says, and she is getting to her feet angrily and awkwardly. Her cheeks are flushed. When she's gone, Hannah sits there in the hideous, quiet after-math of her own hostility. But then Allison comes back. She stands in front of Hannah, her eyes narrowed. 'Mom sometimes asks me if I think there's something wrong with you. Did you know that? She says, 'Why doesn't Hannah have a boyfriend, why doesn't she have more friends? Should I be worried?' I always defend you. I say, 'Hannah marches to the beat of her own drummer.' But it's not that. It's that you're completely stubborn and bitter. You think you have everyone figured out, all of us with our stupid little lives, and you might be right, but you're a miserable person. You make yourself miserable, and you make the people around you miserable, too.' Allison hesitates.

Just say it, Hannah thinks. *Whatever it is*.

'The irony is,' Allison says, 'you remind me of Dad.'

It is their last night in the backcountry. They're on another island tonight, the third and final one (the trip is almost finished, it's almost finished, it's almost finished). Hannah has no idea what time it is but senses only that she has been deeply asleep, probably for several hours, when she awakens to Elliot's weight on top of her, his hand clamped over her mouth.

'You need to stay calm,' Elliot says. He is whispering directly into her ear, more quietly than she's ever heard anyone whisper; it's like he's thinking the thoughts into her. 'Something's trying to get at our food. You can't scream. Do you understand?

I'll take my hand away, but if you make noise, I'm putting it back.'

Though he does not use the word, she understands – once she understands that he is not raping her – that he's talking about the bear. Finally, as she knew it would, the bear has come.

She nods, and he lifts his hand. The sound from outside the tent is a scratching, as against bark, and an unself-conscious huffing. The scratching stops, then begins again. Are Sam and Allison awake as well? Elliot remains on top of her. She is lying on her side in her sleeping bag, and he is out of his, propped on his arms, the center of his torso pressed to her shoulder, his abdomen against her hip, his legs straddling her. Is he staying in this posture because he doesn't want to risk even the slippery noise of climbing off? Because, in the event of the bear's approach to the tent, he is protecting her? Or because it feels nice, and surprisingly normal, for them to be entwined like this? The pressure of his body is not unpleasant at all.

Elliot's breath carries onions from dinner and would probably strike her as disgusting if she were confronted by it at a party. In this moment, it is not disgusting. She wonders if they will die. She thinks of the exhibit in the Anchorage airport: *The bear shows its anger by growling and snapping its teeth, and the fur on its neck stands up as its ears flatten. When threatened, a bear may charge.* And yet she is almost glad that the bear came; it means she wasn't paranoid.

Then the bear crosses between the moon and the tent's triangular screen, and she sees it incompletely but definitively – its dark, silver-tipped fur and the hump of muscle on its shoulder. It's a grizzly; a grizzly is outside the tent. It is on all fours (she'd been picturing it standing), less than ten feet away. How can they *not* die, so close to a grizzly bear? Maybe the reason Elliot has remained in this posture is that it doesn't matter what he does right now – he could grab her breast or spit in her eye, and no one will ever find out. Her heart thuds against her chest. A wave of unhappiness sweeps over her, and she feels her features contort; she starts to cry. A stopped-up sniffle escapes, and Elliot immediately collapses his arms so his face, too, is pressed to hers, his nose under her chin, his forehead at her ear. He shakes his head. He wraps his arms around the top of her head, pinning and suppressing her. Against his face, Hannah breathes the word *Allison*. He shakes his head again. If he were anyone else, anyone whose own sibling was not in the other tent, she wouldn't trust him. Somewhere deep in her backpack is a key ring – how abruptly your keys become irrelevant out of your home city – and attached to the key ring is a whistle, which perhaps would scare off the bear if she blew it. It would be something to try, if she didn't trust Elliot about staying still.

And then the bear leaves. Like a person – she can feel this – it is glancing vaguely around, checking that there's nothing to attend to before it departs. But its focus is already gone from here, directed at the next thing. It is leaving, and then it has left. Neither she nor Elliot moves at all. How long do they not move? Maybe six minutes. It is Sam who breaks the silence. He calls out, 'Holy fucking shit!'

'Are you okay, Hannah?' Allison says. 'You guys are fine, right? We saw it near your tent.'

'I'm okay,' Hannah calls back. 'Elliot made me stay quiet.'

'I want to come give you a hug,' Allison says. 'But I think I'll wait until morning.'

'Did we not hang the food high enough?' Elliot calls to Sam. He says this in an ordinary voice while still on top of Hannah. His breath has started to bother her.

'I did it the same as the other nights,' Sam says. 'I don't think it got anything. I think it was just curious.'

'Or trying to be friendly,' Elliot says dryly. Underneath him, Hannah laughs – not because the comment is particularly funny, but because of her bottled-up energy. They all are willing the moment to turn, and it *is* turning, it's starting to contain the mood it will contain later, as a story they tell to other people.

'It didn't want to disappoint Hannah,' Sam says. 'It knew she'd feel gypped if we didn't get at least one sighting.'

'It wasn't even a real bear,' Allison says. 'It was

that guy from the store in Anchorage, dressed up in a bear suit. Otherwise, he was afraid you'd demand a refund for your pepper spray.'

Now they all are laughing. Also, Elliot has an erection. If she were a different person, not a virgin, this is when Hannah would – what? Unzip her sleeping bag, pull off her sports bra? To get things rolling, she'd probably need to do very little. Plus, there would be the giddy aspect of trying to keep Sam and Allison from hearing. On the plane home, she'll kick herself for not going with the moment. Elliot was hot, they were in Alaska, and for Christ's sake, they'd just escaped being mauled by a grizzly. The fact that things don't shake out for her with guys – who, really, does she have to blame but herself? At critical moments, she can't seem to summon the appropriate energy. But if she keeps thinking of this particular episode, thinks of it in any depth rather than breezing by it as part of a larger list, she must admit that if she had the situation to relive, she would make the same decision. She was tired. He had bad breath. There was a rock beneath her right thigh, poking into her through the bottom of the tent, her sleeping pad, and her sleeping bag. It would have been awkward the next day, or maybe for years to come; she'd wonder obsessively if he had been able to tell she was inexperienced, if he'd thought she was a horrible kisser. And besides, her sister was the one he really wanted. Just because he'd settle for her, just because the proximity of the bear had made him horny – it didn't seem like enough of a reason.

She shifts as if to lie on her stomach, and he rolls off her.

In the morning, there is the requisite debriefing, the repeated reenactment of the bear's trajectory through their campsite. They pack up for the last time and paddle out. In the afternoon, they will meet the captain on the same beach where he first delivered them.

After lunch, the sky drops and darkens. 'Hannah,' Allison says, and abruptly, Hannah is waiting tensely, every strand of hair on her head electrified. 'I know things went wrong in a big way on this trip, right off the bat,' Allison says. 'I wish I could fix them, or maybe we never should have all come here. But you have to accept that I'm marrying Sam. He's honestly a good person, and he likes you. And if you refuse to make an effort, things will be unpleasant for everyone.'

'I'm not disagreeing with you,' Hannah says. 'But can you just explain *why* you're marrying him? I swear I'm not being a bitch. I'm genuinely curious. I want to understand what qualities he has that you like so much.'

'I'm marrying him because he makes me happy,' Allison says, and all at once it begins to rain. Real rain, not drizzle. Hannah can't entirely turn around – she can turn her head so she's facing the side and Allison is in her peripheral vision, but that's it. 'I feel better when I'm with him than I feel when I'm alone,' Allison adds, and because of the increasing volume of the rain, she is almost yelling. Far away – how far it's hard to say, being on the water like this – a flash of lightning splits the sky. Hannah is not sure if Allison notices. 'I know it's wimpy,' Allison says, 'but Sam takes care of me. It's not that I don't see any of his flaws, because I do. But I love him anyway.'

It is pouring; raindrops bounce off Hannah's jacket and soak her face and hair. 'My glasses are steaming up,' she says. 'I can barely see.'

'Take them off. If you already can't see, it won't be any worse.'

When Hannah removes them she doesn't know what to do with them. If she puts them in one of the pockets of her raincoat, she's afraid they'll get crushed when they're landing the kayaks, so finally, she slips them inside the neck of her shirt. In the rain, everything in front of her is gray and indistinct.

'See the guys?' Allison says. 'They're heading toward that beach on the right. Just keep paddling, and I'll steer us.'

Hannah's teeth are chattering, and her hands are cold and slick with water. The rain is almost solid, like sleet. She turns partway around. She says, 'I don't really think Sam's a dick. I hope you know that.' (As if calling him a dick is the worst thing Hannah said. What she really should apologize for is *I guess I just don't see him as very special.*

175

But the sincerity of that comment makes it unerasable; it is better just to move on.) 'And I know that I am like Dad in some ways. But I feel sort of like, of course I am. It's in my genes. Isn't it weirder that you're not like him than that I am?'

'You give too much attention to things that make you unhappy,' Allison says.

No doubt she is right. And yet attending to things that make Hannah unhappy – it's such a natural reflex. It feels so intrinsic, it feels in some ways like who she is. The unflattering observations she makes about other people, the comments that get her in trouble, aren't these truer than small talk and thank-you notes? Worse, but truer. And underneath all the decorum, isn't most everyone judgmental and disappointed? Or is it only certain people, and can she choose not to be one of them – can she choose this without also, like her mother, just giving in?

They paddle through the rain, and when at last they reach the island, the brothers, who have landed already, come into the water to help. 'I put up a tarp,' Sam says. After they've secured the second kayak, Elliot unrolls another tarp on the ground. They lie on it, all four of them flat on their backs.

'Does anyone else have raisin fingers?' Allison asks.

'I have raisin you-don't-even-want-to-know,' Sam says.

Prostrate on the tarp, sore and chilled and not

making eye contact with anyone, Hannah smiles. She is, after all, no longer waiting for the bear, and they are leaving tomorrow. She pushes a clump of wet hair off her forehead and abruptly sits up. 'I don't know where my glasses are,' she says.

'When did you last see them?' Sam asks, and Allison explains to him that Hannah took them off when it started raining.

'Fuck,' Hannah says. She stands and pats her chest and stomach. 'They must have fallen out as we were pulling in the kayak.'

She ducks under the tarp, back into the rain, and jogs toward the water. Where the waves hit the shore, she peers down. She kicks at the black sand and the small rocks with the toes of her rubber boots, but this makes the water murkier. She goes in deeper, stopping when the waves are just below her knee, threatening to wash over the tops of her boots.

'Hannah. Hey, Hannah.' Allison has ventured out from under the tarp. 'I'll help you look,' she says.

They search, shoulders and heads tipped, squinting into the water. They follow separate paths, passing sometimes as they comb over nearby sections, and don't speak. The rain is a huge and violent whisper.

Perhaps ten minutes pass, and Hannah knows she will not find them. But they keep looking, or at least they keep trudging through the water. She glances sometimes at Allison, a blurry figure in a green raincoat, her light curly hair straight and dark, plastered to her head. Hannah will have to be the one to give up searching; Allison won't, by herself. 'They must have washed away,' Hannah says. 'It's all right. I'll get new ones.'

'I feel terrible,' Allison says.

'It was dumb of me not to put them in a pocket.'

'Maybe we could get you glasses in Anchorage.'

'No, I'll be fine. Really.' And she will. Airports, optometrists – these Hannah can handle, even without all her faculties she can handle them.

Allison squeezes Hannah's forearm. 'You can be my maid of honor,' she says. 'I totally want you to. I was being ridiculous before.'

Back under the tarp, they decide to make hot chocolate, and Sam is the one who finds Hannah's cup for her, then washes out the oatmeal remnants from breakfast – he insists – and pours in the cocoa powder and the boiling water from the pan. 'I'm nearsighted,' Hannah says. 'It's only faraway stuff I can't see.' But he wants to wash her cup again after she's used it, and she acquiesces with minimal protest. As she passes the cup to Sam, their fingertips touch. *I give you my sister*, Hannah thinks, *because I have no choice. But you will never catch up to us; I will always have known her longer.*

If he understands, he does not acknowledge it.

Back in Ander, they return their kayaks and life jackets and spray skirts and rubber boots, they take pictures of one another standing on the dock

178

against the backdrop of the mountains, and that night they stay at a bed-and-breakfast – Davida's B&B – which is inside the old army bunker. It's an apartment that smells of cigarette smoke, and Davida herself, a warm woman in her fifties wearing acid-washed jeans, a pilly lavender sweater, and a blue windbreaker, escorts them up in the elevator to their apartment and proceeds to energetically spray air freshener until Hannah can taste it in her mouth, a sour mist. When Davida's gone, Elliot says, 'Who'd have guessed one of the Bs stands for Bunker?' and Hannah laughs extra. Since Elliot's quasi-come-on last night, she felt first generously pitying toward him, then she felt like maybe there was sexual tension between them, and now she feels like probably he's not interested in her at all but she definitely has a crush on him. For the last three hours, the crush has been thriving.

In the morning, they board the train back to Anchorage and take a taxi to the airport, where they will all leave on night flights. Hannah will arrive in Boston at six thirty in the morning. In the airport bathroom, Allison gets her period and doesn't have a tampon and Hannah must buy one, sticking dimes into the machine on the wall, then passing it under the door of the stall. 'Aren't you glad this didn't happen in the backcountry?' Allison says. 'A bear would have sniffed me out in no time.'

Then Hannah *is* back at Tufts, the school year

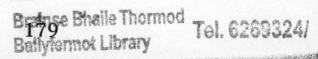

has started. She's safe and alone again, as she is always safe and alone. The following May, Allison and Sam will marry in a simple ceremony at the Palace of the Legion of Honor in San Francisco, and though in the weeks before she flies out, Hannah will not be able to help wondering what her interactions with Elliot will be like, he'll mostly ignore her. He'll bring as his wedding date a very thin, very blond woman who is not only far prettier than Hannah but far prettier than even Allison. The woman will, apparently, be an ER doctor.

For a long time – more frequently than she'll wish she hadn't told Allison Sam wasn't special, way more frequently than she'll regret not having fooled around with Elliot – Hannah will think of her glasses on the floor of the North Pacific. It is dark and calm down there; fish slip past; her glasses rest untouched, the clear plastic lenses and titanium frames. In the stillness without her, the glasses see and see.

CHAPTER 6

SEPTEMBER 1998

Hannah meets the guy in the financial aid office when she's waiting to see the director. This is her third visit to the office since returning from Alaska; the financial aid system is starting to feel like an additional class for which she gets no credit. On a piece of paper, she makes the same calculations she has made more than once, as if this time they will yield a different answer: If the tuition for the year is $23,709, and if her mother increases the amount she pays per semester from $4,000 to $6,000 ('You really don't have to,' Hannah said, and her mother said, 'Oh, Hannah, I'm just sorry it can't be more'), and then if Hannah gets $4,300 as a student loan, and if she works thirty hours a week at the veterinary library instead of twenty – in the middle of her calculations, she senses that the guy behind the desk is watching her. She looks up.

'While you're waiting, maybe I can answer your question,' the guy says. She's pretty sure he's an undergrad. He's only an inch or two taller than Hannah, with brown hair and glasses, and he isn't particularly cute.

Hannah shakes her head. 'It's kind of complicated.'

'Try me. I've worked here a few years.'

'I'm an exceptional case,' Hannah says, which is verbatim what the director of financial aid told her – the exceptional part is that Hannah didn't know until late last May, after the end of the school year, that she'd need aid – but the guy smiles.

He says, 'Oh, I could tell that already.'

He's either flirting with her or making fun of her; whichever it is, it's annoying. She looks down again and resumes writing.

Less than a minute has passed when the guy says, 'I went to that exhibit at the M.F.A.'

The book she's holding on her lap beneath the piece of paper is a biography of Pierre Bonnard. Hannah is considering writing her thesis on him.

'He does all the paintings of his wife in the bath, right?' the guy says.

Hannah nods. She's a little impressed. 'Did you see the last one?' she asks. 'His wife died while he was in the middle of painting it, but it turned out to be the best one by far. The interplay of warm and cool colors is really incredible, the tiles on the floor and the wall. It's, like, luminous.' Right away, she feels embarrassed. That *luminous* – it sounded very art-history-major-ish.

But the guy is nodding. He seems interested. He says, 'When I was at the exhibit—' and this is when the director of financial aid opens his office door and sticks his head out. 'Hannah Gavener?' he says, and she stands and enters the office behind him.

During the last three years, the places Fig has stood Hannah up are two Starbucks (the one at Kenmore Square and the one at the corner of Newbury Street and Clarendon); the Clinique counter on the second floor of Filene's; and now, on a Sunday morning, at Fig's own off-campus apartment. They are supposed to go out for brunch, and standing in the dingy lobby of Fig's building, Hannah presses the intercom button three times in a row. After the third time, a sleepy, unfriendly female voice – one of Fig's three room-mates, presumably – says, 'Who is it?'

'It's Hannah, and I'm looking—' Hannah begins, but the voice cuts her off.

'Fig's not here. She never came home last night.' In the ensuing disconnection, there is something final; to buzz again, Hannah can tell already, would serve no purpose.

Back in her dorm, Hannah sends Fig a sarcastic e-mail (*Don't worry about not being there, because I really enjoyed the early morning T ride . . .*), but after several days pass with no reply, Hannah begins to worry that maybe something bad has happened.

On Wednesday afternoon, Hannah calls. 'Oh my God, I've been dying to talk to you,' Fig says. 'Can we get together immediately? Are you free for dinner tonight? Or, wait, not tonight, because I said I'd go out for drinks with this law student. A law student is the only thing worse than a lawyer, right?'

'What happened to you last weekend?'

'Don't ask. Do you remember my freshman roommate Betsy?'

Hannah remembers her well. The first time Hannah ever visited Fig at BU, Betsy said, 'Did you jog over here?' and Hannah said, 'I took the T. Why?' and Betsy said, 'Because you're so sweaty.'

'Betsy was having this big party Saturday and basically wigging out,' Fig says. 'She begged me to help her get ready when, believe me, the last thing I wanted was to get sucked into the vortex of her insanity. But we ran all over the place, getting food, cleaning up, and then the party just went on forever. People seriously didn't leave until like six in the morning. You should have come.'

'That would have been difficult, given that I didn't know about it.'

'Betsy's new boyfriend has braces. Can you imagine a guy with braces going down on you?'

'If you were hungover, Fig, all you had to do was call me.'

'I know. I'm the most horrible person in the world. But I was just about to call you right now. And I'll make it up to you – I'll *make* brunch for you.'

'You don't know how to cook,' Hannah says.

The staples of Fig's diet are cocktail onions from the jar, a blend of cottage cheese and ketchup, and, occasionally, chocolate bars. At restaurants, she orders food but she rarely takes more than a few bites, and Hannah and Allison have speculated for years about whether she's anorexic.

'Don't be cranky,' Fig says. 'Come over this weekend and I'll whip up some French toast.'

'You've never made French toast in your life.'

'That may be,' Fig says, and it strikes Hannah that there is something undeniably comforting in knowing her cousin so well that even when she wants to be wrong about Fig, she isn't. 'But I've seen my mom do it about a thousand times,' Fig is saying. 'It's eggs and bread.'

'I'm not coming back over there,' Hannah says.

'Ooh, playing hard to get. I like it, Hannah, I like it. It's a bold direction for you to go in. No sweat, though, I'll come to you. Should we say noon on Sunday?'

'I'm busy this weekend,' Hannah says.

'It'll be grand. We'll giggle and tell secrets.'

'I said I'm busy.'

'Then we're set,' Fig says. 'Can't wait to see you.'

The guy is working behind the desk again when Hannah returns to the financial aid office to drop off a form. When he sees her, he says, 'Hannah, right?'

'Hi,' she says.

'I'm Mike,' he says. 'FYI. How've you been?'

There are two other people waiting – an athletic-looking guy reading *The Economist* and a middle-aged woman just sitting there – and it seems slightly weird to carry on a chatty conversation in front of them.

'I've been fine,' Hannah says.

'Big plans for the weekend?'

'Not really. Can I give you this?' She passes him the form, a single sheet of paper.

But after she has left – she's gotten about twenty feet down the hall – he follows her. He says, 'Hey, Hannah,' and when she stops, he says, 'I was wondering if you like jazz. I heard about this place called Aujourd'hui that has jazz on the weekend.'

If you're doing what it seems like you're doing, Hannah thinks uncomfortably, *I just can't help you.*

'I don't know if you're free this Friday,' Mike adds.

Though she tries, she can't come up with a reason to say no. She says, 'I guess I am.'

On Friday, they meet outside her dorm and walk through the warm fall night to the restaurant. He is from Worcester, Massachusetts, he tells her. He's an only child. His parents are divorced, too. When he finds out she's from Philadelphia, he says, 'Don't tell me you're Amish.'

'They're more out in the country,' she says.

'I'm just teasing,' he says quickly.

186

Their table is in a corner far from the stage. Hannah wonders if this is a desirable table, with privacy, given to them because they're young and it's obvious they're on a first date, or if it's an undesirable table and they're being hidden away because they're not glamorous. Even in the corner, the music is so loud that Hannah feels as if she's screaming every time she speaks. Eventually, she and Mike take to nodding at each other, half smiling.

Out on the street again, it's comparatively quiet. He says, 'Live music can be so great,' and he seems in this moment like a person who will never say a surprising thing. In the summer, he will ask, *Hot enough for you?* and on the first day of November, he'll complain (but not even fervently – he'll complain cheerfully, conversationally) about how Christmas decorations go up earlier and earlier every year, and if a scandal occurs involving a politician, he'll say that the press is just trying to be sensational, that it's boring to read about it in the paper day after day. (Hannah herself never feels bored by such scandals.) He will eventually propose marriage – not to Hannah but to someone – by showing up at the girl's door with a dozen red roses, taking her out to a nice restaurant, and arranging with the waiter to hide the ring in the crème brûlée so she'll find it with her spoon, and that night, after she says yes, they'll have sex – he'll call it making love – and he'll look deeply into her eyes and tell her she's made him the luckiest guy in the world. The engagement ring will be a gold band with a small, earnest diamond.

Then they start walking and he says, 'But that sucked. You didn't like it, did you? I could tell.'

'I was a little worried the saxophonist would pop a blood vessel,' Hannah admits.

'Maybe he should have,' Mike says. 'Put us out of our misery. You want to get a cab?' He steps away from her, toward the street.

'We can walk,' Hannah says. 'Or you can get a cab if you want to, and I can walk. I mean, we're not – you're not coming back to my dorm, right?'

He grins. 'Those are some nice manners you have.'

'I just meant that I didn't think we were going to the same place. You can come to my room if you want to.' Why has she made this offer? 'But I should warn you that I don't even have a TV.'

He laughs, and maybe she seems offended by his laughter, because then he touches her shoulder. She can feel his gaze on her face. 'You look very pretty tonight,' he says, and the first true feeling she has experienced all evening shoots through her chest. Is she really this easily swayed?

'Hey,' he says. She looks at him, and he smiles and takes her left hand with his right one. (Their hands are roughly the same size, though his finger-nails are narrower than hers, and so are his knuckles. Later, Hannah will think that if someone took a picture of their hands side by side and showed it to strangers and told them to guess whose were the man's and whose were the woman's, most of the strangers would guess wrong.) They begin walking, their hands linked.

'I'm glad we're hanging out,' Mike says. 'It's a nice night.'

Hannah says in a very quiet voice, 'Yeah, it is.' Intermittently, over the course of the last few hours, she has imagined telling Jenny or Fig about her bad date with a cheesy guy from the financial aid office, but it occurs to her that she doesn't have to tell them anything. In her dorm, they sit side by side on the edge of her bed, and he rides his thumb down her bare forearm, and the tenuousness of the moment leaves her unable to speak. Mike seems so kind and hopeful (surely this will all go wrong somehow) that she wants to weep. He turns her jaw with his fingertips, and when they kiss, his tongue is warm and wet.

They don't end up doing much more than kissing, but he stays over, sleeping in his T-shirt and boxer shorts with both his arms around her; he asks her permission before removing his button-down shirt and jeans. The all-night spooning surprises Hannah. *I don't regret what has happened between us*, Mike's arms seem to say. And then, toward dawn, *I still don't regret what has happened.*

But in the morning, when he again sits on the edge of the bed, this time tying his shoes before he leaves – she lied and told him her shift at the library starts at eight o'clock – she stands there with her arms folded. When he also stands, he sets his hand on her back, and though it's a nice gesture, it feels arbitrary and unnatural, as if he could just as easily have placed his hand on the top of her head or gripped her elbow. It feels *symbolic*; they are actors in a play, and the director has told him to touch her so the audience will understand there's a bond between them. She wants him gone.

Noon on Sunday comes and goes. When Hannah hears a pounding on her door at 1:20, she briefly considers not answering, and then of course she does. Fig is wearing fitted black pants, a black sweater, and black high-heeled boots. She tosses her bag on the floor, and in one fluid movement – Hannah smells cigarette smoke clinging to Fig's long auburn hair as she passes – is lying under the covers in Hannah's bed.

Hannah, who is wearing jeans and a T-shirt, says, 'That's so gross, Fig. Take your shoes off.'

Fig throws back the covers and lifts one leg into the air.

'No,' Hannah says.

'Pretty please,' Fig says.

'You're ridiculous.' Hannah takes hold of Fig's right ankle, unzips the boot, pulls it off, then does the left boot.

'Thanks, donut blossom,' Fig says as she pulls

the covers back up to her chin. 'So I've decided to become a cat burglar. I'd be good at it, right?'

'I was thinking maybe we could go to a movie,' Hannah says. 'Is there anything you want to see?'

'I actually need to get home pretty soon, because Henry is supposed to call.' Fig turns to look at Hannah's clock. 'What time is it?'

Just his name – it's like remembering you have a wonderful party to look forward to. How unreasonable, really, for her to expect that she'd feel for someone like Mike, whom she barely knows, the certainty of affection she feels for Henry. His best e-mail ever arrived a few weeks ago: *You should think of paying a visit here. Fig has talked about it, but I'm not sure she'll make it over. There is lots to do in Seoul (most of which I have not taken advantage of), and we could also travel. It would be so great to see a familiar face, and I hear Korean Air has some relatively cheap tickets.* Relatively cheap – she checked – turned out to be nearly a thousand dollars, which was out of the question. Still, it was an excellent e-mail.

'How's Henry doing?' Hannah asks. She has never known if Fig is aware she and Henry communicate – it doesn't seem like it, but it's safer to assume she is. Perhaps not surprisingly, Fig tends to be a better source of information about Henry than Henry himself, regularly dropping some detail about his life that makes it apparent how sanitized his communications with Hannah are. The most recent tidbit was that he and a few colleagues went to a nightclub where, if you asked your waiter to bring a girl to you, the waiter would find the most attractive woman in the club and, by force if necessary, deposit her at your table. This phenomenon, according to Fig – who appeared utterly unthreatened by the idea of other women being tossed at Henry – was called 'booking.'

'He sounds tired,' Fig says. 'Half the time when he calls, it's three in the morning there and he's still at the office. So aren't you curious about my cat burglary?'

'Should I be?'

'I stole something.'

'That's great, Fig.'

'Look in my bag.'

Hannah has taken a seat in her desk chair, and she doesn't move.

'Go ahead and look,' Fig says. 'It won't bite. You'll get a kick out of it.'

Hannah reaches for the bag. Inside are several one-dollar bills fastened with a rubber band to a driver's license, a tube of lipstick, a pack of cigarettes, and a small silver picture frame containing a black-and-white photo of a woman in an apron and cat's-eye glasses. 'Who is this?' Hannah asks.

'It's Murray's great-grandmother.'

'Who's Murray?'

'The law student. I was trapped in his apartment until half an hour ago.'

'I thought you didn't like law students.'

'I definitely don't now. He was a total snooze. But he's obsessed with me, so I threw him a bone.'

'Does Henry know?'

'It's don't ask, don't tell. Remember? Anyway, after last night, no more bones for Murray.'

'Do you think Henry is involved with any women over there that he hasn't told you about?'

'Mmm . . .' Fig seems to consider the possibility in an entirely disinterested way. 'Nah,' she finally says, and Hannah feels a warm, surging relief. The idea that Henry could just find someone else and be whisked out of both their lives is worst of all. At least as long as he is bound to Fig, he's trackable.

'The picture's so kitschy, right?' Fig says. 'I couldn't resist.'

Hannah looks again at the framed photo. The woman has a broad smile and eyes that crinkle behind her glasses; she looks perhaps sixty. 'Don't you feel guilty?' Hannah asks.

'I feel horribly guilty. Unspeakably guilty.'

'You should.'

'I'm wearing a hair shirt right now to punish myself. You can't see it because I'm under the covers, but it's itchy as hell.'

'Fig, it's his grandmother.'

'Great-grandmother.' Fig grins. 'And the sex sucked, so I thought I should get something out of Murray.'

'It sucked? Really?' The idea of Fig having bad sex is novel.

'It must have taken an hour for me to come. Speaking of which, any progress on your epic dry spell?'

'I really don't feel like talking about this right now,' Hannah says. The irony is that Fig has no idea how epic it had gotten, prior to Ted from the summer – she has never paid close attention to Hannah's life. But to tell Fig about Mike, to tell her about him not as a joke, is unthinkable.

'You've got to put yourself out there,' Fig says. 'God gave you big ta-tas for a reason, Hannah.'

Hannah closes her eyes. 'Didn't you say you had to get going?'

'There's something I want to talk to you about,' Fig says. 'I think I've met the man of my dreams.'

'Fig, please.'

'For real,' Fig says. 'I'm serious.' She seems in this moment to be on the cusp of having genuinely hurt feelings.

'I assume it's not Henry or Murray?' Hannah says.

'His name is Philip Lake. I met him over the summer at Tracy Brewster's sister's wedding – do you remember when I went home for that? It was when you were in Alaska.'

Hannah nods.

'I didn't even talk to him at the wedding, but that was the first time I saw him. He was wearing a seersucker suit, which not every guy can pull off, but he has this air of total confidence. He was with a kind of clingy woman, so that's why I didn't go up to him. But after the wedding, I couldn't get him out of my mind. I finally asked Tracy for his address, and I should have saved a copy of the letter I wrote. It was really good.'

Did she enclose a photo, too? Knowing Fig, probably, and a dirty one at that. Also, thinks Hannah, it's unlikely the clingy date was the reason Fig didn't talk to this guy at the wedding. If she'd wanted to, she would have approached him. What she must have wanted instead was the mystery of contacting him later, luring him from afar.

'He works in television in L.A., and it's not like he brags, but I can tell he's successful,' Fig says. 'He wants to buy me a ticket out there. We were writing to each other for a while, and this week we've started talking on the phone. Why are you looking at me like that?'

'You see this as a good idea? The guy is basically a stranger.'

'Hannah, unless you go out with your own brother, everyone you date is a stranger at some point.' Hannah thinks of Mike – Fig is not wrong. 'But I've thought about safety,' Fig is saying, 'and I've decided you should come with me.'

'To L.A.?'

'We'll get a hotel room. I know you're stressing about money, so we can split the cost.' Does Fig think she's making a generous offer? 'If everything goes well, I'll stay at his place. If he turns out to be some Mark Harris-type scumbag, which I'm almost positive he won't, then I'll stay at the hotel with you. We can stalk movie stars together.'

'How are you so sure Philip Lake *isn't* another Mark Harris?'

'He's practically related to the Brewsters. He used to be married to Mr Brewster's sister.'

'He's divorced? How old is this guy?'

'He's forty-four.' Fig smiles lasciviously. 'Hannah, trust me, older men know what they're doing. Maybe we should try to find one for you, too.'

'When would this trip be?'

'Undecided, but probably the second or third weekend in October. You don't have Friday classes, do you?'

'No, I do this semester.'

'Then live a little. You've never been to California, right?'

In spite of herself, Hannah feels the rise of flattery she experiences whenever Fig issues an invitation. As much as she pretends otherwise, she knows she will go. She will always go. Fig might change her mind and not want Hannah's company, and Hannah still will go.

Fig sits up in bed and swings her feet onto the floor. 'Just think about it,' she says. She raises her arms into a Y, stretching; clearly, she's about to leave. She looks around the room. 'It's so cute that you still live in a dorm even though you're a senior,' she says.

★　★　★

196

The weird part is that Hannah and Mike continue hanging out. He keeps calling her, and as with their first date, there is never a reason to decline his invitations. Their second date is a movie; after no physical contact during the entire evening so far (unsure what to do, Hannah waved hello when they met up), in the last five minutes before the credits roll, he reaches over and takes her hand. On their third date, they eat at a Vietnamese restaurant, on their fourth they get cheeseburgers. He always pays, which she appreciates now more than she once would have; he ignores her half-hearted protests. On their fifth date, they go to Harvard Square, then walk along the Charles, which Hannah imagines will feel fake-romantic, like they're trying too hard, but instead it just feels nice. Also, after their relatively chaste first encounter, every single subsequent night ends with them in Hannah's dark dorm room (he has roommates), both of them stripped entirely naked. He does not try to convince her to have sex, but he often tells her how attracted to her he is; this is pretty much the extent of their conversation during these sessions. When she's on the verge of falling asleep, he'll say, 'Is it okay if I take care of myself?' and when she nods, he'll roll onto his back, take hold of his penis, and pull his wrapped fingers up and down. She lies on her side against him, while he keeps his other arm around her and rubs her top breast. He does this until he comes. She would expect the arrangement to seem either gross or extremely awkward, but he is so matter-of-fact and unself-conscious that it's neither; in the middle of the night, with her curled up to him and close to sleep, it actually feels tender. Sometimes she thinks if she were Fig, she would do it for him, but then she thinks if she were Fig, this would be unnecessary because they'd probably be hanging upside down from a trapeze somewhere, licking whipped cream off each other.

More and more, she does touch him. He'll say, 'You don't have to be gentle. You're not going to hurt me.' But his tone in making these remarks is always – this is very weird and she has no idea why – one of enchantment; he seems to find everything she does highly cute, endearingly girlish. The first time he kisses a trail from her sternum down her belly to between her thighs, she says, 'You don't need to.'

He says, 'I know I don't need to. I want to.'

She says, 'I thought guys didn't like it.'

In the dark, he raises his head. He says, 'Who told you that?'

At first she doesn't mention that she's a virgin – she's learned her lesson – but one night more than two weeks in, when things have tapered off and he is spooning her from behind, she says into the silent room, 'I was thinking about it, and I was wondering how many people you've had sex with.'

He doesn't hesitate. He says, 'Four.'

A silence begins to build on the other side of this exchange.

She cuts it off. She says, 'The number of people I've had sex with' – she pauses, then keeps going – 'is zero.'

There is a millisecond of stillness, of frozen time. She remembers Ted from over the summer. Then Mike tugs at her shoulder to turn her over. When they are facing each other, the length of his body against the length of hers, he takes her arms one by one, slipping the first under him and pulling the other around his back. Then he wraps his own arms around her in the same position. He doesn't say anything.

In the student center, Hannah runs into Jenny. 'I never see you anymore,' Jenny says. 'Where are you hiding?'

Hannah bites her lip. 'I've been hanging out with this guy.'

Jenny's face lights up. 'Who?'

'I doubt you know him. And it's not serious.'

'Are you free right now? Want to get yogurt?'

After buying the frozen yogurt, they carry their Styrofoam cups to a table among the clatter of other students checking mailboxes, walking in and out of the bookstore. Hannah describes the sequence of dates. 'He's nice,' she says. 'But he's not really my type.'

'What's your type?'

'I don't know. Taller.'

Jenny makes an appalled expression. 'Seriously,' she says, 'I don't see what the problem is. He sounds great.'

For the most part, they have just been tumbling onto the mattress and groping each other until they fall asleep – not changing into pajamas, not washing their faces or brushing their teeth – but that night Mike pulls out a new toothbrush, still in its packaging. He holds it up. 'Okay?' he says.

She nods.

'Cool,' he says. 'I guess we're taking it to the next level.'

When they are getting into bed, he climbs over Hannah, and his penis brushes her knee, and this contact seems utterly ordinary. That their bodies, it turns out, are just bodies is either deeply reassuring or deeply disappointing. He lies flat on top of her, and they both are still, and after a minute he says, 'Am I your first boyfriend?'

'You're not my boyfriend.' She says it flirtatiously, she pats his butt twice. But she is not really kidding. 'I could never have a boyfriend.'

'Why not?'

'Because I'm Hannah.'

'What does that mean?'

Are they having the relationship talk? As much as she's heard about it, she's always seen it as akin to going on safari or joining a bowling league, an activity practiced by others that she herself would probably never participate in. That she is now participating does not feel like a relief, it does not feel like proof of anything she yearns for proof of. It feels unreal, and provokes that sense of being actors in a play.

'So how should I introduce you to people?' Mike asks.

'As Hannah,' she says.

Fig calls on a Tuesday afternoon. 'I just got off the phone with a travel agent,' she says. 'I need to call her back by five o'clock. You're coming, right?'

It is four forty. 'Tell me again what weekend this is.'

'Hannah, does it really matter? What else do you have going on?'

She just can't give Mike to Fig to destroy. She says, 'Maybe I'll have a paper due.'

'It's the third weekend in October. The ticket is a little over three hundred.'

Hannah sighs. Now that she's in debt, money has started to seem pretend – what's the difference between being $11,000 in the hole and $11,300? 'That's fine,' she says.

The third weekend in October – the Saturday – is Mike's twenty-second birthday. He says, 'I told you that. It's when we talked about going to my mom's.'

He's right. Once reminded, she remembers the

conversation perfectly. She says, 'Well, at least it's not a big birthday, like twenty-one.'

'It's nice to know you care so much.'

This is the first time he has been displeased with her, and his petulance seems childish. She rises from her bed, where they have been lying clothed above the duvet – they are about to go have dinner – then takes a rubber band from the dish on her dresser and pulls her hair into a ponytail; it's an excuse to move away from him.

'Based on how you talk about your cousin, it doesn't even sound like you like her,' Mike says. 'You make her sound awful.'

'She is,' Hannah says. 'But she's great, too.'

Mike looks disbelieving.

'Once when we were little, someone gave Fig's parents chocolate truffles for Christmas, and we snuck the box up to her room and ate the entire thing,' Hannah says. 'Afterward, we realized they had some kind of liqueur in them, and Fig convinced me we both were drunk. She believed it herself. We started stumbling around her room, sort of rolling on the floor – we had no idea how drunk people really acted. And I was all freaked out, but it also was fun. Fig is never boring, and life is never boring when you're hanging out with her.'

Mike still appears unimpressed.

'Also,' Hannah says, 'she once tried to set me up with a guy at BU.'

'I don't know if I want to hear this.'

'It was the beginning of last year. She was going to a fraternity formal, and she arranged for me to go with a friend of her date. I'm sure my date imagined I'd be really pretty because I was Fig's cousin. She told me if I drank a lot and didn't say anything weird, he'd definitely hit on me, but that I shouldn't go back to his room unless I was prepared to have sex. And he sort of pawed me on the bus, but I just couldn't do it. I couldn't go through with it.' Hannah also cannot remember the guy's name. He was a lacrosse player, and his defining characteristics to her were that he wore a tight, ropy necklace with brown wooden beads and that he told her he hoped to be making a hundred Gs – that was how he phrased it – within five years of graduation. 'The night was a bust,' Hannah says. 'But this is the thing: Fig brought me a corsage. She knew the guy wouldn't, so she got me one herself, an iris with baby's breath. Fig's not all bad.'

Mike shakes his head. 'First of all, you *are* really pretty,' he says. 'And you know what else? You're your own worst enemy.'

Mike attended an all-boys' Catholic high school, and Hannah suspects it is particularly gratifying to him to be at such a liberal university: He is a registered member of the Green Party, and he doesn't eat grapes because of the migrant workers who pick them. She says, 'Because of what about the migrant workers?' and he provides a detailed

203

response, which surprises her; she asked partly because she doubted he'd be able to. But she's not sure if the fact that his idealism is well informed makes it better or worse. It just seems a little silly. Growing up, when she still lived with her father, any given day was about not stirring the pot, and so people who stir the pot voluntarily, who define themselves in these vocal ways – she can't shake the sense that they're playing a game, even if they're not aware of it.

Mike also seems to get a particular kick out of the fact that one of his closest friends is a lesbian named Susan who has a dainty black cross tattooed on the back of her neck. The night they go to a bar with her, Hannah thinks she can hear in Mike's voice an extra catch of pleasure while he comforts Susan about having just run into her ex-girlfriend.

But then – they do this a week early, because of Hannah's trip to L.A. – Hannah and Mike take the bus to his mother's house in Worcester, and it turns out his mother is a lesbian, too. So, no, that evening at the bar when Mike was talking to Susan, the subtext wasn't *Look how down I am with your gayness.*

Mike's mother's house is a tidily maintained two-bedroom colonial with white aluminum siding. Mike, Hannah, and Mike's mother eat dinner on the back deck, and when Hannah calls his mother Ms Koslowski, she says, 'Don't be silly, Hannah.

Call me Sandy.' She is an accountant, divorced from Mike's father since Mike was four. She's short, like Mike, and trim, with chin-length gray hair and a mild Massachusetts accent. She's wearing a sleeveless plaid button-down shirt, jeans, and penny loafers. She owns a lethargic bulldog named Newtie, short for Newt Gingrich. 'Is that a tribute or an insult?' Hannah asks, and Mike's mother says, 'To the man or the dog?' A certain wiliness in this exchange – on Mike's mother's part, both a withholding of information about herself and a suspension of judgment of Hannah, or a pretense of suspension – makes Hannah realize that his mother sees her as a rich girl. Which, though it feels untrue these days, is not entirely wrong.

Mike touches Hannah frequently in front of his mother, and when they are finished with dinner, he moves next to her on the bench and drapes his arm around her shoulder. When he stands to clear – he won't let Hannah help – he holds up her left hand and kisses the back of it. They have ice cream for dessert. 'Hannah, do you want mint chip or butter pecan?' Mike asks as he carries the pints out from the kitchen, and when Hannah says, 'Can I have a little bit of both?' Mike's mother says approvingly, 'Atta girl.'

She lets Hannah and Mike sleep in the same room, in his boyhood bed; Hannah assumed she'd end up on the living room couch. In the middle of the night – they both are wearing boxer shorts and T-shirts – Mike says, 'Let's take off our clothes. I want to feel your skin.'

'What about your mom?' Hannah asks.

'She sleeps like a log.'

Soon, of course, they are kissing and entangled; he is on top. 'You're sure she can't hear?' Hannah whispers.

'Shh.' Mike smiles in the dark. 'I'm trying to sleep.'

When he says he has a condom, she nods – really, the surprising part is that it has taken this long – and then he is plunging into her; the entry hurts the most, and Hannah thinks of Fig saying, back in high school, 'You just grit your teeth and get it over with.' After the entry, when it is actually happening, it's neither as painful nor as pleasurable as she imagined. As he thrusts, there is mostly a kind of juicy friction, and she thinks how this, allegedly, is the reason people stand in crowded bars on Saturday nights, the reason for marriages and crimes and wars, and she cannot help thinking, *Really? Just this*? It makes people, all of them – all of *us*, she thinks – seem so strange and sweet. She can see how every other act that unfolds between a man and woman in a bed together might vary, but mustn't this always feel more or less the same? For the first time since she met Henry almost a year and a half ago, it occurs to her that maybe he's not an answer to anything in particular. Maybe Mike is as much an answer as Henry.

After Mike collapses on her, he whispers, 'How do you like sex, Hannah?'

What is there to say? She squeezes his hand.

He whispers, 'It's going to get better and better,' and though she doesn't cry, this is when she gets the closest, because of his sureness in their future. Does he not have any doubts at all about her? He says, 'Now let me take care of you,' and he uses the tips of his forefinger and middle finger. She squirms and squirms (surely this is one of the acts that is not identical from couple to couple), and when she comes, she whimpers softly, and he murmurs into her ear, 'You're so beautiful. I'm so lucky to have a beautiful, wonderful naked woman in my bed.'

The night before Hannah leaves for Los Angeles, Mike's friend Susan holds a dinner party for his birthday. Susan lives off campus with two other women, and they serve gnocchi on paper plates and red wine in plastic cups, and everyone smokes pot except for Hannah and, possibly out of deference to Hannah, Mike. Hannah has brought a sheet cake she got at the supermarket and on her computer has typed up a certificate for dinner at the restaurant of Mike's choosing. She considers this present lame, what an unimaginative boyfriend who hadn't planned ahead would peeve his girlfriend by giving her, but when she hands it to Mike before they leave for the party, he hugs her and says, 'Thank you, baby.' (Being called baby: like safaris and bowling leagues, a phenomenon she never thought she'd experience firsthand.)

At the party, Hannah doesn't drink, but Mike has six or seven beers. Back in her dorm, she climbs in bed after he has, turns off the light, and lies on her side. He leans over from behind her and pulls the covers up around her shoulders. 'Thanks,' she says.

'I hope you feel warm and loved.' He pauses. 'Because I do love you, you know.'

It is two in the morning and entirely dark in the room. Previously, it has occurred to Hannah that this moment will come to pass with Mike, and she has not known whether or not she wants it to. Either way, she did not expect it now. She is quiet for perhaps thirty seconds and then says, 'How do you know?'

She hears him, she feels him, smile. 'I took a quiz on the Internet,' he says and wraps his arms around her; he rubs his nose in her hair.

Saying it back is not an impossibility, but the sentiment hasn't emerged spontaneously, and then more time passes. Has he fallen asleep? The front of his body curves against the back of hers, and she lies with her eyes open. After fifteen minutes, in a small but completely awake voice, he says, 'Do you love me?'

The reason she says nothing is that nothing she can think of is exactly right. Finally – she feels mean, but she also feels like he's backed her into a corner – she says, 'We've been together less than two months. That's not that long.'

He rolls away from her. 'Do me a favor,' he says. 'Check your emotional calendar, and let me know what kind of schedule we're looking at here. Maybe throw out a couple dates that might work for you.' She has never heard him be sarcastic.

'Mike, maybe I do,' she says.

'Maybe you do what?'

Again she says nothing, and then she says, 'If I said it because you'd forced it out of me, would it really mean anything anyway?'

She feels him roll over another ninety degrees, so they're back to back. 'Thanks for making this such a great birthday,' he says, and she begins to cry.

Immediately, he rolls back toward her (so some males really are softened by female tears). 'What could be different between us that would make it better?' he says. 'I don't think it *could* be better, except it seems like you don't want it official. The I'm-not-your-boyfriend bullshit – what is that? Are you embarrassed by me?'

'Of course I'm not embarrassed by you.' Sometimes she's embarrassed by him. She wishes that he didn't unironically pronounce the word *genuine* gen-u-wine, like a used-car dealer; she wishes he'd just eat grapes, or shut up about not eating them; she wishes she didn't suspect that, should she introduce him to her family, they'd probably think he's not that cute. She realizes she can never express these sentiments, but is she supposed to pretend, even to herself, that she doesn't feel them? 'I'm just getting used to everything,' she says.

'You know what?' Mike says. 'You can get used to it without me. I can't sleep here tonight.'

'It's two thirty in the morning!'

'I'm too riled up. I don't want to fight with you.'

'I'm going to L.A. tomorrow,' she says. 'Don't leave.'

'You know what else?' he says. 'The vet library doesn't open until ten on Saturdays.'

'What are you talking about?'

'The first time we got together, you told me you had to go to work at eight the next day.'

'Mike, we barely knew each other. I was freaking out.'

'You're right, though,' he says. 'Why would I want to convince you of anything?'

Carrying her backpack and duffel bag, Hannah rides the T to Fig's apartment. She has agreed to come over before they head to the airport in order to help Fig pick out clothes to take. In Hannah's head, the fight with Mike is a bowl of soup she is carrying down a long hall, and to think about it at all is to shake the bowl; it is best just to walk forward. At Fig's, her cousin's bedroom is open, and Fig stands in front of the closet in a black thong and nothing else. Instinctively, Hannah lifts her hand in front of her eyes, and Fig says, 'Don't be a prude. Will I look like a college student if I wear a halter top?'

'You *are* a college student.' Fig's double bed is unmade and covered with clothes, so Hannah sits on the floor, her back against the wall.

'But I don't want to give Philip Lake a vibe of, like, keg parties,' Fig says. 'I want to seem classy.'

'Your black boots are classy,' Hannah says. 'Wear those.'

'They're Mindy's, but that's not a bad idea. Hey, Mindy—' Still in only her thong, Fig walks out of the bedroom and into the hall.

When she returns, Hannah says, 'How will you decide if you stay with Philip Lake tonight or stay in our hotel?'

'I'll play it by ear.'

'How about this – definitely stay in the hotel tonight, and then think about staying with him tomorrow?'

Fig steps into a black suede skirt, pulls it up over her hips, and zips it. She stands in front of a full-length mirror hanging on the wall and looks at herself intently. 'How about this?' she says. 'I wear a collar, and you attach a leash to it, and when I get too frisky, you yank.'

'Fig, you're the one who asked me to come on this trip.'

'I didn't ask you to babysit me.'

You sort of did, Hannah thinks, and says nothing.

Fig steps out of the skirt and flings it back on the bed. She glances over at Hannah, and when

211

their eyes meet, Fig says, 'Are you checking out my tits?'

Heat rises in Hannah's cheeks. 'Of course not,' she says. In fact, observing Fig, she'd been thinking she could understand for the first time in her life why men are drawn to women's breasts. In the past, breasts always seemed to her an odd-looking and unwieldy part of the anatomy – she included her own in this assessment – but on her cousin, they make sense. Fig's are small but firm-looking, her dark skin (Fig lays out in the summer and goes to a tanning bed the rest of the year) accented by darker nipples. Sometimes when Mike is sucking away, Hannah is unclear who's doing whom a favor – she thinks it's more for his benefit but isn't sure in precisely what way. In Fig's breasts, though, she sees a certain festivity; hanging there so visibly, they're a kind of invitation. Aloud, Hannah says, 'So what's the exact plan? Is he picking us up at the airport?'

'Oh God, no,' Fig says. 'I thought we'd take a taxi. I mean, Hannah, it's not like Philip knows you're coming.' Fig is spritzing perfume on her wrists, then rubbing her wrists behind her ears. She is no longer looking at Hannah, and so, Hannah thinks, Fig will not see what is surely an expression of dismay crossing Hannah's face. Of course Philip Lake doesn't know Hannah is coming; she had only assumed otherwise because she hadn't given it real thought. There was a time when this whole trip would have loomed larger to

Hannah, consumed much more anticipatory energy, but she has been so distracted lately. She's not even certain what time their flight is leaving – it's either 1:20 or 1:40 – and she unzips her backpack and reaches into it for the airplane ticket. When she pulls it out, the yellow Post-it note is stuck to the ticket sleeve. In blue ink, in Mike's handwriting, it says, *Hannah is Great!*

For at least a minute, she holds the square of paper between her thumb and index finger, looking down at it, stricken. She doesn't know if he put it there before or after their fight, but either way, how has she been so foolish? Why exactly is she flying to Los Angeles? Why, as Allison might put it, is she giving attention to something that makes her unhappy, why is she still choosing Fig when she finally has the privilege of making a choice?

She stands. She says, 'Fig, I'm not going with you.'

'What are you talking about?' Fig says.

'You'll be fine. If you think Philip Lake isn't sketchy, I bet your instincts are right. You don't need me.'

'Are you offended because I didn't tell him you were coming? If it matters that much to you, I will.'

'It's not that,' Hannah says. 'There's stuff I need to take care of here. This was never a good idea.' She has pulled on her backpack, she's holding her duffel. Fig is regarding her with both curiosity and confusion. Perhaps, unprecedentedly, Fig is entertaining the thought that Hannah's life contains its own dark corridors and mysterious doors. 'You do have great tits, though,' Hannah says. 'I'm sure Philip Lake will love them.'

'What's gotten into you?' Fig says, but Hannah is already backing down the hall, waving with her one free hand.

'You'll have to tell me all about it,' she says.

'You've lost your fucking mind,' Fig says, 'and I hope you don't think I'm reimbursing you for your plane ticket.'

Hannah sits on a bench waiting for the T, holding the Post-it note in her hand. She's within view of Fig's apartment, but Fig doesn't come after her. The train has just appeared in the distance when it occurs to Hannah that she can't possibly wait for as long as it will take to transfer lines and then walk from the Davis Square stop back to campus. She's pretty sure Mike is working until noon, so what she should do instead is catch a cab and ride it straight to the financial aid office. But he almost certainly wrote the note before their fight, and what if it doesn't still apply?

Next to the T tracks is a pay phone. Hannah sticks in the change and presses the number keys. When Mike answers, he says, 'Student Financial Services,' and she is on the verge of tears as she says, 'It's me.'

His silence is long enough to let her feel afraid.

214

In this silence, she thinks that if he is glad to hear from her – she'll be devastated if he's not glad to hear from her – she'll say she loves him, too; she'll say it immediately, in this conversation.

She hears him swallow.

'Hi, baby,' he says.

PART III

CHAPTER 7

FEBRUARY 2003

On the morning of her mother's wedding to Frank McGuire, Hannah sleeps until quarter to nine and awakens to Allison saying, 'Get up, Hannah. Aunt Elizabeth is on the phone, and she wants to talk to you.' When Allison opens the curtains – they are pink-striped, the same ones their mother first decorated Hannah's room with when they moved into the condo twelve years ago – Hannah blinks in the light. White flakes appear to be sailing past the window.

'Is it snowing again?' she asks.

'It's only supposed to be a couple inches. Hurry up and get the phone. Elizabeth's waiting.' Allison pauses in the door. 'When you're done, you might want to come rescue Oliver. Aunt Polly is here, and I think she's talking his ear off.'

Of course – Oliver. Hannah knew there was some reason she was feeling unsettled even in sleep. 'I'll be down in a second,' she says.

There is no longer a phone in Hannah's old bedroom. She walks into her mother's room, lifts the receiver from its cradle, and stands in front

219

of the mirror that hangs on the inside door of the open closet. She is wearing cotton pajama pants and a long-sleeved T-shirt, and she watches herself say hello.

'Can we just discuss for a minute what that gorgeous Jennifer Lopez is doing with that squirrelly Ben Affleck?' Elizabeth says. 'Every time I see him, I want to wipe the frat-boy smirk off his face.'

'I think they're sort of cute,' Hannah says.

'Darrach and I just rented – now I can't even remember the movie. Hannah, this addled brain of mine. But here's why I'm really calling. You need to go see your dad.'

'I think I'd rather not,' Hannah says.

'How long has it been? Five years?'

'I saw him at Allison's wedding, and that was less than four years ago. Anyway, that was when I last saw *you*.' This is true. Since the summer she stayed with Elizabeth and Darrach, Hannah has seen her aunt twice: once on a Sunday during Hannah's freshman year in high school (this was Hannah's idea) when Elizabeth and Darrach and Rory met her and her mother at a restaurant halfway between Philadelphia and Pittsburgh; and then a few years after that, when Elizabeth came to Philadelphia for Hannah's father's fiftieth birthday. Hannah and Elizabeth still talk every two or three months, and Hannah thinks of her aunt more than that – she finds herself remembering things Elizabeth told her,

220

intimations Elizabeth gave of adulthood – but Hannah has never returned to Pittsburgh. She is pretty sure it would remind her of too much.

'Come on, now,' Elizabeth says. 'His ex-wife is getting married today, and the guy she's marrying sounds, pardon my French, pretty stinking rich. You don't think your dad deserves a break?'

'How's Rory?' Hannah says. 'Is he still working at that restaurant?'

'Don't you try to change the subject.'

'My dad can get in touch with me as easily as I can get in touch with him. Why is it my responsibility?'

'Didn't you tell him never to call you?'

Hannah says nothing. A few days after she and her father had that last lunch, he forwarded her a postcard from her dentist, a reminder to schedule her annual visit, which had somehow been sent to his apartment. On the outside of the envelope he'd stuck the card in, he'd scrawled, *Nice to see you last week, Hannah*, and she had no idea if he was being sarcastic or just oblivious. At Allison's wedding, it was impossible to avoid him completely, but she did so as much as she could. To this day, Allison claims that their father inquires after her, and Hannah doesn't know whether this is true. That he didn't end up paying any of her Tufts tuition senior year seemed a message of sorts – it would have been easy enough for him to go above her head and just send in a check.

Hannah has never regretted her decision, but she is still in debt.

'I'm not asking you to go see your dad,' Elizabeth says. 'I'm telling you. Do I have enough authority to do that?'

'He and I have never had that much to say,' Hannah says. 'Maybe this is how things are supposed to be between us.'

'No one's suggesting you pretend you don't have problems with him. But just go drink a cup of tea, ask him how work is. Give him a reason to think he hasn't destroyed everything good in his life.'

'He kind of has,' Hannah says, though she is arguing as much on reflex as on conviction. The freshness of her anger toward her father, what she felt that afternoon at the restaurant, has faded; she knows she's mad at him more than she feels it. 'If I were to go see him,' she says, 'I'm sure he'd expect me to apologize.'

'Tough shit for him. You're going over to be sociable, not to grovel.'

'Why are you so confident this is a good idea?'

'I'm tempted to say you wouldn't even be doing it for him, you'd be doing it for you. But maybe you'd really be doing it for me. Here's the bottom line, though. Are you ready for the bottom line?'

'Probably not.' Hannah has moved to a window over-looking the driveway. Outside, the snow is still falling, and she can see her mother, in a pink quilted bathrobe and boots, talking to Aunt Polly as they walk toward Aunt Polly's Volvo. At least this means Aunt Polly is no longer trapping Oliver.

'The bottom line is he's lonely,' Elizabeth says. 'And he's your father.'

In the kitchen, there are bagels and muffins in a basket on the table, and Sam is grading his sixth-grade students' papers while Allison rolls forks and knives into dinner napkins and ties them with thin blue ribbon. There will be nineteen wedding guests, including family; the ceremony will happen at five o'clock this afternoon. When Hannah asked her mother whether she would avoid Frank during the day – it wouldn't be that hard, since Frank still has his own house – Hannah's mother said, 'Oh, honey, I'm fifty-three. That's more for your age.'

When Hannah sits down, Sam says, 'It's Sleeping Beauty. Are you hungover or something?'

'Where's Oliver?' Hannah asks.

'He took Mom's car to run an errand,' Allison says. 'He said he'd be gone about twenty minutes.'

'Wait,' Hannah says. 'He drove?' Oliver does not have a driver's license. When Allison looks at her curiously, Hannah looks away. To Sam, she says, 'I'm not hung-over at all. I didn't even drink last night.'

'You should have,' Allison says. 'The champagne looked delicious.' Allison is six months pregnant and glowing even more than usual.

223

'Hannah, if you're dating an Aussie, you have to step up,' Sam says. 'Become more of a lush.'

'Oliver's from New Zealand,' Hannah says. 'But thanks for the tip.'

Sam grins, and Hannah thinks of the energy she used to expend feeling irritated by him. She didn't understand back then that you don't ask a person to defend her significant other, that she never should have asked Allison to. Not because of the sanctity of couplehood (as far as Hannah can tell, there are only ever fleeting, split-second episodes of sanctity between any couple) but because maybe the person *can't* entirely defend her mate, because maybe – probably – the person has her own ambivalence, and your criticisms are undermining. And not even of the couple but of this individual trying to move forward in her life, making choices that she hopes are the right ones when, really, how does anyone ever know? Forcing Allison to stand up for Sam, Hannah thinks now, was naïve as much as obnoxious. Hannah used to imagine a greater merging between two people, a point beyond which you felt an unquestioning certainty in each other.

'Did you sign the card for Mom and Frank?' Allison asks.

Hannah nods, taking a sesame bagel. 'Dad's in town, right?' she says.

'Yeah, we saw him yesterday. Are you thinking of . . .' Allison trails off, her expression encouraging.

'Maybe,' Hannah says. 'But please let's not have some big conversation about it.'

Oliver returns after closer to forty minutes than twenty. When Hannah hears the car in the driveway, she grabs her coat and goes outside. Oliver kisses her on the lips, and she can taste cigarettes, the purchase of which she assumes was his errand. He is wearing a plaid flannel shirt and over it a black down parka that definitely doesn't belong to him – it's Sam's or maybe even Allison's. Hannah gestures toward it and says, 'Cute.' Hannah and Oliver flew in last night from Boston, and then – Hannah's mother apologetically insisted – Oliver slept on the pullout couch in the den. It's slightly bizarre to have his handsomeness set down here by daylight in her mother's familiar, comforting, unexciting condo.

'So Aunt Polly offered to show me her art class portfolio,' Oliver says. He perches on the porch railing, lights a cigarette, and takes a puff. 'But I sense that it's filled with giant penises, and I'm afraid I'll feel inadequate.'

'Aunt Polly's taking an art class? Like adult ed or something?'

'Ask her yourself. She'll be more than happy to tell you. They're currently studying the human form, and she said the male model is quite well hung.'

'Aunt Polly did not say *well hung*.'

Oliver holds up the hand with the cigarette in

225

it, palm facing her. 'As God is my witness.' He has that little pre-smile on his face, though.

'Aunt Polly would never say that. Or if she did, she must not know what it means.' Polly is Fig's mother, fifty-eight years old, with graying black hair that's usually pulled back in a bun. Every year on Thanksgiving, she wears an enamel turkey pin.

'Of course she knows what it means,' Oliver says. 'Do you think she was referring to his earlobes? She also said she finds his scrotum exquisite. She's never considered herself partial to the scrote, but something special's going on with this guy.'

Hannah shakes her head – they both are smiling – and she says, 'You're such a liar.'

'Your aunt's appreciation of the male sex organs is healthy. Don't be judgmental.'

Oliver is still seated on the railing, and she has a strange urge to butt her head against his chest, like a goat. She's not into the sex with him, but she's always reassured by his arms around her. When he lights another cigarette, she feels a leap of happiness – she thought he would smoke only one, but now they get to stay out here longer, alone on the back porch. Oliver's smoking doesn't bother her at all, which is something that actually does sort of bother her. But the smoke reminds her, even when they're together, of him.

'I might go see my dad today,' Hannah says. 'Do you think I should?'

Oliver shrugs. 'Sure.'

'Do you remember that I haven't spoken to him for several years?'

'Not since he tried to force-feed you pasta, if I'm not mistaken.' Oliver often seems like he's not particularly listening, yet he has an excellent memory. It's both insulting and flattering.

'If I go, do you want to come?' Hannah asks.

'Do I want to or will I?'

'Either, I guess.'

'Will, yes. Want to, no.' Perhaps he senses that she's displeased, because he reaches out and pulls her toward him so she's leaning sideways against his chest. Although his cigarette must be perilously close to her hair, this configuration is pretty much what she was thinking of before, with herself as the goat. 'You don't need me to go with you, Hannah,' he says, and his voice is one of affectionate indulgence. 'You're a big girl.'

After stepping off the elevator on the fourth floor, Hannah walks down the carpeted hall until she finds her father's apartment. This is where he has lived for almost ten years, since selling their house on the Main Line. Though her heart is thudding, she knocks without hesitation; the gesture of knocking is habit. When her father opens the door, he smiles in a pleasantly superficial fashion, as he might for the adult daughter of a neighbor, and says, 'Come on in.' She follows him and accepts his offer of Diet Coke, which is what he is drinking. (It's weird – it's practically girly – to see her father drinking Diet Coke.) Hannah is struck by, of all things, his good looks. At fifty-eight, he remains fit and lean; his gray hair is neatly combed; he is wearing Top-Siders, khaki pants, and a blue polo shirt with the collar visible above the neck of his gray sweatshirt. If he were a stranger Hannah passed on the sidewalk, wouldn't she assume he had a life attendant to such looks? She'd think he had an attractive wife, with whom he would attend a benefit dinner at the art museum that night.

When they are settled in the living room, he says, 'Long time, no see, Hannah. I have to confess, I was surprised when I got your call this morning. To what do I owe the honor?'

'Well, I'm in town for the weekend,' Hannah says.

'Indeed. And your mom's becoming a real estate heiress, huh? Who'd have thunk?'

'Frank seems like a good guy.'

'I'll tell you what Frank McGuire is, and that's one shrewd businessman. He's not afraid to get his hands dirty. I'll say that about him.'

'Have you ever met him?'

'Oh, sure. Not for years, but I've met him. He's a well-known fellow in this city.'

'He's pretty low-key with us,' Hannah says.

'And how about yourself? I trust you're gainfully employed these days.'

If he really does ask Allison about Hannah, it seems impossible that he doesn't know what her

228

job is. 'I work at a nonprofit that sends classical musicians into public schools,' she says.

'Now, there's some irony. I remember when you wouldn't practice piano to save your life.'

'You're thinking of Allison. I never took piano lessons.'

'I beg your pardon? You took them from that witch of a woman on Barkhurst Lane.'

'That was definitely Allison.'

'You never took piano lessons? I guess you had a deprived childhood.'

'Anyway,' she says, 'I'm on the fund-raising side.'

'A nonprofit, huh? Both you and your sister turned out to be bleeding hearts.'

'You were in the Peace Corps, Dad.'

He makes a kind of cheerful grimace. 'Hard to believe, isn't it? I always thought one of you would go to business or law school. It's not too late, you know. You're about to turn twenty-six?'

She nods. She can't imagine anything she'd be less suited for than business or law school.

'You'd probably be right in the middle. An MBA in particular, that opens up a lot of options. If I were your age, I'd go for that, forget about this law crap.'

She nods some more. If she stays another fifteen minutes, that ought to be enough. 'Have you been traveling much for work?' she asks.

'Less and less. I've got a case over in King of Prussia, if you consider that toilet bowl travel. Where I did go, not for work but for some R and

R, is down to Florida last month.' Her father leans forward. 'Grab that album on the shelf, will you? You'll enjoy these.'

When she's holding the album, he waves her toward him. Meaning they're supposed to sit on the couch side by side? And since when has her father taken pictures? He always showed impatience when her mother had them pose; as her mother waited hopefully for the sun to reemerge, or perhaps for Hannah to smile, he'd say, 'Hurry up and just take it, Caitlin.'

'I went with a couple of the guys, Howard Donovan and Rich Inslow,' he says. 'Inslow's separated now, too.'

Hannah does not remember her father having friends, certainly not close ones. The Donovans and the Inslows both belonged to the same country club as the Gaveners – her mother was no longer a member after the divorce, so Hannah rarely went – but the other men hadn't appeared to be more than acquaintances. Interestingly, her father stopped dating around the time her mother started; he was in a few relationships at first, but those all fell away.

'It was a golfing trip, just a long weekend,' her father is saying. 'This is the resort. Gorgeous greens, perfect view of the ocean. It's in Clearwater, over on the Gulf.'

How strange to think of her father purchasing this blue leather album in a store, then sitting on this very sofa, perhaps, and sliding the photos under plastic. He has not labeled the pictures, nor has he done any weeding, including even the shots that are identical or out of focus or show the men with closed eyes. Here are Howard Donovan and Rich Inslow sitting in the waiting area of their gate at the Philadelphia airport, Rich eating some type of breakfast sandwich; here are aerial photos during the plane's descent, a photo of Howard driving while Rich holds a map in the front seat, a shot of them unloading their clubs from the trunk of the rental car in the resort parking lot. On and on, her father's mood steadily climbing as he shows her the pictures, and then comes the clear zenith: photos from what her father refers to as an Oriental restaurant where they ate the night before their departure. There are two shots of Rich with his arm around a young, pretty dark-haired waitress in a navy and white kimono, a few of the decor (heavy on bamboo, with the option – her father and his friends apparently declined – to remove one's shoes and sit on the floor), and her father's favorite shot of all from within this favorite setting, a sushi and sashimi tray ordered by Howard. Her father points out the slimy rectangles of pink and maroon fish draped over rice, the tiny heap of ginger. 'You know what that is?' he asks, jabbing at a lump of pale green.

'It's wasabi, isn't it?'

'That stuff is lethal. It's the Japanese kind of horseradish. Honest to God, it'll bring tears to your eyes.'

She is shocked, and also afraid to look at him. As he turns the page, he's describing a dessert whose name he cannot remember but which arrived at the table in flames. She feels utterly bewildered. This is who her father is: someone tickled by the existence of sushi. Someone who takes pictures inside a restaurant. Her father is *cheesy*. Even his handsomeness, she thinks, looking at one of the few photos in which he appears, is of a certain harmlessly generic sort, the handsomeness of a middle-aged male model in the department-store insert of the Sunday *Inquirer*. Has she only imagined him as a monster? His essential lesson, she always believed, was this: There are many ways for you to transgress, and most you will not recognize until after committing them. But is it she who invented this lesson? At the least, she met him halfway, she bought in to it. Not just as a child but all through adolescence and into adulthood – until this very moment. She realizes now that Allison does not buy in to it, that she must not have for years, and that's why Allison doesn't fight with their father or refuse to talk to him for long stretches. Why bother? Hannah always assumed Allison was bullied into her paternal devotion, but no – it is Hannah who has seen his anger as much bigger than it ever was.

After thirty-two minutes, Hannah carries her Diet Coke into the kitchen to throw away (years ago, Allison tried to get him to recycle, and of

232

course he wouldn't). Hannah wonders, does Sam also recognize that Douglas Gavener is not to be taken seriously? Does Dr Lewin, from a distance? Does everyone except for Hannah and, for a time – for nineteen years, which is how long Hannah's parents were married – her mother?

But not truly threatening isn't the same as not a jerk. He *was* a jerk. Standing in the kitchen, she thinks she will go back out there and ask him just what he had to be so angry about all those years ago. His wife was kind, his daughters were obedient. They had the accoutrements of upper-middle-class life. What more had he expected?

But when she re-enters the living room, he says, 'Tell your sister or Sam to call me if they want the tickets – Eagles versus the Giants. There's a chance I could get hold of one for you, too.' Then he extends his hand for her to shake, and this is why she can't ask him anything. If he is shaking her hand, if he's being this distant and careful, he knows he was a jerk. He doesn't need to be asked or told – beneath his sour jocularity, he knows.

She steps forward and kisses his cheek. She says, 'Bye, Dad.'

Frank McGuire is sixty-one, eight years older than Hannah's mother. He's about five-ten, with both a receding hairline and thinning hair, an ample midsection, pudgy fingers, and full lips; his lower lip in particular is as soft and large as a Hollywood actress's. During the ceremony, holding a bouquet of freesias and roses, Hannah experiences a surge of thoughts, suppressed until this moment. Do her mother and Frank have sex? Is Frank in essence buying her mother's middle-aged beauty, and is he able to buy it only because her mother has put it up for sale? What does his gut look like unclothed, and if you have a gut like that, do you go on top or on the bottom? It seems one thing to age together gradually, like maybe the drooping and expansion would be less obvious as it occurred over the years, but to come to each other for the first time this way – don't you feel terribly apologetic about your own shortcomings, and afraid of what the other person might unveil?

Also, what about the information you disclose? With all that has happened to you by then, you must by necessity be picking and choosing, so do you simply jettison the most excruciating parts of your past? Would Hannah's mother ever mention to Frank that her first husband once forced her and her daughters to leave the house in the middle of the night? Does Hannah's mother remember this? She must. Not that they would ever talk about it, but she must.

'I'm going to tell you something I haven't told anyone,' Fig says, 'but you can't react at all.'

Hannah and Fig are sitting on the living room couch, holding plates on their laps. The food is catered, and Hannah's mother has brought out

234

the blue-and-white china and monogrammed silver, and all around them the other wedding guests, the majority of whom are relatives, talk noisily. The ceremony was brief, and it is now almost six and dark outside the unshut curtains. Inside, the room has a rosy glow: The glasses and silverware are shiny, and people's cheeks are flushed, maybe because of the champagne or maybe because Mrs Dawes, the oldest friend of Hannah and Fig's deceased grandmother, has been dutifully included in the festivities and the thermostat has therefore been jacked up to seventy-five.

'I'm serious,' Fig adds. 'No gasping.'

'Fig, just say it.'

'I'm seeing someone new,' Fig begins, and Hannah thinks, *Of course you are* and is halfway to tuning her out, and then Fig says, 'and it's Dave Risca's sister.'

At first Hannah thinks she didn't hear correctly. 'His *sister*?' she repeats.

'What did I just tell you about reacting?'

'I'm not reacting,' Hannah says. 'I'm clarifying.' Fig is dating a *woman*? 'You don't mean seeing-seeing,' Hannah says. 'You mean you made out at a party.'

When Fig says, 'No, I mean we're in a relationship,' Hannah thinks how this news will force her to reconsider the world. 'I ran into her a few months after I moved back to Philly,' Fig says. 'We were talking on the sidewalk, and I start to get this vibe, and she asks if I want to have a drink. And then one thing led to another.'

'What does she look like?'

'She's stylish.' In Fig's charmed, protective tone, Hannah can hear her attraction to the woman. The relationship might be partly a lark for Fig, but not completely. 'She has, like, a delicate jaw and green eyes. Her name's Zoe.'

'Long or short hair?'

'Short.'

This relieves Hannah. It would be somehow unfair, though not unsurprising, if Fig were dating a lesbian with long blond hair. 'Is it really different from being with a man?' Hannah says.

'Not especially. I always found it easier to climax through oral sex than penetration anyway.'

'Fig, ew. That wasn't what I was asking.'

'Sure it was.' Fig smirks. 'Everyone's curious about girl on girl. How's your sex life with Oliver?'

'Never mind,' Hannah says.

'Oliver's cute,' Fig says, which depresses Hannah. Mostly, it depresses her because soon after she introduced Fig and Oliver – Fig is wearing a low-cut black blouse – Oliver whispered in Hannah's ear, 'Your cousin has magnificent breasts.' Probably right now, with Oliver across the living room, he and Fig are exchanging some sort of extrasensory signals that only the highly attractive are privy to: *You're hot, bleep bleep. Yes, I know, same to you, bleep bleep. I can't believe I'm sitting next to Hannah's snooze of a stepfather.* In

236

that moment when Oliver remarked on Fig's breasts, Hannah said, 'You should ask her if you can touch one,' and Oliver replied, 'Why ask? It would ruin the surprise.'

'My mom thinks he's cute, too,' Fig is saying. 'Hey, Mom.'

Aunt Polly is by the fireplace, talking to Allison.

'Hannah's boyfriend is cute, right?' Fig says.

Aunt Polly cups one ear.

'Hannah's boyfriend,' Fig repeats and gives a thumbs-up gesture. (*Hannah's boyfriend* – they will always be the weirdest words Hannah can imagine. *Jumbo shrimp*, she thinks. *Military intelligence*.)

'Oh, he's fabulous, Hannah,' Aunt Polly calls. 'That Australian accent!'

'Actually, New Zealand.' Hannah feels like she's screaming.

'Allison told me you two met in the office. Let's—' Aunt Polly angles her head to the right and points. *We'll talk later in the kitchen*, she means. *Or at least we'll pretend we will, so we can stop howling at each other*.

'Have you noticed that Mrs Dawes has obscenely bad breath tonight?' Fig asks, and Hannah can feel it abruptly, that she needs to check on Oliver. Maybe she has the extrasensory perception after all, maybe it's not tied to personal hotness. Talking to her mother and Frank, Oliver has grown restless, he wants a cigarette, and he wants Hannah to keep him company while he smokes. She knows it. 'It's like she ate a garlic clove before coming over,' Fig says.

Hannah touches Fig's forearm. 'Hold on,' she says. 'Sorry. I'll be back.'

This is why Hannah fell for Oliver: because he took out her splinter.

She sometimes thinks to herself, as if it's some kind of excuse, that before he became her boyfriend, she didn't even like him. She knew him, she shared an office with him, and she didn't like him. But does her initial resistance, given what's happened between them, mean she's even more of a sucker?

At work, their desks faced opposite walls, and when she'd hear him on the phone or, worse, when some youngish, attractive female colleague who often was new to the organization would come and linger in the doorway, clearly either gearing up for or giddily descending from an extra-office sexual encounter with Oliver, Hannah would ignore both him and the woman. The game of it all, the pattern of their words, the way the woman was either as jaded and crass as Oliver, or else the way she was entirely uncynical, ready to be swept away – either possibility was nauseating. Except that after a while, Hannah mostly stopped noticing. That was how much Oliver didn't interest her, how unable he was to upset her. (Later, she felt the nostalgia of remembering the time before she took him seriously.)

One day after a woman named Gwen had stopped by – she and Oliver were, apparently, heading to a bar in Downtown Crossing that evening – Hannah said, 'I just hope you know that it's ninety percent your accent.'

'My sex appeal, you mean?' Oliver was smiling. In the space between when she'd spoken and when he'd responded, she'd imagined maybe he wouldn't know what she was talking about, and she'd been relieved. But he did not appear offended.

'That's not what I'd call it,' Hannah said. 'But suit yourself.' If he hadn't understood and she hadn't offended him, she'd have stopped. The fact that he had understood and that she hadn't offended him – yet – only meant she needed to try harder.

'Animal magnetism,' Oliver said. 'You could call it that.'

'I could.'

Had they ever had a conversation before? It suddenly seemed like they hadn't. They'd been sitting eight feet apart for four months, over-hearing every word out of each other's mouths while directly exchanging only the blandest of pleasantries: *Did you beat the rain? Enjoy the weekend!* And now she could see, he was slimy but also intelligent.

'Of course,' Oliver was saying, 'you raise two questions, or two to start with. Undoubtedly, you raise many more, and we'll have to spend the rest of our lives untangling them. But the most pressing question is, is it safe to assume you don't include yourself in the category of women seduced by anything as superficial as an accent?'

'Obviously not,' Hannah said, 'and the other ten percent is basic aggression. That was your second question, right?'

'You're clairvoyant!' Oliver exclaimed. 'Which is just as I always suspected. But aggression has predatory overtones, and I'm such a peaceful chap.'

'Assertive, then,' Hannah said. 'You're a skirt-chaser.'

'Now, that I don't mind – it sounds charmingly old-fashioned.'

'A cad,' Hannah said. 'How about that?'

'A swashbuckler.'

'In your dreams.'

'If I'm a skirt-chaser,' Oliver said, 'then you must admit that every woman wants to be chased.'

'And *no* always secretly means *yes*, right? And if you're riding the T next to a hot woman and you want to cop a feel, you should, because I'm sure she'd be totally into it.'

'*No* doesn't always mean *yes*,' Oliver said. 'But it probably does with you more than most. Under your prim exterior, I'm sure there beats the heart of a lusty animal.' In spite of herself, Hannah felt flattered, and then he added, 'Perhaps a gerbil.'

Had he been waiting, these last few months, for her to start a conversation with him? Had he *wanted* to talk to her? No. He's cocky – if he'd wanted that, he'd have initiated it. It must just have been that in the moment of her insulting him, he, too, was bored, ready for some minor conflict. It was three thirty in the afternoon, the deadest part of the office day. Why not?

But it felt like maybe the conversation had soured; the gerbil insult seemed personal. They were sitting at their desks, each half turned toward the other, and she said, 'I have to make a call.'

She was dialing when he said, 'Inside me, there beats the heart of a skirt-chasing lion.'

It was weird, Hannah thought, that Oliver was entertaining, because it didn't seem like he particularly needed to be. It wouldn't matter to the Gwens of the world if he were or not. In addition to his accent, it was the tone and rhythm of such conversations that counted, wasn't it? Not the actual insights. Also his handsomeness, which was considerable: Oliver was six feet tall and broad-shouldered, with hair that had been brown when he'd started at the organization and, three weeks after that, bleached blond. Hannah had asked at the time if he'd gone to a salon to have it dyed or done it himself, and she'd been disappointed when he'd said he did it himself, with help from a female friend. Later, she could see how she had wanted to be scornful of a guy who'd spend hundreds of dollars on his hair. She'd been warding off his handsomeness; it was so easy to see that she'd be damned if she was falling for it.

After their post-Gwen conversation, Hannah and Oliver talked a little more but not much. Probably within three minutes, or maybe even before she turned back to her own desk, Hannah was already nervous about whether the dynamic between them had shifted. Was she supposed to act different now? Like, cranky but up for repartee? The next morning, riding the elevator to the eighth floor, she felt panicky; while panicking, she assumed a greater and greater degree of stoniness. Oliver typically arrived about forty minutes after she did, and she kept making half-necessary phone calls because it would be better if she were on the phone when he walked in; there would be less pressure to form a particular facial expression or say anything. But she ran out of calls to make, so when he arrived, she was pretending to be deep into paperwork. She glanced up in the direction of his face without making eye contact and said, 'Hey,' then returned to her work.

In a voice that was perfectly friendly but not overly, notably warm, he said, 'Hello, Miss Hannah,' and nothing else. So maybe – maybe he didn't really want to talk to her, either, he didn't want yesterday's conversation to have set a precedent. Maybe yesterday's conversation *hadn't* set a precedent. Maybe he didn't give a shit. Whatever. The more time that passed – days passed – the more it felt like a relief not to be wound up about nothing.

The retreat was a few weeks later, in Newport.

It was in October, and they were staying overnight, courtesy of one of their major donors. Everyone had boarded the bus that morning in Boston, with lots of cracks about how early in the day they could start drinking, and Hannah noticed when they checked into the hotel that Oliver's room was three down from hers. Presumably, he would not be sleeping alone; Hannah was pretty sure a new assistant named Brittany had sat next to him on the bus.

In the evening, after the meetings but before dinner, Hannah showered and dressed and went to stand on her deck, which overlooked the ocean. The temperature was in the sixties, the sky a streaky pink and orange, the air fresh and sweet-smelling, and Hannah felt the hopeful sadness of being in a perfect setting. It may have been the distraction of this sadness, or the indulgent quality of it, that caused her to carelessly rub one hand against the wooden railing. She yanked it back immediately, but it was too late – the splinter's tiny brown tip protruded from her palm with the rest securely embedded.

Hannah hates things like this, an eyelash in her eye, a gnat in her mouth, any foreign object where it's not supposed to be; she just wants time to pass, to be at the part where it's all cleaned out and you're moving forward, even if you're bruised or cut. Without thinking, she hurried, almost running, back into her room and then into the hallway toward Oliver's door.

He was there. If he had not been there, would they not have ended up together? 'I have a splinter,' she said, and held her hand out to him while he stood in the doorway. She wasn't so distraught that it didn't occur to her she might seem prissy, but the splinter *was* in her right palm, and she's right-handed. How could she have gotten it out herself? He ushered her in – she thought but was not positive that he touched her back as she passed – and they sat on the edge of one bed. Her room had a king-size bed, but his had two doubles. Below true consciousness, she had the flickering thought that if he was nice about helping her with the splinter, maybe she'd offer to switch rooms so that he and Brittany could have more spacious sex.

He bent his head over her extended arm and spread the flesh of her palm in both directions, using his thumbs. 'It's pretty well in there,' he said.

Right away, her awareness of him, of their proximity, had become greater than her distress over the splinter. She didn't care about the splinter at all. Maybe it had only been an excuse to begin with. His hair was back to brown again, the dyed part had grown out, and she liked his bent head, she liked his man's fingers, she liked how they barely needed to speak, how unsurprised he'd seemed to find her outside his door. It felt *inevitable*. In their lives together, he'd recognize her as a member of his tribe: He wouldn't mistake her quietness for niceness, her

244

sense of responsibility for humorlessness; he wouldn't even mistake her prudishness for real prudishness. He'd be boisterous and obnoxious, and he wouldn't think (Mike had thought this) that talking about other people was slightly immoral. She wouldn't feel the loneliness of being the only one who had opinions. When leaving a restaurant where they'd eaten with a group, if she remarked on what a small tip one person had left, or on how long and dull another person's story about his trip to France had been, Oliver would have noticed these things, too. He wouldn't say in an aggressively pleasant way, 'I really enjoyed hearing about the trip.'

'I need some tweezers,' Oliver said.

It seemed a little embarrassing that she had some, but they were necessary. In the time it took for her to return to her room, find the tweezers, and walk back down the hall, her realization about their destiny reversed itself – clearly, she was insane – and back in his room, it reversed itself again. Yes. *Soul mate* struck her as a dumb term, but whatever the non-dippy equivalent was. They could always keep each other company, she could take care of him, she could keep him on track. Surely he needed to be kept on track. Maybe, she thought brightly, he'd been trying unsuccessfully to kick cocaine.

'Hold still,' he said. 'I've almost got it. Ah, there we are. Would you like to see?' He held the tweezers aloft; the splinter, in its stubby brown spindliness, almost did not exist, it almost was nothing.

When he looked at her, she knew she was looking back at him too heavily. He smiled – heartbreakingly – and said, 'Remember, Hannah, that I'm a skirt-chaser.'

'I remember,' Hannah said.

'Well, then.' Still, neither of them moved.

Finally, she said, 'If I were another woman, you'd kiss me right now.'

'True,' he said.

'So kiss me.'

Leaning in, his mouth close to hers, Oliver said, 'I always knew you were a dirty slut.'

After wedding cake, the younger generation – Hannah, Oliver, Allison, Sam, Fig, and Fig's twenty-two-year-old brother, Nathan – end up in the den, watching ESPN. Allison asks, 'Fig, where's your beau?'

'What beau?' Fig sounds blasé.

'You know who I mean. The hottie you introduced me to last year.'

'Oh, that guy,' Fig says. 'Ancient history.'

'Geez,' Allison says. 'They can't hold on to you, can they?'

'You're a man-eater, then,' Oliver says over his shoulder. He is sitting on the edge of the couch between Hannah and Fig, leaning toward the TV, his elbows set against his knees and a Scotch (his fourth? his ninth?) in his hand. Fig is slouched all the way back against the cushions, her feet propped on the coffee table. This is the couch, pulled out, that Oliver slept on last night.

'Sometimes I am,' Fig says. 'When I'm hungry.'

No, Hannah thinks. *No, no, no!*

'Why are you called Fig, anyway?' Oliver asks, and Hannah thinks, *I forbid it. This is not negotiable.* Plus, Oliver's question is bullshit, because Hannah has told him about the origins of Fig's nickname not once but twice. She told him early on, when she was first describing her family, and she told him about it again on the plane to Philadelphia. Fine if he doesn't remember the first time, despite his excellent memory, but he must remember the second.

'It's Hannah's fault,' Fig says. 'She couldn't pronounce *Melissa.*'

'Yet you choose the nickname now,' Oliver says. 'You could change it if you wanted.'

'It suits me,' Fig says. 'I'm figgy.'

'You mean flaky,' Nathan says without turning away from the television. Fig balls up the napkin beneath her glass of wine and throws it at him, and it hits the back of his head. Still without turning around, he swipes at the place it landed.

'In ancient Syria, the fig was considered an aphrodisiac,' Oliver says, and Hannah stands and leaves the room. She's pretty sure that the comment is, among other things, not even true. It's not that she didn't know bringing Oliver home for her mother's wedding was a questionable idea – it's that she

247

couldn't help herself. This good-looking, charismatic man is, sort of, hers; she wanted witnesses.

In the kitchen, Hannah's mother and Aunt Polly are washing dishes. Hannah's mother is wearing an apron over the beige satin dress she got married in. 'Mom, you shouldn't be doing that,' Hannah says. 'Let me.'

'Oh, I don't mind. You know what you can do that would be a huge favor to me, though, is go with Frank to take Mrs Dawes home. Just ride along so he doesn't get lost. They're in the front hall.'

This feels decidedly dicey – leaving Oliver and Fig in the house together without her supervision – but what can she say? Also, she doesn't really want to be around them.

As Hannah, Frank, and Mrs Dawes make their way down the eight steps from the condo to the car (it stopped snowing in the early afternoon, and Hannah was the one who shoveled the steps clean), Hannah thinks that an observer, someone standing across the street, would assume they are close family members – Hannah as twenty-something daughter, Frank as middle-aged son, Mrs Dawes as grandmother – when the truth is that none of them know one another well. Mrs Dawes holds on to Frank's arm, and Hannah walks just in front of them. They move excruciatingly slowly. Mrs Dawes wears low black heels with black grosgrain bows on the front, sheer flesh-colored stockings, and a black-and-red wool suit currently obscured by a full-length black wool coat. She carries a black leather pocketbook. Her ankles are as thin as Hannah's were in elementary school, and her hair, a dry gray bob that flips up in a little curl at the bottom, is thinning in such a way that slivers of her pink scalp show through. She should be wearing a hat or scarf, Hannah thinks, though she herself is wearing neither.

Thanks to Frank, the car is running already, the heat on. At the foot of the steps, they negotiate Mrs Dawes into the front seat, and just before Frank shuts the door, Hannah says, 'Mrs Dawes, do you want your seat belt on? I can do it for you.'

'That won't be necessary,' says Mrs Dawes.

Hannah gets in back, directly behind Mrs Dawes, and Frank gets in front. His car is a Mercedes. Where her father, like a Doberman pinscher you want to keep entertained, well fed, and unthreatened by disagreement or surprise, has always been the defining presence in every situation, Frank is so agreeable that Hannah is not sure what his personality is like. Before this weekend, Hannah had met Frank twice: first in the summer and then when Frank, Hannah's mother, Hannah, Allison, and Sam went to Vail for Thanksgiving, the five of them staying in three separate rooms paid for by Frank. Prior to this, Hannah's mother had not skied since 1969, but she did so pretty much all day, every day, starting with lessons the first morning on the bunny hill, then quickly joining Frank; Allison had skied only a few times with Sam up at Lake Tahoe but also enthusiastically took to the slopes, even snowboarding a few times; Hannah had never skied before and did not choose to do so after the single lesson with her mother. Observing her mother and sister as they returned to the lodge in the evening, their faces burned a healthy pink, their spirits high, Hannah felt impressed and betrayed. That trip was designed to help Frank, Allison, and Hannah get to know one another, as Hannah's mother expressed repeatedly, even when all of them were in the same room – she'd say, 'I hope you're getting to know one another!' Hannah and Frank's conversations were the type you'd have with a pleasant-seeming person sitting next to you on a plane: weather, movies, the meal presently being consumed. Frank was in the middle of a large hardcover biography of an early-twentieth-century British member of Parliament. Frank enjoyed crosswords. He wore ties to dinner, except on the night when Allison announced, 'We're taking you to a dive, Frank!' and led them to a restaurant she'd read about in a magazine where horns and antlers hung from the walls and the waitresses wore tight jeans and even tighter long-underwear tops or flannel shirts. To this place, Frank wore his usual blazer and button-down but left the collar open. The bill for the five of them at the so-called dive was (Hannah peeked) $317, and as always, Frank picked up the check.

Sometimes when she and Allison are talking in front of Frank about, say, perfume, Hannah wonders if he finds them amusingly gabby or just frivolous. He has no children of his own. He was married for twenty-nine years to a woman who was either mentally ill or extremely difficult (Hannah's mother speaks of the woman so briefly and mysteriously that Hannah has not been able to tell which), and he became a widower four years ago. 'He's a little shy,' Hannah's mother said initially, though Hannah is not sure this is true – just because he isn't chatty doesn't mean he's shy. Mainly, Frank is rich. This is the ubiquitous fact about him, the reason why his marriage to Hannah's mother is, barring any as-yet-unrevealed psychotic streaks in him, a positive development. All things being equal, why not be married to a rich man? (Somewhere, Hannah thinks, there must be a needlepoint pillow asking this very question in a cleverer way.) Now there's a guarantee that Hannah's mother can, for the foreseeable future, keep wearing pleated pink pants and soft pastel cardigan sweaters, keep preparing shrimp fettuccine Alfredo (her signature dish) for special occasions. It's not that Hannah's mother is materialistic, per se, just that Hannah isn't sure she knows how to live another way. And Frank possesses a certain competent, comforting quality that Hannah suspects comes partly from his

251

money. She gets the sense that, under pressure, he could take care of problems – say, if Allison or Hannah had an eating disorder and needed to be hospitalized, or if one of them got a DUI. The likelihood of either is pretty much nil, but if one did occur, Frank seems like he'd acknowledge the problem and go about addressing it without getting bogged down in a lot of talk or blame. Plus, Frank doesn't seem to be trying to prove anything, he seems the opposite of edgy. Even the fact that he's driving Mrs Dawes home – Hannah takes it as a good sign for Frank's marriage to her mother that he doesn't feel the need to bask in newlywedded attention, he doesn't have to stay all night at his wife's side so that he can see himself, or other people can see him, as someone who stayed all night at his wife's side.

Frank turns on the radio, set to the public station, and a polite volume of classical music fills the car. 'Mrs Dawes, how's the temperature for you?' he asks. 'It'll get warmer in a minute or two.'

'I'm never warm,' Mrs Dawes says. 'You could turn it up to ninety-five degrees and it wouldn't be enough.'

'Well, I'm certainly glad you could join us for the wedding,' Frank says. 'It meant the world to Caitlin.'

Hannah has never been all that fond of Mrs Dawes, but it's probably true that her attendance meant something to Hannah's mother: the older generation sanctioning the union.

'It's remarkable how Caitlin's kept her figure,' Mrs Dawes says. She turns her head ninety degrees to the left. 'I'll bet you girls have to watch what you eat, but your mother has always been naturally slim. I don't think I'm imagining that Allison is heavier than when I saw her last.'

'Allison is pregnant,' Hannah says, and Frank snorts in a way that might mean he is suppressing a laugh – in which case, he's aligned with Hannah – or might just mean he swallowed a piece of dust. 'She's due in May,' Hannah adds.

'I hope she won't have any trouble. They have a lot more trouble when they're older, you know.'

'She's only twenty-nine.'

Mrs Dawes chortles. 'That's not so young, Hannah. I had four little ones by the time I was twenty-nine. But you girls with your careers, running about.'

Mildly, not even vehemently, Hannah thinks, *Oh, fuck you.* In the abstract, Hannah considers herself evil to dislike an eighty-two-year-old. And Mrs Dawes's physical weakness is a sobering sight. But whenever Hannah talks to her for longer than a minute, she remembers immediately why she feels this antipathy: Mrs Dawes complains and criticizes in an upbeat way, suggesting, perhaps, her own good-humored tolerance of others' deficiencies. She never asks Hannah much of anything, nor is she particularly loquacious, yet you can feel her waiting for you to attend to and engage her, all of which makes talking to her work.

253

Hannah knows that other people (Allison, for one) would not consider it fair to judge an octogenarian on the same criteria you'd apply to people much younger, which is why Hannah has never mentioned to anyone else her dislike for Mrs Dawes. Also, Mrs Dawes isn't quite critical or grouchy enough to seem like a certified old crank.

'Tell me,' Frank says, 'is it sons or daughters you have, Mrs Dawes?'

'I have two of each, and would you believe they all live in California? All four of them.'

Yeah, I would believe it, Hannah thinks. Then, though presumably her mother sent her on the ride less to provide directions than to relieve Frank of some of Mrs Dawes's unrelenting company, Hannah tunes out and lets Frank pull the weight of the conversation.

Mrs Dawes lives fifteen minutes from Hannah's mother's condo, in a wooded area where you can't see most of the houses from the road. You take a driveway a quarter of a mile back through the trees, and then a house – invariably, a large one, though of the old-fashioned shingled variety rather than the immodest newer developments – appears at the end. Mrs Dawes is describing to Frank her late husband's interest in bird-watching – she refers to him as Dr Dawes – when she interrupts herself to tell Frank to make a left into her driveway. Hannah has a dim memory of coming here years ago to the birthday party of one of

Mrs Dawes's California grandchildren, which featured a magic show. Though Hannah couldn't have been more than six or seven, she remembers thinking it was strange to attend the birthday party of a person she'd never met.

The house is completely dark. Allison and Sam picked up Mrs Dawes before the wedding ceremony, and Hannah thinks irritatedly that her sister should have left on at least one light. Frank suggests that Hannah help Mrs Dawes from the car onto the brick walkway leading to the front door, and then he will back up a few feet and illuminate the walkway with his headlights. Hannah climbs from the backseat, opens Mrs Dawes's car door, and extends her right arm. Mrs Dawes sets her feet on the ground, which is to say she sets her heels in the snow, since the walkway is not cleared at all. (Allison and Sam also should have done that – it would have taken Sam about three minutes.) Mrs Dawes takes hold of Hannah's arm, and Hannah can feel the old woman pulling herself up. When Mrs Dawes is next to her, Hannah catches the scent not of garlic, as Fig claimed, but of a pleasant lilac perfume. Hannah leans around her to shut the car door, and Frank sets the car in reverse. Only a few seconds pass when the car doors are closed and Hannah and Mrs Dawes are standing by themselves out in the night, but Hannah feels that primal fear of the dark – the house and woods and sky are black around them, all stealthily watchful and indifferent to an individual's vulnerabilities, or possibly preying on such vulnerabilities. Even when Frank has parked and emerged from the car, Hannah's tension dissipates only slightly. As when they left Hannah's mother's condo, they walk in tiny steps, but this time Hannah is the primary escort.

'If you'll give me your keys, Mrs Dawes,' Frank says, 'I can go ahead and open the door for you.'

They pause while Mrs Dawes rummages in her pocketbook. Her key chain proves to be a brown leather strap, not unlike a bookmark, beaded in turquoise, red, and black. *Why, Mrs Dawes,* Hannah thinks, *how ethnic of you*. The confusion of explaining to Frank which of the twelve or so keys corresponds with which of the two locks means that by the time Hannah and Mrs Dawes have arrived at the door, it still is not open. 'Give them back to me,' Mrs Dawes says sternly, but she spends no fewer than four minutes fiddling with them herself. 'You've gotten them turned around so I can't tell up from down,' she says to Frank more than once. During this interval, Frank and Hannah make eye contact several times. The first time he raises his eyebrows, and the second time he smiles the saddest smile Hannah has ever seen. He is not impatient right now, she realizes; he feels only sympathy for Mrs Dawes.

At last the door opens. Frank finds a light switch, and they are standing in a hall with a wooden floor covered by an Oriental rug. To the right of the door is a mahogany bureau with a mirror hanging over it; to the left is a staircase with a shiny banister. The hall opens onto a shelf-lined living room filled with dated-looking but nice furniture – a white sofa, several large chairs covered in floral fabrics, marble end tables, a coffee table with a porcelain ashtray on it and a silver vase containing no flowers – as well as a brown La-Z-Boy stationed about six feet from a plasma TV.

'Can I help you upstairs, Mrs Dawes?' Frank asks. 'I'd love to get you settled in before we take off.'

Hannah glances to see if the staircase features a motorized chair. It doesn't. And she knows from her mother that Mrs Dawes has refused to get help outside of a housekeeper who comes three times a week. Hannah's mother always mentions this refusal whenever she has reason to discuss Mrs Dawes: Mrs Dawes, *who won't even think of giving up that big house;* Mrs Dawes, *who still won't consider a night nurse, even a woman who just sits downstairs and Mrs Dawes wouldn't have to see her* . . . For several years, Hannah's mother has dropped off food for Mrs Dawes once or twice a week – a few cookies, say, or a pint of soup – and the smallness of the quantity has made these deliveries seem to Hannah almost not worth the effort. Or, even worse, like maybe Hannah's mother is simply passing on leftovers, when in actuality she purchases the items at an upscale deli. But now, imagining her mother driving out

257

here, Hannah understands the minuscule portions. Also, possibly, she understands why her mother is willing to overlook Frank's gut.

'You two ought to get back so the others don't think you've been buried in a snowbank,' Mrs Dawes says.

'No hurry at all,' Frank says. 'May I make you some tea? I don't know if you like a cup of tea at night.'

'I'll tell you what I've been planning to drink since we left Caitlin's, and that's a glass of water. The duck was extraordinarily salty. Didn't you find it salty, Hannah?'

'It tasted okay to me,' Hannah says.

'I typically don't care for duck. If you'd like some water, you can come this way.'

There is another slow progression, this time down a hall, and then they're in the kitchen: white-and-red-checked linoleum floor, a rounded refrigerator and sink Hannah thinks are from the fifties, but maybe it's the forties or the sixties. When Mrs Dawes turns off the faucet, Hannah becomes aware of the absolute quiet of this house. The only noise is the noise they're making. Mrs Dawes has provided clear juice glasses with faded nickel-sized orange polka dots. She offers no ice, and the three of them stand there, audibly gulping the luke-warm water. Hannah realizes she was sort of thirsty. She watches – she sees that it's about to happen, then she sees it happen, but she doesn't think of it until after as something she might have

258

prevented – as Mrs Dawes sets her glass on the edge of the drain board. Two thirds of the glass's base are hanging in the air, as if over a cliff. The entire glass tips to the floor and shatters.

Frank yelps, a high, embarrassing cry. Then he is hunching over, bending from the waist rather than the knees, to blot the spilled water with paper towels from the roll by the sink. Looking up, his face reddened because of either yelping or bending, he asks, 'Mrs Dawes, where's your broom? We'll get this up in no time.'

When Mrs Dawes pulls the broom from the closet in the corner, Frank tries to take it, and she won't let him. 'I made this mess, Frank,' she says. 'I'll clean it up.' She sweeps slowly and a bit shakily, and Hannah feels as if she is observing a private act; she should turn away or pretend to be preoccupied by something else. But she also wants to intervene. She waits until the shards of glass are in a pile, then says, 'Let me do the dustpan. May I?'

Perhaps Mrs Dawes lets her because Hannah is a woman, or perhaps Mrs Dawes can't crouch over the floor in the way the dustpan requires. Is she getting all the tiny pieces, Hannah wonders, or is she leaving some tiny sparkle of glass? She hopes Mrs Dawes wears slippers, because if she were to cut herself, it would all be such a complicated process – bending to press a piece of tissue to her foot, making her way to wherever she keeps Band-Aids, discerning whether the glass was embedded in her skin or somewhere still on the floor.

'Be careful,' Mrs Dawes says, but she doesn't say anything else, and neither does Frank. Hannah feels them watching from above. A few seconds ago, she was thinking how enormous her thighs look as she squats, but she has a sudden realization that what is most prominent about her right now is probably her health. Her youth, her vigor, her resilience – the effortlessness for her of squatting to sweep up broken glass, and the preoccupied quality of her attention to the sweeping. They might imagine that she has plans to go to a bar after this with her cousins and Oliver, that the wedding was the first part of the evening but for her there will be another part. As far as she knows, there won't be, but it's true that there could. In Mrs Dawes's kitchen, Hannah feels a hot bright awareness of the many flexibilities her life still contains, the unpredictabilities. Bad or painful things will occur for her, surely, but she will bounce back from them. A lot is going to happen.

When the glass has been disposed of, Mrs Dawes leads them to the front door, and Frank says to her, 'You're sure one of us can't help you to the second floor? Either Hannah or I would be delighted—' Very quickly, he glances toward Hannah, then glances away. In that glance, she thinks he apologizes to her, and later, Hannah will remember this as the precise moment when she first loved her stepfather. The kindly presumptu-ousness of his volunteering her services as well as his own, and then his immediate unspoken apology for having done so, for possibly delaying their departure when he can tell she is restless – it feels so family-ish.

Hannah is glad when Mrs Dawes again rejects Frank's offer. She does, however, allow him to remove her coat and hang it.

'Truly, many thanks for sharing our wedding,' Frank says, and Hannah can tell he is debating whether it would be too forward to embrace Mrs Dawes. He must conclude that it would be, or that Mrs Dawes would think it was, because he settles for patting her shoulder three times. Before Hannah has consciously decided to, she leans in and kisses Mrs Dawes's cheek, not unlike the way she kissed her father several hours ago. It is possible, she thinks, that she'll never see Mrs Dawes again.

Before Hannah and Frank walk out of the house, Mrs Dawes turns on the outside light, and the illuminated brick pathway now staves off the sorrow and danger of the night. But also the sorrow and danger are held at bay, beyond the perimeter of the light, because Hannah and Frank have left Mrs Dawes inside. Hooray! It's not rude to feel this way, is it? They did everything they could for her. They were totally patient, they went overboard. How many times did Frank offer to help Mrs Dawes upstairs? At least twice!

But as they are fastening their seat belts, a mournful symphony emanates from the radio, and Hannah loses her brief giddiness. Abruptly, she and Frank no longer exist in contrast to Mrs Dawes; they are just themselves, contained in a car. She glances to her left. Frank is focused on the curving driveway. They come to the road, and sitting there, perhaps feeling her gaze on his face, Frank shakes his head. 'I never want to grow old, Hannah,' he says.

She looks at him in astonishment. She thinks, *But you already are.*

At home, Frank parks in the driveway, and as they are walking inside, she can see through the back porch window that her mother and Aunt Polly have been joined in the kitchen by Oliver and Fig. If Oliver weren't here, she could go to sleep now, but because he is here, because he is Oliver, she will have to entertain him. This morning he asked her where they could rent porn, and she said, 'This is my mom's house, Oliver.'

'There you both are,' Hannah's mother says, and Oliver exclaims, 'The chauffeurs!'

Hannah takes a seat at the kitchen table and glares at Oliver – this is the look she was saving from hours before – but he merely smiles glassily, then returns his attention to tying shut a trash bag. (She is shocked he's helping clean up.) Fig stands a few feet from him, drying dishes. 'Did Mrs Dawes settle in?' Hannah's mother asks.

'She's certainly strong-willed,' Frank says. 'She wouldn't even let us help her upstairs.'

'Maybe she didn't want you to see her dildo collection,' Fig says, and Aunt Polly says, 'Honestly, Fig.' Fig, presumably, is drunk as well.

Oliver pauses by the door before carrying the trash bag out to the back porch and says, 'Fig, don't be naughty.' Hannah was right a million years ago – that it really is his accent.

Aunt Polly says, 'Caitlin, the duck was fantastic. Were there cherries in the glaze?' At the same time, Hannah hears Fig say to Oliver – quietly but not that quietly – 'Maybe I should be spanked for my bad behavior.'

'Cherries and also apples,' Hannah's mother is explaining as Oliver steps outside. Really, it is all Hannah can do not to jump up and lock the door. 'I wondered if it would be too sweet, but the caterer said it's one of their most popular dishes.'

'I'll bet,' Aunt Polly says.

'The other way they prepare it is sort of Asian-style, with cabbage and snow peas and whatnot' – here, Oliver re-enters the kitchen – 'but I was afraid that might be a little outré for Mrs Dawes. She isn't the most adventurous of eaters. Hannah, was it you or Allison who offered her hummus that time and she just didn't know what to make of it?'

'I don't remember,' Hannah says, and she is barely listening because she is watching – this is only half surprising – as Oliver creeps up behind

263

Fig, pulls at the neck of her blouse, and drops a snowball down her back.

Fig shrieks, and Hannah stands. 'Just quit it,' she says.

They all turn toward her. Fig is groping behind her back, and Oliver's expression – the heat must still be turned way up – is one of sweaty glee.

'Don't bother,' Hannah says. 'It's a waste of your time. She's batting for the other team.'

No one reacts at all. Hannah can't help making eye contact with Fig for about a second. Fig appears confused. Hannah glances back at Oliver. A look of curiosity has replaced his glee.

'She's a' – Hannah pauses – 'a dyke.' She has never used this word before. She is hideous to herself. Her disloyalty to Fig and her prejudice are unattractive, but her awkward delivery is truly grotesque. They are staring at her, the five of them. In the end, there is nothing so strange as a human face. And several at once – how did all of them arrive at this dreadful moment?

'That's why you shouldn't hit on her,' she says to Oliver as she backs out of the room. 'Not because she's my cousin.'

The rules for Oliver are:
   He cannot hire prostitutes.
   He can have sex with the same woman twice but not more than twice.
   He can receive oral sex but not perform it.
   He has to use condoms.

He has to take a shower before he meets up with Hannah again.

Does she believe he abides by any rules apart from the shower one? Most of the time, of course not. Please. He probably does nothing except eat out hookers, and Hannah herself is probably filthy with STDs.

At other times, she doesn't think the rules are so unrealistic. It seems possible they offer enough wiggle room even for Oliver. Once Hannah looked up sex addicts online, but after glancing at a couple of websites, she just felt weary. What does it matter if that's what Oliver is? Or if he's an alcoholic? Call it what you like – his behavior is the way it is, he has no plans to change it. It's not like he hates himself, at least no more than everyone else hates themselves. He just happens not to believe in monogamy.

This is the rule for her (there's only one):

She is allowed to ask him anything as long as she remembers that the answer won't make a difference; as long as she remembers that it's better for them both if she doesn't act on this privilege but saves it, like a coupon, for an indefinite future; as long as really, in point of fact, she never asks him anything.

The first time this all came up was the second week Hannah and Oliver were together. After eating lunch outside, they'd walked into their office, and when she sat down at her desk, he said, 'Turn around. I want to tell you something.' He seemed nervous in the way of someone who urgently needs to urinate. 'You know the skirt-chasing?' he said.

'The what?'

'Debbie Fenster gave me a blow job this morning.'

She thought he was kidding. She didn't think it completely, but she thought it more than, at first, she thought he was serious. She said, 'Here?'

'In the handicapped bathroom.'

What she felt more than sadness or anger was distaste. Debbie had been kneeling in there, on that dirty tile floor? Hannah knew the bathroom well; it was the one she preferred because the regular women's bathroom had multiple stalls, but this one allowed you to use the toilet alone, in peace. And what, had Oliver's ass been pressed against the grimy wall? Under neon lights, at ten A.M., or whenever it had been?

'What do you think?' he said.

'I think it's gross.'

'Are you breaking up with me?' he asked. Neither of them had, since Newport, used the terms *boyfriend* or *girlfriend*; they'd just been sending flirty e-mails to each other from a few feet apart, going to bars after work (getting drunk with Oliver, especially on a week-night, seemed festive then), and spending the night together. That short week she'd felt uncomfortably happy.

'I'd be kind of stupid if I didn't break up with you,' she said. 'Don't you think?' It occurred to her that she should feel more devastated than she did. Receiving the news was strange and unpleasant but not devastating.

He was still standing there, regarding her anxiously, and then he swooped forward, knelt, and placed his face in her lap, his arms around her calves. The door to their office was open; she could hear two of their coworkers talking about soccer from perhaps twelve feet away.

'Get up,' she said, which she didn't want him to do at all.

He pressed his nose against her pubic bone.

'Oliver—' Although she'd have been genuinely mortified if anyone walked into their office, she did love this inappropriate posture. And then she saw a flashing image of Debbie Fenster kneeling before Oliver, not unlike the way he was at present kneeling before Hannah. 'Really,' Hannah said. 'Get up.'

When he lifted his face and rocked back so his weight rested on his heels, she stood. 'I'm leaving for the day. If anyone is looking for me, say I had a doctor's appointment. This is too weird.' From the doorway, she said, 'I know you gave me fair warning in Newport. But it's still weird.'

They did not talk the rest of that day or night, and when she got to work the next morning, ahead of him, there was an envelope with her name on it set on her keyboard. Not a business envelope but one for a card, which, when she opened it, turned out to have on its front a dark-hued painting from 1863, of a kingfisher. Inside, in his customary capital letters, it said, *DEAR HANNAH, PLEASE FORGIVE ME FOR NOT BEING GOOD ENOUGH FOR YOU. LOVE, YOUR RECALCITRANT OFFICEMATE, OLIVER.* Only after several weeks did it occur to her that the note might have represented his gracious farewell, that he believed it was over between them. She had been the one to see the Debbie Fenster incident as a temporary flare-up. But even realizing this, she does not regret her lack of harshness toward him. Harshness then would have felt like a resolution rather than an organic reaction.

Later that day, as they sat at their desks, Hannah asked enough questions to figure out what the basic routine would be, and then she established her ground rules. The conversation was much less fraught than she'd have imagined; maybe it was the setting, but it felt awfully similar to an amicable business agreement, complete with moments of levity.

Lying on her back atop the bedspread, Hannah hears a knock and then the door opens, yellow light from the hall bisects the bedroom, the door closes again, and Fig is saying, not in a deferential whisper but in a normal voice, 'You're awake, right?' Up until the moment Fig speaks, Hannah still thinks the person might be Oliver. (All women want to be chased.) Is he out in the backyard now, smoking pot with Fig's brother? Or still in the kitchen, regaling her mother and aunt with tales about life as a Kiwi?

But maybe this is what Hannah has always wanted: a man who will deny her. A man of her own who isn't hers. Isn't it the real reason she broke up with Mike – not because he moved to North Carolina for law school (he wanted her to go with him, and she said no) but because he adored her? If she asked him to get out of bed and bring her a glass of water, he did. If she was in a bad mood, he tried to soothe her. It didn't bother him if she cried, or if she didn't wash her hair or shave her legs or have anything interesting to say. He forgave it all, he always thought she was beautiful, he always wanted to be around her. It became so boring! She'd been raised, after all, not to be accommodated but to accommodate, and if she was his world, then his world was small, he was easily satisfied. After a while, when he parted her lips with his tongue, she'd think, *Thrash, thrash, here we go.* She wanted to feel like she was striving cleanly forward, walking into a bracing wind and learning from her mistakes, and she felt instead like she was sitting on a deep, squishy sofa, eating Cheetos, in an overheated room. With Oliver, there is always contrast to shape their days, tension to keep them on their toes: *You are far from me, you are close to me. We are fighting, we are getting along.*

Hannah has not responded to Fig, and without

warning, Fig flings herself onto the bed next to Hannah. As Fig rearranges the pillows, she says, 'So I didn't know *dyke* was in your vocabulary. Pretty racy.'

'I'm sorry about outing you to our moms,' Hannah says. 'Now will you leave?'

'My mom already knew, and yours did, too,' Fig says. This shouldn't come as a surprise. When Fig said earlier that she hadn't told anyone, she didn't really mean *anyone*. Probably she herself told Oliver, and probably he ate it up. 'They both read some article in *Newsweek* about bisexual dabbling, so they've decided that's what this is.'

'Is it?'

'Well, I've been dating Zoe since June. What do you think?'

'You've been dating Zoe since June? That's twice as long as I've been dating Oliver.'

'How about that?' Fig says. 'Maybe I really am a big lesbo.'

'Fig, if you are, I'll support you. Obviously, there's nothing wrong with being gay.'

'Whatever,' Fig says, and she seems to mean it. How does she go so unanxiously about her life? For some reason, Hannah thinks of the summer after they were in fourth grade, when the public library sponsored a program for girls in which, if you read biographies of all the first ladies, your name was printed on a paper star and pinned to the corkboard in the children's section. (If you were a boy, you read about the presidents.)

Hannah loved these books, their cheerful, orderly recounting of lives – Martha Washington was a poor speller, Bess Truman threw the shot put – and by August she'd read all the way up to Nancy Reagan. Meanwhile, Fig, whose dyslexia would not be diagnosed for several years, was stalled around Abigail Fillmore. For Hannah, things had seemed good then, it had seemed like she was headed somewhere.

'Anyway,' Fig says, 'I came to tell you Oliver and I were just joking around. It was totally harmless.'

Hannah says nothing.

'And it wasn't like anything was going to happen,' Fig adds.

Both of them are quiet for nearly a minute, and then Hannah says, 'He cheats on me all the time. It's not even like it's cheating. It's our normal lives. It's like saying that I'm breathing oxygen, or, oh, I think I'll go swimming in water.'

'He's having an affair or it's different women?'

'The second one.'

'I know I haven't always been the poster girl for fidelity, but maybe you should dump him.'

'Lately,' Hannah says, 'I've been thinking I'll marry him.'

'You just think that because he's the first guy you've gone out with since Mike. You've always taken men far too seriously.'

'That's easy for you to say now.' And yet this assessment is not inaccurate. All these years, Hannah has seen Fig as defined by men and her

271

attractiveness to them, and that is part of why it's shocking – almost wasteful – that Fig is now involved with a woman. But in reality, perhaps it is Hannah who has allowed herself to be defined by men: first by worrying about what it meant that she wasn't dating them, then by making up new worries when she was.

'If you won't break up with Oliver,' Fig says, 'at least you should confront him.'

'He knows I know. We've talked about it plenty.'

'No shit – you're in an open relationship?'

'I'm not sure I'd call it that. It's not open for me. On the plane, I asked him to restrain himself here, and I was thinking of you. I didn't want to mention you specifically because I didn't want to plant the idea in his head, but I was thinking of you.'

'Hannah, give me some credit. When we were teenagers, I might've kissed him or something, but it's not like I would now.'

'Well, he definitely would have kissed you. And I almost admire him for how he acts – for not altering his behavior depending on circumstances. I mean, he was pawing you in front of my mom. If he behaves this badly, isn't that a form of honesty?'

'You're cutting him a lot of slack,' Fig says. 'There are decent guys out there.'

'Yeah, and I used to be going out with one. When Frank and I were at Mrs Dawes's house, I was thinking about how Oliver would never take care of me if I were old and feeble. And then I was thinking, hell, Oliver wouldn't even help me take care of someone else, like my mom. But Mike was a total caretaker, and I had complaints about him, too. Oliver and I have a good time together. It's not as if it sucks nonstop. Maybe this is the best I can do.'

'Oh my God,' Fig says. 'That's so depressing.' She turns her head to look at Hannah. 'Don't take this the wrong way, but it's time for you to lose your low-self-esteem shtick. It's gotten kind of stale, you know what I mean?'

'I don't have low self-esteem,' Hannah says.

'Right.'

'I don't,' Hannah says.

'Listen carefully,' Fig says, 'because I'm only doing this once. You have a lot of integrity. That's one of your good qualities. And you're not fake. Probably you'd enjoy yourself more if you *were* fake, but you're not. You're very reliable and trustworthy. You're not that funny – no offense – but you do have a good sense of humor, and you appreciate other people's funniness. You're just overall a sturdy presence, and that's something very few people are.'

'Please tell me,' Hannah says, 'that you mean a steady presence.'

'That's what I said.'

'You said sturdy, which is what a dining room table is.'

'Hannah, I'm heaping compliments on you. Quit

273

pretending you don't realize it. Oh, also, when you rescued me from my creepy professor on Cape Cod, that was one of the top three nicest things anyone ever did for me. I knew I should call you that day because you were the only person who would just get in the car without making me go through some massive explanation.'

'Yeah, but then I abandoned you when you went to see Philip Lake.'

'Who's Philip Lake?' Fig says.

'Are you serious? He's that man in L.A., the man of your dreams.'

'No, I knew the name was familiar.'

'Don't you wonder what became of him?'

'Not particularly,' Fig says.

They both are quiet.

'As long as we're soul-baring,' Hannah says, 'I should also tell you that the Cape Cod rescue mission was the beginning of my obsession with Henry. I had a huge crush on him for years after that.'

Fig sits straight up in bed. Hannah assumes her cousin is angry – in spite of time and everything else, Fig is angry – but she sounds practically joyful when she says, 'Of course! I can *completely* see you and Henry together. We should call him right now.'

Hannah pulls her back down toward the mattress. 'Fig, I haven't been in touch with Henry for years. I lost track of him when he was living in Seoul.' She pauses. 'Do you even have his number?'

'I'm sure I can get it. I think he's in Chicago now. This is so perfect. I was always way too insane for him, but you guys would definitely be compatible. I can't believe I didn't think of this before. Did I ever tell you he has a huge penis? He'll rearrange your internal organs, but you'll enjoy every minute of it.'

'You seem to be forgetting that I already have a boyfriend.'

'I thought we just decided you're breaking up with Oliver.'

'*You* decided it. Anyway, why are you so sure Henry would want to date me?'

'This is exactly what I mean,' Fig says. 'Enough with the defeatist crap. Why not assume from now on, until you have evidence to the contrary, that every man you meet finds you irresistible?'

Lying next to Fig – their heads are now on the same pillow – Hannah cannot help smiling. 'So that's your secret,' she says. 'I always wondered.'

Hannah doesn't leave her room again before going to bed, and she sleeps fitfully. Each time she wakes up, the idea of having to face her mother, Frank, or Aunt Polly after her outburst seems increasingly mortifying. Oliver she doesn't worry about – she knows by now she's incapable of offending him.

She rises at seven thirty, thinking she will eat a quick bowl of cereal before anyone else is up, and finds her mother already in the kitchen, standing at the sink in her pink quilted bathrobe and fiddling with one of the bouquets from the wedding. Immediately, it is clear that her mother is willing to pretend that Hannah did not mar the festivities last night with her personal vileness. 'You cut the stems on the diagonal so they stay fresh,' her mother says and holds out a single flower toward Hannah, stem first. 'Like so,' her mother says. 'And you want to change the water in the vase if it starts getting cloudy.'

Hannah nods. Her mother has always been a font of tidbits useful for a life Hannah is pretty sure she'll never have: Don't use too harsh a cleaning agent on marble; when you're stacking good china, put a flat paper towel on top of every plate.

'You just missed your sister going for a walk,' her mother says. 'Would you think of saying to her that she should be careful exercising in this kind of temperature, especially while she's pregnant?'

'You don't want to tell her yourself?'

'I already have. I'm an old nag, aren't I? But I worry.' Her mother opens the cabinet beneath the sink and tosses a handful of flower stems into the trash. 'Hannah, I hope you know how appreciative I am to both you girls for coming home.'

'Mom, of course.'

'Well, I know you're busy. You two work long hours.' Perhaps because their mother has not had much of a career, she is, in Hannah's opinion, overly respectful of her daughters' jobs. For Christmas she even gave them monogrammed leather briefcases. *I'm mostly just sitting at a desk*, Hannah wants to say, but she suspects her mother takes pleasure in the idea of Hannah and Allison as on the go, conducting important business.

Her mother dries her hands on a dish towel. 'You and Oliver fly out around three, right?'

Hannah nods again.

Her mother hesitates – possibly she's blushing – and then she says, 'You know, honey, I've met Fig's friend, and she seems quite nice.'

'You've met Fig's girlfriend?'

The blush deepens. 'I didn't realize at the time that they were an item, so to speak. But Frank and I ran into the two of them at Striped Bass, oh, probably in November. We all had a drink.' Her mother as stealth gay sympathizer? Hannah can't wait to tell Allison. 'She seemed like an appealing young lady,' her mother says. The toaster pops up then, with a little ding. 'How about an English muffin?'

Hannah says okay before realizing her mother intends to give her this English muffin, the one that's ready now. 'I can fix my own,' Hannah says.

'Oh, honey, don't be silly. It will take me one second to make another. Sit down and eat this while it's warm.'

Hannah obeys because it seems easier, it seems like what her mother wants. Passing Hannah the plate, her mother says, 'I think the important thing is to find someone you feel comfortable around.' Then – her mother has always been both tentative and not subtle – she adds, 'Oliver is a little eccentric, isn't he?' She's lowered her voice; presumably, Oliver is asleep in the den.

'In what way?' Hannah says.

'Well, I'm sure he's had a lot of interesting experiences. I take it he's traveled the globe. We all grow up differently, don't we?' This is definitely her mother's version of a condemnation. The question is, did Oliver do something explicitly inappropriate in front of her, something besides the snowball, or was it a general vibe her mother got? 'And he's very handsome,' her mother continues, 'but you know, your father was handsome, too, when he was a young man.'

Hannah is more intrigued than insulted. Because her mother is truly without malice, she'd make such remarks only due to a nervousness on Hannah's behalf, a concern for her future.

'Is that why you fell for Dad, because of his looks?' Hannah asks, and unexpectedly, her mother laughs.

'That was probably part of it. God help me if that was all of it. I was twenty-two on our wedding day, which seems extraordinary to me now. I moved right from my parents' house into a house with your father. But Hannah, I would never consider my marriage to your father a mistake. I used to beat myself up, thinking what a bad role

278

model I must have been for you and Allison, but eventually, I realized, well, I'd never have had you girls if I hadn't been married to your father. Sometimes it's hard to say what's a bad decision and what's not.' There is a silence, and then her mother adds, 'It's nice you went to see him yesterday. I know it made him happy.'

'Who told you?'

'He mentioned it when he called to wish me luck.'

'That was uncharacteristically gracious of him.'

Her mother smiles. 'Let's hope it's never too late for any of us.'

Hannah bites into the English muffin, which is excellent: It is perfectly browned, and her mother buttered it about three times more thickly than Hannah would have, meaning it tastes three times better. 'Mom,' Hannah says.

Her mother looks over.

'I really like Frank,' Hannah says. 'I'm glad you married him.'

She was not planning to, but as she passes by the closed door to the den on her way back upstairs, she impulsively stops and turns the knob. Inside the den, the curtains are pulled and the room is dim; Oliver is a vertical lump beneath the covers. She also is acting on impulse when she joins him. He lies on his back, and she curls up against him, her face in the hollow between his shoulder and neck, one of her arms against the left side of his rib cage and one across his chest. He does not seem to wake completely as he shifts to accommodate her, encircling her waist with his arm. She glances up at his face, relaxed in sleep. He is breathing audibly without quite snoring.

There is a way he smells in the morning, beneath the ever-present smell of cigarettes; he smells, she thinks, like a baby's spit-up. If she ever expressed this, he'd make fun of her. It's a scent that's of the body yet completely clean, coming from some blend of his hair and mouth and skin, and it's her favorite thing about him. Inhaling it in this moment, she feels an urge to somehow store it, to save it up for remembering, and this is how she knows she's going to end things with him after all. Of course she is. Isn't she the only one who's ever thought that to do otherwise would be a good idea?

And how heartbreaking, because if it were all just a few degrees different, she is pretty sure they could be quite happy together. She really does like him, she likes lying next to him, she wants to be around him; when you get down to it, can you say that about many people? But also, what a relief: When he awakens, she knows, he'll be talkative – he is in the morning even when hungover – and after a few minutes he'll pull her hand toward his erection. *Look what you've done*, he'll say. *You're a vixen*. Not that long ago, in spite of everything she knew, his constant horniness was sort of flattering, but at this point it makes her feel depleted. Staving him off or giving in – both options are equally unpleasant.

And so who knows what will happen next, how exactly it will unravel? For now, she thinks, this is the trick: to pay such close attention to him that she is able to stay until the last possible second before he opens his eyes.

CHAPTER 8

AUGUST 2003

When Hannah tells Allison they need to go by her doctor's office in Brookline before getting on the highway, what Allison says – this is highly un-Allison-like – is 'Are you fucking kidding me?'

It is just after eleven A.M., a sunny morning on the last day of August, and they both are sweating. Hannah's apartment is empty, all the furniture and boxes loaded onto the truck; last night she and Allison slept in separate sleeping bags on the same air mattress. Between trips out to the truck this morning, Hannah ate handfuls of stale animal crackers from a carton she'd unearthed in a cupboard, but Allison declined them.

'Brookline really isn't that far away,' Hannah says. 'It's sort of parallel to Cambridge.'

Allison looks at Hannah. '*Parallel?*' she repeats.

Because Allison has agreed to drive the moving truck out of the city, Hannah is not in a position to be anything but diplomatic. In eight years of living in Boston, Hannah has driven here exactly once – that time her freshman year when she and Jenny came back from the engineering school in the middle of the night – and she has no wish to do it again, regardless of the fact that the truck is the smallest size available. When Hannah first broached the topic, Allison hesitated a little because of her daughter, Isabel, who is only a few months old, but Allison appeared not to see the driving part of Hannah's request as a big deal. In San Francisco, Allison and Sam share a standard Saab, and they blithely back into parking spaces midway up hills.

Hannah inserts three more animal crackers into her mouth and then, while chewing, says, 'Should we go?'

She's not certain how to find Dr Lewin's – she has always come by T – and is relieved they don't get lost. They are a few blocks from Dr Lewin's office, which is in the basement of her house, when Hannah realizes her mistake. When she told Allison she'd forgotten her sweater after a doctor's appointment, Allison presumably thought she meant a doctor-doctor, which of course is what Hannah intended for Allison to think. To pull up in front of Dr Lewin's gray stucco house will require explanation, and Hannah doesn't feel like announcing, at the start of a two-day drive from Boston to Chicago, with Allison in a ragingly bad mood, that she sees a shrink. Allison is a social worker and thus officially supports the pursuit of mental health, but Hannah suspects Allison would think it was kind of weird, borderline unsavory, for her own sister to go to a psychiatrist. Hannah would not be surprised if Allison is the kind of person who thinks only crazy people go to psychiatrists.

'Sorry,' Hannah says, 'but I've gotten really mixed up. I know how to get us onto Ninety from here, but I don't know how to get to' – she pauses – 'the hospital. I think I'll just have them send me the sweater.'

'Can't you look at the map? We might as well figure it out if we've gotten this far.'

'No, you were right that this was a bad idea. If you turn on Beacon, we can go around the block.'

'Your doctor doesn't have anything better to do than mail you sweaters?'

'Allison, I thought you wanted to get on the road.'

Allison does not respond, and Hannah thinks, *This is for your sake as much as mine*. 'Sorry,' she says. 'I thought I knew the way.'

Allison makes the turn that will lead them back to Ninety, but instead of acknowledging Hannah's apology, she leans forward and tunes the radio until she finds the public station. Then she turns it up, which is pure Allison: aggression by NPR. Hannah eats several more animal crackers and looks out the window.

Amazingly, until yesterday Hannah had never once, during seven years' worth of appointments, cried in Dr Lewin's office. What prompted yesterday's tears was, as much as anything, the

284

logistics of moving: Earlier in the afternoon, Hannah had gone (for the fourth time in a week) to the shipping store, planning to buy more medium-sized boxes, and the store was out. Back at her apartment, she waited on hold for nearly half an hour in an effort to get her gas turned off and her account closed, then finally hung up the phone when she needed to leave for Dr Lewin's. At the T stop, she arrived just in time to see a train pull away, and the next one took so long to come that she was six minutes, or $12.60, late for the appointment. (Dr Lewin's sliding fee has slid up over the years.) Plus, it was a grotesquely humid ninety-five degrees, the sun blazing overhead and air conditioners everywhere straining to keep the indoors even moderately cool. Why on earth had she brought along this pink cotton sweater? Hannah set it on the floor next to her chair, which was thick and leather. Her damp skin stuck to it.

'I'm sorry for being late,' she said for the second time.

'It's really all right,' Dr Lewin said. 'How are moving preparations?'

In reply, Hannah burst into tears. Dr Lewin passed her a box of tissues, but in the moment, it seemed like a better idea to Hannah just to yank up the neck of her shirt and use it to wipe her eyes and nose.

'You have a lot going on,' Dr Lewin said.

Hannah shook her head; she couldn't speak.

'Take your time,' Dr Lewin said. 'Don't worry about me.'

For another two or three minutes ($4.20 to $6.30), Hannah collected herself but then thought of, well, everything, which started new tears streaming, which necessitated recollecting herself. Eventually, there appeared to be no more tears forthcoming, the cycle sputtered out, and Dr Lewin said, 'Tell me what's worrying you most.'

Hannah swallowed. 'Moving to Chicago isn't a terrible idea, is it?'

'Well, what's the worst that could happen?'

'That I get fired, maybe. I mean, probably I could find another job then.'

Dr Lewin nodded. 'Probably you could find another job.'

'I guess the truly worst thing would be if it doesn't work out with Henry. Am I psycho for moving there if we're not dating?'

'Do you think you're psycho?'

'With all due respect' – Hannah sniffled a little – 'aren't you in a better position to answer that question than I am?'

Dr Lewin smiled dryly. 'As far as I can tell, you recognize there are no guarantees with Henry or with anyone else. What you're doing is taking a risk, which is perfectly healthy and reasonable.'

'Really?'

'You're twenty-six,' Dr Lewin said. 'Why not?' This *why not*? type commentary had been a

286

relatively recent development, mostly since Hannah's breakup with Oliver: Dr Lewin had, after all these years, gotten a little jaunty. Once when Hannah told Dr Lewin that whenever she and Oliver had sex, she imagined that she could feel herself getting an STD in that moment, Dr Lewin said, 'So why don't you quit having sex with him and buy yourself a vibrator?' Hannah's eyes must have widened, because Dr Lewin added, 'They're not against the law, you know.' Hannah could not help wondering, was it possible, even in a small way, that Dr Lewin might miss her?

'Twenty-six isn't *that* young,' Hannah said. 'It's not like twenty-two.'

'The point is that you're unencumbered. It's not irresponsible for you to take a chance.'

The chance Hannah was taking – is taking – is that she is moving to Chicago to see what might happen with Henry. It had all come about rather quickly. Fig's wedding (that's what Fig herself called it, a wedding – she'd say, 'A commitment ceremony sounds so *gay*') happened in June. It was small and elegant and took place in a private room at a restaurant on Walnut Street in Philadelphia. Zoe wore a white pantsuit, and Fig wore a simple white dress with spaghetti straps, and they both looked hiply beautiful. Allison and Hannah were Fig's bridesmaids, and Nathan and Zoe's brother were – well, not groomsmen – but the really clever idea on Fig's part was to ask Frank to officiate, thereby eliciting a tacit generational endorsement that Fig's own parents went along with. Frank was both dignified and warm, and Fig's parents seemed to enjoy themselves. Afterward, at the dinner, Nathan had several martinis and gave a toast that started 'Given what a slut she's always been, who ever thought Fig would go lezzie?'

And also: Henry was there. Hannah had not seen him since her junior year in college, but there he was; she was pretty sure Fig had invited him solely as an act of generosity. He and Hannah were seated next to each other at the reception and he was completely easy to talk to. Instead of the conversation whittling away, getting closer and closer to nothing the longer they spent in each other's presence, it enlarged and enlarged. There was an infinite amount to cover, and nothing he said bored her at all – one of his stories was about how, after he'd checked in to his hotel that afternoon, he'd gotten trapped in an elevator with an eighty-nine-year-old Russian woman who was soon feeding him piroshki and scheming to set him up with her granddaughter, though actually, Henry said, he'd stepped off the elevator feeling slightly in love with the eighty-nine-year-old herself; her name was Masha. They also discussed what Henry called Fig's 'change of heart,' and he did not seem personally disgruntled. He said, 'How can I not be happy for her? She's the most at peace I've ever seen her.' When Hannah told him all about Oliver, he said, 'Hannah, the dude sounds like a total jackass. He doesn't sound worthy of you.' They'd both drunk a fair amount, and this was sometime after midnight, as the reception was winding down. 'And you still share an office with the guy?' Henry said. 'What a drag. You need to get out of Beantown.'

'I'm not sure where else I'd go.'

'Go anywhere. It's a big world. Come to Chicago. Chicago is definitely better than Boston.'

She looked at him sideways, pursing her lips a little. She was so much better at this than she'd been back in college – also, she was pretty sure she looked considerably better. She'd cut her hair to chin-length, she was wearing contact lenses, the strapless bridesmaid dresses Fig had picked out showed her shoulders and arms to flattering effect. As it happened, this was the first time in her life that Hannah had worn a strapless dress. She was thinking she might do it again.

In perhaps the most coquettish voice she'd ever used, she said, 'You think I should move to Chicago?'

He was smiling. 'I think you should move to Chicago.'

'What would I do there?'

'You'd do what people everywhere do. Work. Eat. Have sex. Listen to music. But all of it would be better because it'd be happening there.'

'Okay,' Hannah said.

'Really?' Henry said. 'Because I'm holding you to this.'

As the night proceeded, it seemed harder and harder to believe something physical wouldn't happen between them, but the logistics were complicated – his hotel was downtown, she was getting a ride back to the suburbs with her mother and Frank. Everyone in her family knew Henry as Fig's ex-boyfriend. It would have been tricky to explain. On the street, with her mother and Frank waiting in the car, Hannah and Henry hugged, and he kissed her cheek, and she thought that this was how it would be when they were husband and wife and saw each other off at train stations and airports. It almost didn't matter that nothing more happened. As she sat in the backseat riding home, her heart kept clenching with how much she liked him.

And what was to stop her from moving? If Fig was married to Zoe, then Fig and Henry weren't going to reconcile; they were definitely and absolutely finished. Besides, if Zoe could get Fig to fall in love with her when Zoe wasn't even the *gender* of person Fig believed she was attracted to, then why was it so far-fetched to think Hannah and Henry might end up together? Really, Zoe and Fig's courtship was emboldening; it gave Hannah hope.

Of the five nonprofits she sent résumés to in Chicago, one – the educational outreach arm of a medium-sized art museum – asked for an interview. She flew out in late July, and the interview was fine (she wasn't entirely paying attention, anticipating her evening with Henry), and then she had dinner with him and his friend Bill and it was great again, the three of them went to a billiards hall on Lincoln Avenue and played pool and darts for six hours straight, Henry was touchy-feely, Hannah turned out to be okay at darts, and when, after her return to Boston, she was offered the job, it was hard to think of a reason not to take it. Dr Lewin didn't disapprove – ahead of time, Hannah had felt sure she would, but later Hannah couldn't remember why.

Yesterday at their last session, which Dr Lewin let run over by an unprecedented eight minutes, Hannah wrote her a check that had two softly lit frolicking yellow Lab puppies superimposed on the 'pay to the order of section. 'I know you probably don't care,' Hannah said, 'but I just want to say, obviously these aren't my usual checks, and the reason I have them is I ran out of normal ones but there was no point in getting another whole set since I'll be opening a new bank account in Chicago, so they just gave me a bunch of samples. See, they don't have my address.' Hannah ripped the check from the book and held it out, and Dr Lewin glanced at it for half a second before taking it. Then Hannah extended the whole book; now the check on top featured an orangutan with a forearm resting atop his head, his right armpit on full display. 'Look,' Hannah said. 'This one is even worse.'

'Hannah.' Dr Lewin stood, and her voice seemed

to contain both fondness and a kind of warning. 'I know you well enough to know you'd never order checks with furry animals on them.'

Hannah stood, too. She should have brought Dr Lewin a present of some sort, she thought. Did clients do that on bidding farewell? Fancy chocolates might have worked, or a geranium. 'Thank you for meeting with me ever since I was a freshman in college,' Hannah said. This felt absurdly inadequate.

'It was a privilege.' Dr Lewin reached out and squeezed Hannah's hand – more than a handshake, less than a hug. 'I want you to take care of yourself, Hannah, and I want you to let me know how things turn out.'

'I definitely will.' Hannah nodded several times before saying goodbye and turning to walk outside into the stifling heat, without her sweater.

It's after four o'clock when Hannah says, 'I kind of need to pee, so if you want to take one of the next few exits, that would be great.'

'Maybe if you didn't snack so much, you wouldn't need to pee so often,' Allison says.

It's not untrue that Hannah has been snacking most of the afternoon, but that's because Allison didn't want to stop for lunch, after they already didn't have breakfast. 'Can't you just buy something here?' Allison asked when they last got gas, so Hannah gathered up pretzels, caramel popcorn, and a little packet of cheese and crackers. The

292

cheese was the texture of mud and came with a red plastic stick for spreading.

'It's not food that makes you pee,' Hannah says. 'It's drinks.'

'It's food, too,' Allison says, and before Hannah can respond, Allison adds, 'This is a stupid conversation.'

'Fine,' Hannah says, 'but unless you want me to wet my pants, you have to stop.'

At the gas station, Allison uses the bathroom after Hannah does (*See*, Hannah thinks, *you needed to go, too*), and when her sister emerges, Hannah says, 'Want me to drive?' She hopes Allison will say no. Besides the unwieldiness of the truck, they've just passed signs for construction up ahead.

'Sure,' Allison says. As she hands Hannah the keys, she says, 'Watch the temperature gauge. If the traffic gets too slow, we should probably turn off the AC.'

The worst part, as Hannah expected, is the lack of rearview visibility. The second worst part is sheer size. It has never occurred to her until now that whenever she sees one of these move-it-yourself trucks on the road, there's a strong possibility that it's being driven by someone as incompetent as she is. No matter who gets in front of her, she thinks, she's definitely staying in the right-hand lane.

Allison mashes up her sweatshirt and presses it against the window, then sets her head against it and

293

closes her eyes. *Thanks for the moral support,* Hannah thinks, but after a few minutes, she's glad her sister is asleep, or at least faking it; Hannah can get her bearings without an audience. The one good part of the truck is height. Really, way up here, how can anyone not start to feel superior to some little Honda?

About forty-five minutes have passed, and Hannah has settled into the rhythm of the road (the first round of construction turned out not to be lengthy) when something – a thing that is brownish and has a tail, a neither large nor small thing – scurries in front of the truck. 'Oh my God,' Hannah says aloud and then, almost immediately, she has run over it: a low bump under the left wheels. She brings her hand up to her mouth, making a fist in front of her lips. 'Allison, are you awake?'

Allison stirs. 'Where are we?'

'I think I just ran over a possum or a raccoon. What am I supposed to do?'

'Just now you did?'

'Should I turn around?'

Allison sits up straighter. 'You don't do anything,' she says. 'You keep driving.'

'But what if it's not fully dead? What if it's suffering?'

Allison shakes her head. 'You still don't do anything – it would be really unsafe. Have you never hit roadkill before?'

'It's not like I drive that much.'

'Are you sure you even hit it? Did you see it in the rearview mirror?'

'I hit it,' Hannah says.

'Then don't think about it.' Allison's voice is nice but firm. 'This happens all the time – did you see that deer on the median a couple hours ago? That was a lot worse than any possum.'

'Have you ever hit something?'

'I think so.' Allison yawns. 'I actually don't remember, which must mean I'm not as compassionate as you are.'

'You're the one who's a vegetarian.'

'Well, I've never *eaten* roadkill, if that's what you're asking. Really, Hannah, quit thinking about it. Do you want me to drive?'

'Maybe.'

'I promise it's not a big deal. I bet the critter had a good life, and now it's gone on to a better place.'

They're quiet – *I'm sorry, possum,* Hannah thinks – and then Allison says, 'You know what I was kind of thinking about while I was asleep? Remember the Mexican restaurant we used to get that seven-layer salad from? Mom would pick it up for us if she and Dad were going to a dinner party or something, but actually in no way was it a salad – it was like sour cream on top of cheese on top of beef on top of guacamole.'

At the same time, Hannah says, 'Yeah, that was good,' and Allison says, 'It's amazing how unhealthily we ate when we were little.'

'It did have lettuce,' Hannah says.

'Barely. And that beef was nasty. I can't believe I ever ate meat.' Allison and Sam now eat almost exclusively organic food, and this, Hannah realizes, must be the subtext of Allison's comments – the miracle of her growing up to be such a wise and authentic person in spite of a childhood spent chowing on pesticides and hydrogenated oils. There are products Hannah didn't even know you could buy organic versions of until she saw them in Allison and Sam's apartment: ketchup, say, or pasta.

'You know what you loved, though?' Hannah says. 'That super-greasy pizza from the place on Lancaster Avenue.'

'Oh, that place was the best. You're right. And I was obsessed with the bread sticks – I thought they were really classy for some reason.'

'It was the dipping sauce,' Hannah says. 'Because Mom told us about fondue, remember? We thought we were like Parisians sitting in a bistro. So why were you in such a bad mood before?'

'When was I in a bad mood?'

'You mean besides for the last five hours?'

'Hannah, you have to admit you could have been more responsible about getting directions to the hospital.'

In Allison's voice, Hannah can hear the bad mood again. She shouldn't have brought it up, especially when she's just pulled Allison back from the precipice of organic righteousness and into a reverie about the bleached carbs of their youth. 'Aren't you starving right now?' Hannah asks. 'You haven't eaten all day.'

'I haven't been that hungry,' Allison says, and for the first time, it occurs to Hannah that Allison could be upset about something having nothing to do with Hannah, that Allison's foul humor could be more than sibling annoyance. Under stress – it's inconceivable to Hannah – Allison loses her appetite.

Hannah thinks of saying *What's wrong*? Instead, she says, 'There's some popcorn left.' She gestures toward the seat between them.

'I'm really not hungry. Besides, we'll stop for dinner soon enough.' Allison yawns again. 'Has anyone ever told you that you grip the wheel like a little old lady?'

'You have.'

'Well, you do. I should call you Esther. Or maybe Myrtle. I can see you as a Myrtle.'

Hannah glances across the seat. 'Would it be rude,' she says, 'if I told you I liked you better when you were asleep?'

That night they stay at a motel outside Buffalo, Hannah's treat, if a Days Inn in western New York can be considered a treat. Allison's cell phone rings while they are watching television before bed. It is Sam. First he apparently holds up the phone to Isabel's ear.

297

'Mommy misses you so much, Izzie,' Allison says. 'Mommy can't *wait* to see you again.'

Not for the first time, Hannah is struck by her sister's generous and unself-conscious affection for her daughter. Clearly, Allison is a good mother and also, she is lucky. Has time ever elapsed between Allison being aware she wants something and the thing becoming hers? That she got married, and that she now has a child – it all seems like proof that Allison is loved, Allison's life is proceeding apace. What Allison desires is normal and appropriate.

After saying good night to Isabel, Allison says in her adult tone, 'Yeah, just hold on a second.' She stands, walks into the bathroom, and closes the door. Does she think Hannah is going to eavesdrop? Besides the fact that eavesdropping is unavoidable, that is – does Allison think Hannah is still thirteen and infinitely titillated by everything her older sister does?

The worst part is that Allison's coyness makes Hannah curious; it brings out her inner thirteen-year-old. They've been watching a sitcom, and at the next commercial, Hannah mutes the television and lifts her head off the pillow. At first she can hear only voice, no distinct words, but there does seem to be an edge to Allison's tone. Are they fighting? What would Allison and Sam fight about? Then, loudly and unmistakably, Allison says, 'At some point I'm not sure it even *matters* if it's true.' She pauses. 'No. No. Sam, I'm not the one—' He must be interrupting her, and when she speaks again, it's incomprehensible.

The television show comes back on, which feels like a sign to Hannah to stop listening. She turns on the volume. Surely, after this, Allison will not pretend that nothing is wrong, but she stays on the phone for so long that Hannah falls asleep before her sister emerges from the bathroom.

They're just west of South Bend, Indiana, and about to start their fourth round of twenty questions – a game they have not played, quite possibly, for twenty years – when Allison's cell phone rings again. It is three o'clock, overcast but even hotter than yesterday, and Hannah is driving. She is trying to suppress a rising anxiety at the appearance of more and more signs for Chicago. Ninety-one miles, the last one said, and they've agreed they'll switch places when they get to forty. They will drive straight to Hannah's new apartment – which she rented sight unseen – unpack with Henry's help, and return the moving truck tonight. Allison's flight back to San Francisco is tomorrow afternoon.

'Is it a woman?' Allison asks.

'Yes.'

'Is she famous?'

'Yes,' Hannah says. 'You can answer your phone, by the way.'

'That's all right. Is she an actress?'

'No.'

'Is she a politician?'

'Not really, but I won't count that one.'

'That's not fair. She either is or she isn't.'

'Then she's not.'

'Is she living?'

'No. That was question five.'

'Is she American?' Allison asks, and her cell phone starts ringing anew.

'Yes. Really, answer it. I don't mind.'

Allison pulls the phone from her purse, looks at the ID on the screen, and puts the phone away.

'Who is it?' Hannah says, and Allison ignores her.

'Okay, so, female, dead, American, not a politician but sort of. Is it Harriet Tubman?'

'You aren't already pregnant again, are you?'

'Not that I'm aware of. Should I take that as a no on Harriet?'

'Is this about Sam's brother being in love with you?' Hannah asks. 'Is that what it is?'

'The only person who ever thought Elliot was in love with me was you. He had a tiny crush on me before Sam and I got married, and that was years ago.'

'Then did Sam cheat on you? If he did, I could maybe cut off his balls.'

'That's very sweet, Hannah. I'll keep it in mind. Okay, I've got it – is it Amelia Earhart?'

'Why won't you tell me what's going on?'

'Why do you assume something *is* going on?'

'Because I'm not a complete idiot. You never tell me anything. I'll tell you something. You want to know the real reason I'm moving to Chicago? You know Henry, the guy who's helping us unload the truck? I think he's the love of my life.'

Allison is quiet at first, and then she says, 'You're dating Fig's ex-boyfriend?'

Right – this is the reason Hannah shouldn't try explaining herself to other people.

'I'm not dating him,' Hannah says. 'But we're friends.'

'You're moving to a different state to live near a guy you're not dating?'

'Never mind,' Hannah says.

'Have you told Mom?'

'Have you told Mom you're having marital problems?'

Looking straight ahead, Allison says, 'The family of one of the girls on Sam's track team filed a complaint with the school, saying he made inappropriate remarks. Are you happy now?'

'As in sexually inappropriate?'

'Is there another kind?' Allison's voice is sour. 'He coached the seventh-and eighth-graders last spring, and they're so hormone-crazy that they're out of control. It's different from when we were that age – these girls wear little sports bras and prance around in their little shorts and ask him all these questions about blow jobs, and then they say that he made them uncomfortable.'

'What does the school think?'

'They're having meetings now to decide what'll happen. He might have his coaching duties suspended for the fall, which is just ridiculous. He's basically guilty until proven innocent.'

'You're not mad at *him*, though, are you?'

'Well, I'm not thrilled by the situation. Do you smell a burning smell?'

Hannah sniffs, then shakes her head. 'Do you know the specifics of what they're saying Sam said?'

'The girls were pretending to be prostitutes or something, and he made a joke about them selling themselves in the Tenderloin.'

'Yikes,' Hannah says.

'Thank you, Hannah,' Allison snaps. 'He used bad judgment. He's not a pervert.'

'That's not what I meant at all. I know he's not. You and Sam are the ideal couple – you're Mr and Mrs Perfect.'

'I'm sure our marriage counselor would be fascinated to hear you say that.'

'Wait, you guys see a marriage counselor?'

'We've been going to her since before we got engaged. She costs a fortune.'

'You went to a marriage counselor before you were even married?'

'She's a couples therapist. Whatever. Honestly, Hannah, take your blinders off. Perfect couples don't exist.'

This reminds Hannah of some other conversation; what other conversation does it remind her of? Just as she remembers that it was Elizabeth who made similar remarks when Julia Roberts and Kiefer Sutherland canceled their wedding, just as Hannah is recalling sitting beside Elizabeth on her aunt's front stoop in Pittsburgh twelve years ago – this is when Allison says, 'Jesus Christ, Hannah, there's smoke coming out of the hood! Pull over!' As Hannah slows down and turns on the right blinker, Allison leans toward the steering wheel. 'Look at the temperature gauge!' she says. 'Didn't I tell you to keep an eye on it?'

The needle can go no higher; it is in the bright red zone. Also, the smoke is now billowing from the hood, and Hannah definitely can smell it – it smells like burnt seafood. When they are parked on the shoulder, Allison climbs out, and Hannah slides across the seat to get out from Allison's side. They stand a few feet away from the hood, the afternoon's humid air pressing against them, the cars whizzing by. 'Should I pop it open?' Hannah asks, and Allison says, 'The engine is overheating. You should wait for someone to get here.'

After calling AAA – thank God Allison belongs, because Hannah doesn't – Allison says, 'You didn't have the emergency brake on, did you?' Sweat has beaded above her upper lip.

'Of course not. Why do you assume this was my fault?'

'I'm not saying it was, but I do think it's interesting that both the incidents of the trip so far have occurred while you're driving.'

'Allison, you bent over backward to tell me the road-kill thing happens all the time.'

After a pause, Allison says, 'This is absurd. We're an hour from Chicago.'

'Are you in a hurry? Were you hoping to go to a museum tonight?'

'I was hoping not to get stuck in Nowhere, Indiana.'

'It could just as easily have happened when you were driving,' Hannah says.

Allison doesn't respond.

'You're such a bitch,' Hannah says. She takes a few steps down the grassy hill that abuts the highway shoulder. She doesn't like being visible to the passing cars, doesn't like the sense of herself as someone the other drivers are glad not to be right now. She folds her arms, then looks back up at her sister. 'By the way,' she says, 'it was Eleanor Roosevelt.'

So they are staying for a second night in a motel. It's not even five o'clock when they check in; the guy who towed the moving truck drops them off. The garage says the truck will be ready by noon tomorrow, which means Hannah and Allison will have to drive straight to the airport if there is any chance of Allison making her plane. Then Hannah will drive alone into the city, through the scary Chicago traffic, to meet Henry and unload the truck, and then, presumably, she'll return the truck alone. It's not until she knows it won't happen that she realizes she wanted Allison to be there when she greeted Henry, when she officially moved to his city. This never happens with Fig because Fig and Hannah look nothing alike, but sometimes when Hannah and Allison are together, Hannah feels like Allison's prettiness rubs off on her. Two cars pulled over and offered to help while they were waiting for AAA; both of the drivers were men, and Hannah wondered if they'd have stopped were she not with her sister.

They are in the town of Carlton. The motel is family-owned and one-story, with parking places in front of the rooms. On one side of the building are modest houses; on the other side are woods so lushly green that Hannah assumes there has been lots of rain lately. According to the woman who gives them their room key, the closest stores and restaurants are about a mile beyond the woods along a road with no sidewalk. As soon as Hannah and Allison have set down their bags, Allison announces she is going jogging. She is gone for nearly an hour and comes back with a dripping, ruddy face. By then Hannah is watching her second talk show. After showering, Allison leaves the room again and returns a few minutes later with a pack of vending-machine potato chips that she does not offer to share. She lies on the other bed, reading a book about raising children with self-esteem.

If she and her sister didn't hate each other right now, Hannah thinks, being stranded might almost seem fun – the randomness of it, the annoying-ness, even. As it is, Allison is making her so tense that Hannah is tempted to tell her to just take a bus to the airport now. Go ahead, see if Hannah cares. But she says nothing. There is a brief thunderstorm around six, and when the rain stops, Hannah says, 'What are you thinking for dinner?'

'I'm good for the night. Those chips filled me up.'

Is she serious? Dinner was what Hannah was counting on to give the evening back some shape and purpose. 'Do you want to come with me to find something?'

'No, thanks.'

What Hannah decides to do – this is doubly pleasing, because it will both irritate Allison and make Hannah happy – is order Chinese food. She finds a phone book in a drawer and asks for three dishes (Kung Pao shrimp, string beans Szechuan style, and eggplant in spicy garlic sauce) as well as a serving of wonton soup and two egg rolls. When she gets off the phone, Allison says, 'I hope you're planning to eat all of that, because I certain don't want any.'

'I'm leaving my options open,' Hannah says. 'I didn't know what I was in the mood for.'

'It's going to stink in here.'

'I like the smell of Chinese food.'

'Apparently, you like the taste, too.'

'Oh, how embarrassing that I eat three meals a day. You really got me there. Boy, do I feel awkward.'

'You know,' Allison says, 'there are people who might think me leaving my infant daughter to do you the favor of driving your moving truck cross-country would encourage you not to be so rude.'

The food takes a long time to come, almost an hour. But finally, there is a knock at the door, and a middle-aged Asian man in a short-sleeved button-down beige shirt passes the bags to Hannah. She sets all the containers on the bureau; keeping the lids off will mean the food cools sooner, but it's a small price to pay for circulating the aroma in the room, insinuating it into Allison's nostrils. No doubt assuming this is a meal for a family, the restaurant has provided three sets of chopsticks and plastic utensils, yet there are no plates, so Hannah pulls the room's lone chair to the bureau, her knees flush against the bureau's middle drawer, and eats straight from the containers. There's a mirror above the bureau in which she can observe herself chewing; it's not the most attractive sight. Stretched out on one of the beds behind Hannah, Allison channel-surfs before settling on a reality dating show. This selection is a bit alarming – for Hannah to watch a reality dating show would be normal, but for Allison, it seems like an admission of defeat, possibly a sign of desperation. Where did the earnest parenting tome go? Hannah can't help glancing at her sister in the mirror every few minutes. Once, their eyes meet, and Allison quickly looks away.

Hannah is stuffed and about to start perspiring when she gives up. She's eaten one egg roll, two spoonfuls of soup, one tenth each of the shrimp and eggplant entrees, and half of the string beans. Already, the food seems like a disgusting error. She washes her hands – the sink is not in the bathroom but just outside it – then methodically tidies and closes all the containers.

'You're *not* keeping those in the room overnight,' Allison says.

In fact, Hannah wasn't planning to, but it's tempting, hearing Allison's outrage. 'I thought I'd leave them under your pillow in case you got hungry,' Hannah says. 'If you don't want me to, I guess I'll just throw them away.'

In a small voice, Allison says, 'Thank you.'

The parking lot is wet from the storm, and filled with golden sunlight. There's a breeze, and after the unrelenting heat of the last several days, the air is actually pleasant. Standing outside the motel's main office, Hannah thinks of offering the leftover food to the woman behind the desk, but this seems possibly insulting. She has just dropped the bags into a green metal trash can and turned around when there it is: a massive rainbow, the biggest she has ever seen, perfectly formed and very close. Looking at the half circle of fuzzed colors, she thinks of learning about Roy G. Biv in fourth-grade science. She hurries into the room. 'Allison, come out here. You have to come see.'

Allison, lying on the bed, turns her head; her

308

expression is suspicious, and suddenly, Hannah has trouble remembering what it is they've been bickering about.

But Allison does get up. She follows Hannah back out the door, and they stand side by side in the parking lot.

'It's amazing, right?' Hannah says. 'I've never seen one that size.'

'It is amazing.'

Neither of them have spoken for several minutes when Hannah says, 'When we were little, do you remember we used to say if it was rainy and sunny at the same time, it meant the devil was getting married?'

Allison nods.

'How far away do you think that is?' Hannah asks.

'Half a mile, maybe. It's hard to say.' They keep watching, and then Allison says, 'I don't think Sam did anything wrong. It's just that the whole thing is so distasteful. It's embarrassing.'

'It'll blow over.'

'You don't know that.'

'I really think it will. Sam is a decent person. I'm sure he's good at his job. And maybe you guys aren't perfect, but you're definitely a good couple. He wouldn't jeopardize your marriage – he's way too in love with you. Honestly, that's why I'm moving, because I want what you guys have.' Hannah looks over. Allison's profile is lit by the evening sun, her brow furrowed, her lips tight.

'I don't mean this to be glib,' Hannah continues, 'but I feel like a lot of life is distasteful and embarrassing. And you just push through it. Isn't that the big lesson we learned from living with Dad? You fix what you can, and you let time pass.'

After a silence, Allison says, 'When did you get all wise?'

'I'm not as clueless as you think. I mean, I don't know. I actually see a therapist, too. She knows all about why I'm moving to Chicago, by the way, and she doesn't disapprove.'

'Hannah, I chased boys when I was single. Everyone does.'

'Really?'

'Of course. And it's good about you seeing a therapist. I thought of suggesting it to you a few times.' Allison pauses. 'So you think we should go look for the pot of gold?'

'I know,' Hannah says. 'I keep thinking of "Somewhere Over the Rainbow."'

Allison smiles. She says, 'That song always makes me cry.'

CHAPTER 9

MAY 2005

Dear Dr Lewin,

I have been meaning to write to you for quite some time, but I have put it off first because I've been busy and second because – this feels very silly to say, which makes it no less true – I wanted to wait until I could tell you I'd fallen in love. It's difficult to believe almost two years have elapsed since I left Boston, and this afternoon (it's a Sunday) I thought to myself that I needed to write a letter today, before either you forget who I am or my wish to contact you starts to seem sentimental and pointless even to me.

I now live in Albuquerque, New Mexico, where I am working at a school for autistic children. It's coed, but the classroom I'm in is all boys. (You probably are aware that there's a higher rate of autism among boys than girls.) The boys' ages range between twelve and fifteen. Most are small and appear younger than they are, but one, a student named Pedro, is taller than I am and probably forty pounds heavier. He sometimes slyly calls me by my first name, as if I won't notice. If we're drawing side by side – he's especially fond of drawing guitars – he'll say, 'You like my picture, Hannah?' and I'll say, 'Not Hannah, Pedro. Ms Gavener,' and he'll be quiet for a few seconds and then say, 'Not Pedro, Ms Gavener. Mr Gutierrez.' Pedro is the most conversational. Many of them speak very little and are prone to outbursts and tantrums. There is a particularly temperamental boy, Jason, whose pockets are at all times bulging with miscellaneous items including but not limited to broken pen caps, candy wrappers, rubber bands, two or three pairs of scissors, and a cat brush. (The cat brush is gray plastic, with metal bristles.) Jason might be calmly eating lunch, then drop a grape on the floor and become hysterical, or I'll be talking to him, coaxing him to respond by asking questions – once this happened when I said, 'Does your name begin with a J?' – and he'll make a horribly offended expression before beginning to seethe and spit. By contrast, a boy named Mickey is the most cheerful person I've ever known. I take him to the bathroom once an hour. He recently graduated from wearing diapers to Pull-Ups, and if ever I slip and refer to the Pull-Ups as diapers, he corrects me immediately. When he sits on the toilet (even urinating, he sits down) he looks around the bathroom in such an upbeat, appreciative way that he calls to mind a businessman who has finally taken a long-awaited trip to the Bahamas and is reclining on a lounge chair by a pool, drinking a fabulous drink. Mickey is a curly-haired boy who alternates, no matter the season, between red sweatsuits and blue sweatsuits. Last week, sitting there with his red pants bunched at his ankles, he happened to notice a metal shelf – just a ledge, really – that had been installed to store rolls of toilet paper.

He gestured up at it and said, 'Is that new?'

'Yes, Mickey,' I said. 'I think it is.'

He smiled so widely and shook his head so slowly and blissfully that you might have thought, to continue the businessman analogy, he had just been informed of his million-dollar bonus. He was elated. He asked what the shelf was for, and I told him for toilet paper. Then he asked, as he often does, 'Do you like me, Ms Gavener?' (Mickey slurs his words and pronounces it more like *Ms Gaahv*.) I said, yes, of course, and then a few more minutes passed, and he again gestured above him and said, 'New shelf!' I smiled and said, 'I know, Mickey.' He said happily, pointing, 'Look at it!' and I said, 'I am.'

I live in a one-story adobe house south of the university, and my roommate is a police officer. (I'd never personally known a female police officer before I met Lisa.) About half the time, she stays with her boyfriend, who's also a police officer, but on the nights she's home, we watch TV together. A lot of Lisa's habits would be considered stereotypically feminine – she's always getting manicures, or spending three hundred dollars on shoes at the mall – though she's also a bit of a tomboy and avidly follows the Lobos. In the first week I knew

313

her, she once said, 'No day is so shitty that it can't be salvaged by a good margarita.' She grew up in Albuquerque, and she has never, you might be interested to know, sought therapy.

If it seems like I am avoiding the real topic here, the topic of Henry, that might be correct. But I can say truthfully that at this point I don't think of him from day to day or even from week to week. I do think of him on a monthly basis, but honestly, I think of you far more. Sometimes when I'm trying to make a decision, I wonder what you would recommend, and in my mind you always pick the option that involves either having more fun or standing up for myself. When I try to explain what the disadvantages might be, you remind me to relax; whatever it is, you say, it's worth a shot.

By the way, I'm glad I finally met your husband before I moved from Boston, even if it was just by chance when we all ran into each other outside the movie theater on Brattle Street. I was surprised (in neither a good or bad way – I just hadn't considered the possibility) to learn that he is African American. I used to imagine that he must either be a doctor like you or else some sort of hot carpenter – maybe I came up with this notion because you had such nice moldings in your office, and the floor was so elegantly refinished – but given that he is a math professor, both my guesses were wrong. When you introduced us, you could not reveal to him how you knew me, but I suspect he inferred it. He smiled at me as if to say *I presume you are extremely neurotic, yet I do not hold your neuroses against you.*

Dr Lewin, to this day you remain the smartest person I have ever met. You once used the word *periphrastic* – you used it utterly unshowily, only because it was for you the most precise word for the occasion – and I was enormously flattered by your incorrect assumption that I knew what it meant. I never told you that after each session, as I rode away on the T, I'd take notes about what we'd discussed. I came across my folder of notes when I unpacked after moving here, and while for narcissistic reasons I did find them interesting, I am afraid they gave off a sort of wispy, elusive air when what I'd always hoped for was the snap of revelation – the clarity and permanence of some official knowledge that would feel instantly true and keep feeling true from then on.

In any case: That first night in Chicago after I'd dropped Allison at the airport and then Henry and I carried all the boxes and furniture up the stairs to my new apartment, I said, 'Should we get something to eat?' and he said, 'There's a really good Greek place around the corner, but first let me touch base with Dana,' and I said, 'Who's Dana?'

Oh, Henry said, had he not mentioned his girlfriend when we'd seen each other at Fig's wedding or during my interview trip? He had not. She joined us that night for dinner – I was in a disbelieving agony – and she turned out to be a tall woman with a certain preppy hardness. She'd rowed crew in college, she was Republican, she seemed to be the type of person who, no matter how many drinks she consumed, would never divulge anything inappropriate or endearing. At the end of dinner, she said, 'Why'd you move to Chicago?' I laughed nervously and said, 'I'm trying to remember.'

'She got a job here,' Henry said.

Dana was a paralegal, worked long hours, was rarely around during the week, and was often not around on the weekend, either. This made it easy for Henry and me to quickly develop a pattern of spending large quantities of time together. Though Dana's existence initially prompted in me a sense of betrayal I wouldn't have dared articulate to Henry, perhaps I also preferred it. In college, when he and I had driven to Cape Cod together, Fig's existence had been something of a relief, it had taken the pressure off. Now, in Chicago, I thought Dana would allow Henry and me to get used to each other again, and then she could conveniently make her exit. Such a prospect did not seem entirely unrealistic: On a regular basis, Henry made comments that threw into question the stability of their relationship, and I tried to pretend the comments didn't thrill me. 'I think she secretly has a thing for her boss' was an early one. Also, 'She's not the most compassionate person you'll ever meet.' Unfortunately, not all of his remarks about her were negative, and once he said, 'She's the first girlfriend I've ever had who could literally kick my ass if she wanted to. Is it weird that that turns me on?'

Pretty soon Henry and I were hanging out as many nights of the week as not. He often asked my advice, which surprised and flattered me. At the time, he and his twin sister were squabbling long-distance – her husband had borrowed money from Henry to start a restaurant in New Hampshire, and Henry was having an increasingly suspicious feeling about the whole venture – and so we talked about what, if anything, Henry should do. It took me a few months to realize how many other friends Henry confided in. True, I became the one he sought out most, but perhaps that was because no one else made themselves as available. Although I was unsure why he believed me to be capable of giving advice, I took his problems very seriously and would concentrate on them so hard, genuinely trying to find a solution, that I sometimes had headaches afterward. In addition to talking about his sister and brother-in-law, we talked a lot about his new boss at the consulting firm where he worked, who was, Henry thought, a particular asshole, and sometimes about Dana. Henry had the idea he'd screwed up his last several relationships, and he was determined to make this one work. It seemed so clear to me that he couldn't that I didn't even try to convince him. I figured he'd realize it himself soon enough.

One night in late September – I'd been in Chicago for three weeks by then – Henry and I drove to Milwaukee with his friend Bill to see the Brewers play the Cubs. Though I hardly understood the rules of baseball, Henry had bought my ticket and insisted I come along. At the ballpark, Bill announced that he was going to eat one hot dog for every run the Cubs scored. By his fifth hot dog, Bill was gripping his stomach unhappily, and by the seventh, he could barely watch the game. He was leaning forward, his head in his hands.

After the game, we drove home to Chicago, and Bill fell asleep in the backseat, and Henry and I were listening to a classic-rock station, and it was a warm night in early fall. We were talking about the situation with Henry's sister and then about a new building going up near his apartment. We weren't talking about Dana; those conversations had already become unbearable to me, embedded as they were with the potential to be either exciting or heartbreaking, and on this night it all just felt ordinary and calm. I stuck my hand out the window so the air pressed against my palm, and I felt in that moment that I could never love anyone more than I loved Henry.

I loved how he was both a good driver and a relaxed driver; how he'd gotten me a giant foam finger at the ballpark; how he'd cared that I'd come to the game, he'd *wanted* me to come; how in the first week after I'd moved to Chicago, he'd taught me to open a bottle of wine, to parallel-park, and to say 'You're a tricky bastard' in Spanish, and how these seemed like long-overdue skills that you'd need for a life of happy situations; how, after I said that in high school my sister trained me to sing the Rolling Stones song 'Under My Thumb' by replacing all the *she* and *her* pronouns with *he* and *him*, he sang the song that way, too, unprompted, the next time we heard it on the radio; how he looked cute in his plaid shirt with the pearl snaps and he looked cute in a Brooks Brothers tie and he looked cute when he met me after playing basketball at the gym, still all sweaty, and how he had the good kind of fingers, fingers that are the same width at the top and bottom instead of tapering up; how he knew me really well, and how, once when we ate at an outdoor restaurant, he said, 'You can take the far chair,' because one of the things he knew was that I didn't like having my back to the street. Later, when I'd think of how I ought to cut Henry off, I'd think of teaching another person to know me like he did, and it seemed – with a hypothetical person, especially – like it would be a lot of work.

That night all I wanted in the world was to sit in the front seat next to Henry, driving home from a baseball game in Milwaukee. Back in the city, he dropped off Bill first, even though it was out of the way, because he always dropped off anyone besides me first. Outside my building, he put the car in park and we talked for ten more minutes,

319

still about basically nothing, and I wanted to touch him so badly that I felt like I wasn't a body, I was just an aching propulsive meteor, and then abruptly he said, 'I'm beat. I gotta hit the sack.' He always was the one who made us part, who could; I just couldn't. Once I was inside my building, it was terrible to still be a meteor. I was alone with all my pent-up energy.

I believed, except in the dreadful moments when I didn't believe this at all, that Henry and Dana would break up and he and I would enter a relationship that would lead to marriage, except that I was afraid when he first kissed me, the fact of our being friends would make me more rather than less tense, and after we kissed tensely, he might, unaware that the situation would improve, never want to kiss me again. But the main thing was that I was sure about Henry, certain my real life had finally started, and all that had come before had been preamble.

One Saturday in winter when Dana had gone to Washington, D.C., to visit her parents, Henry and I went snowshoeing – this was his idea – and that night we made tacos and drank beer and sat in his apartment listening to Bruce Springsteen. At three in the morning, while I was slumped on the couch with my feet propped on the coffee table and he was sprawled on the floor, I said, 'Henry, sometimes I feel like things are weird between us.' No one had ever explained to me that such conversations are futile, that you go ahead and kiss him because what's a discussion compared to your warm and moving lips? The guy could still reject you, of course, but he'd be rejecting you because he didn't want to kiss you back, which is a truer reason than anything that can be put into words.

Henry was quiet, and the moment was huge, it still contained two outcomes, and then he said, 'I sometimes do, too,' and even though this was an affirmation of sorts, I could tell immediately that the rest of the conversation would make me sad. There would be bright bursts, but that would be the net of it: sadness. He was quiet for a long time again, then said, 'I don't think you understand how important you are to me,' and I thought he might cry.

'Henry, you're important to me,' I said.

'But Dana's great, too,' he said. 'And she's my girlfriend.'

'I just have to say this,' I said. 'I've liked you since we were in college.'

Henry squinted. 'You liked me back then?'

'Wasn't it obvious?'

'Oh, I don't know. There were times—' He shook his head and exhaled a long breath. 'It's all complicated.'

Looking back, I think, *No, not really*. I also think, *No, Dana was not in fact great*. But I was still inclined then to take Henry at his word.

Henry said, 'When I lived in Seoul, I really wanted you to visit me. Do you remember that?'

I nodded.

'I think I kind of had a crush on you then. And when you e-mailed me saying you had a boyfriend, I felt jealous.' He smiled wryly, and my heart sparked – he'd had a crush on me! – and it is not an exaggeration to say I thought probably a hundred times afterward of my mistake in not having visited him then. It took me until I'd moved to New Mexico to understand that it never comes down to a single thing you did or didn't do or say. You might convince yourself it did, but it didn't.

'Can you imagine us together now?' I asked him.

'Of course.' There was another long, long silence, and he said, sounding pained, 'I feel like I'm making a mess of things.'

'No,' I said. 'I'm the one who's creating awkwardness by bringing this up.'

'It's going to be *really* awkward now. So awkward.' He grinned. We listened to the end of the song – it was 'Mansion on the Hill' – and then he said, 'It's late. Why don't you stay over and sleep in my bed, and I'll sleep on the couch?'

When he'd escorted me to his room, we paused in the doorway and he set his hand on my shoulder and said, 'This isn't because I'm not attracted to you, because I totally am.' And that, of everything, probably hurt my feelings the most. It sounded so *There, there, little sister*. Now I see how he offered opportunities but how, in such opportunities, I had to be the initiator. It had to be my fault, or at least more mine than his. But I didn't understand that as a condition, or I half understood – I understood subconsciously but I was too shy, and it also wasn't how I wanted it to happen, while he was still involved with another girl. I smiled like a good sport and said, 'Thanks for letting me stay here, Henry,' and we looked at each other a moment longer, and he said, 'Sleep tight, Gavener.' His use of my last name hurt, too, at the time.

I suspect you can imagine the rest. It was so repetitive that even if you can imagine only a portion, you know the entire story. I thought that night was a breakthrough when it wasn't a breakthrough at all, I thought a relationship was imminent, I thought the conversation was an outrageous anomaly, but it was a conversation we had over and over and over, and every time it seemed less like an acknowledgment of the mutual attraction between us and more like my reminder to him of my unrequited love, and of my unwavering availability should he ever find himself in the mood to indulge. What he reminded me of was how much he *valued* me, how well I understood him. Sometimes, if our discussion had taken a disagreeable turn, he'd ask, seeming hurt, 'Do you not want to be friends with me if I'm not your boyfriend?' And I'd say, 'Of course I want to be friends!' Hanging around while he noodled over his feelings, while he soaked in the tepid bath of his ambivalence, contorting my face into expressions of concern and sympathy and unjudg-mental insight and unhurt receptivity – that I had no problem with. But what kind of pathetic person would I have revealed myself as if I didn't want to be friends with him because he wouldn't be my boyfriend?

A few times Henry said, 'I love our friendship.' Or 'I love hanging out with you.' Or the closest he got: 'I love you in my life.'

And then there were the evenings I sat on the couch and he lay with his head in my lap while we watched television, and I might set my hand on his shoulder but only in such a way as to treat it like a resting place; I did not run my fingers through his hair. When he lay like that, I was the happiest I had ever been. I was so happy I was afraid to breathe. We never talked about it, and any conversation we had before, during, or after was entirely casual. And we never spoke of it when he stopped doing it, which he did – I don't know for sure that they were related, but it seems plau-sible – soon after a wedding he and Dana attended together. After he stopped, when we sat on the couch, the absence of his head on my lap was bigger than the television program, or my apart-ment, or the city of Chicago.

And where exactly was Dana in all of this? She was working at the law firm downtown, then rowing on the Erg at her gym on Clark Street, then, on Fridays and Saturdays, drinking gin and tonics at gatherings Henry did not invite me to, at swanky bars where I'd never been. Once when I used the bathroom in Henry's apartment, I saw a tampon wrapper in the wastebasket and wanted to weep. A few times he said, 'I think Dana's threatened by you. She's threatened because she doesn't know what to make of you.' And didn't I love the idea that broad-shouldered, gin-drinking Dana could be threatened by me, didn't I, in certain ways, love my own sadness? On weekends, when I walked to the supermarket and the movie rental store at seven-thirty P.M. in corduroy pants and a sweatshirt while around me couples in black clothes held hands and hailed taxis, wasn't I stirred by the poignancy of my loneliness, by how *deserving* I was of Henry's love, by how much more exquisite it would be, coming after my suffering?

On the one hand, I feel that I was the biggest fool ever: If a man wants to be romantically involved with you, he tries to kiss you. That's the entire story, and if he doesn't kiss you, there is never a reason to wait for him. Yes, in the history of crushes, one person has come around for another – during this time, I collected such stories – but it happens rarely. Again, though, no one had told me. And it wasn't that I didn't know spending so much time with Henry was unwise. It was that I didn't really care. I didn't *want* to keep my distance from him, to pick up the pieces and meet some pleasant fellow on the El one day, a guy who'd appreciate me as I deserved to be appreciated. I wanted Henry.

Our wedding, I believed, would not be a victory in and of itself but would be merely a by-product of the fact that we enjoyed each other's company so much, and that it seemed impossible to imagine a time when we wouldn't. My certainty was like a physical object – a telephone, a running shoe, nothing precious or sparkly – and I did not need to be in the same room with it to know it existed. For his twenty-ninth birthday, I bought him a set of twelve orange dinner plates costing over two hundred dollars, and though the purchase felt extravagant, I understood – not in a cute way, not as an inside joke with myself, but matter-of-factly – that the plates would ultimately be both of ours.

Henry and Dana were still going out in February when he met Suzy, a meeting at which, I, too, was present. (I have heard that many of those at Harvard University's 1947 graduation did not realize, in listening to Secretary of State George C. Marshall's commencement address, that they were hearing the announcement of the Marshall Plan.) Henry and I got pizza one evening on Damen Avenue, and Suzy was at the table behind us, smoking by herself, while Henry and I waited for our slices. She looked so, for lack of a better word, undergraduate-ish that it didn't occur to me to feel nervous. She wore a jean jacket, she kept most of her long hair loose but had a few tiny braids in front, and she had silver rings on almost all her fingers. She was small and pretty, and I don't remember that she actually did smell like patchouli, but she seemed like she could have. If you'd asked me that night how we got into a conversation with her, I probably wouldn't have known immediately, but later, I forced myself to remember, and it seemed not coincidental that it was when I went up to the front counter to get a cup of water that she and Henry started talking. Probably he was the one who started talking to her. When I returned, they were discussing gun control. And the next week when I called his office midmorning he announced he was hungover. He'd seen Suzy at a bar, he told me, but I still didn't understand, and I was surprised when he said that they'd stayed until closing time.

'That's weird that you keep running into her,' I said. 'Maybe she's stalking you.'

'No, we met up on purpose,' he said. 'I called her.' There was a silence, the silence of my receiving this information and Henry – what? – dignifying my receipt of it.

'How'd you get her number?' I asked, and I felt that familiar slide down the icy precipice: the slick burn of my hands, the endlessness of the drop.

'When we saw her before,' he said, which didn't really answer my question, while telling me pretty much all I needed to know.

Even when he and Dana officially broke up, I thought it couldn't be serious for him and Suzy. She was nineteen and probably loved giving blow jobs or something. The three of us had dinner once, and she wasn't stupid – I wanted her to be, obviously – but she wasn't particularly interesting. She wasn't someone who asked other people questions, or maybe she just didn't ask me. She was from Madison, majoring in sociology at DePaul, working twenty hours a week as a waitress. At one point Henry said, 'I got the weirdest e-mail from Julie today,' and Suzy said, 'Who's Julie?' and I said, 'Henry's twin.' I didn't say it pointedly, I was just answering the question. Suzy said, 'You have a twin?' and again (Dr Lewin, I hope it does not seem like I am being gratuitously crude), all I could think was *blow jobs*.

I walked home after that dinner, and it was a rainy April evening, and I thought – I was by this point constantly trying to impose these types of limits – that I should never again hang out with Henry in Suzy's company, and that from then on I should see him no more than twice a week and I shouldn't talk to him if he called me at work. Or maybe I am mixing this up, and maybe this was the time I decided I *shouldn't* talk to him at home and should *only* talk to him at work.

Either way, we met for lunch the next week, and I had the feeling I so often had with him, that between us no words or gestures were impossible. I wanted to reach across the table and cup his chin and feel all the bones of his face beneath the skin. He always seemed like mine. Or I wanted to say *I feel gutted like a fish*, without any more explanation. But I didn't cup his chin, I didn't say anything weird, and I didn't ask him about Suzy, because that was another of my resolutions: to quit acting like talking about his girlfriends didn't bother me.

We weren't in touch for ten days. I intentionally didn't call him, and I felt proud for holding out. And then on a Thursday morning when he called me at work, I thought, *Of course, of course, he always needs to check in*, and he said, 'I have some news, and I hope you'll be happy for me,' and then he said, 'Suzy's pregnant.' They had been dating then for less than four months.

I was sitting at my desk, and all the objects on it – the red mouse pad, the mug of pens, the line of plastic binders – seemed suddenly *obvious*; I noticed them in a way I never had before.

'I need your support,' he said, and I observed the fat spine of the Chicago phone book. 'My family is flipping out.'

Finally, I asked, 'How many weeks along is she?'

'Nine.'

'Are you not pro-choice?'

'Do you hear yourself, Hannah? I guess you can't imagine this, but we want the baby. We feel like this happened for a reason.'

'You mean a reason other than Suzy not taking her birth control pills?'

'That's completely sexist,' he said. 'I'm more ready than she is. She's the one who's still in school. But we really are in love.' For a split second, I thought he was talking about us. 'I wish you wouldn't make this weird,' he said.

'I think you already have.'

He was silent.

'Are you guys getting married?' I asked.

'Not for now, but probably at some point.'

'What does her family think?'

'They're cool with it. We were up there this past weekend. They're wonderful people.'

I thought again of the afternoon we'd driven to Cape Cod, and of how Henry had changed since then – I think he'd become less honest with himself – but also how what had been true that day turned out to be true seven years later: that he liked to rescue girls who needed rescuing. He'd been wrong only in predicting his proclivity would change.

And surely Henry would have been disappointed had I not reacted negatively to the news. Wasn't this the pattern we were supposed to follow, that he'd tell me, I'd freak out, I'd calm down, I'd then talk him through how to smooth things over with his family, we'd figure out a way for these developments to reinforce the idea that he was a good, thoughtful guy whose life was headed in the right direction? We'd say his decision was *honorable*; also, he'd mention in passing how gorgeous he found Suzy, so I knew they were having good sex and didn't get the idea he was acting entirely out of duty.

'Well, good luck,' I said, and he said, 'It's not like we'll never see each other again.'

I began to cry as soon as I'd hung up. I was sitting at my desk, and the door to my office was open, but I didn't care. I was crying partly because Suzy got him and I didn't, but more than for the loss of Henry, I was crying for my own wrongness, a wrongness of which there now was incontrovertible proof. My intuition, my gut instinct – whatever you want to call it, it had been wrong. Henry and I weren't each other's fates. We weren't going to spend the rest of our lives eating dinner off orange plates, I wasn't ever going to actually rub his head while he rested it in my lap, we'd never travel together to a foreign country. None of it. It was over. Or maybe it wouldn't work out with him and Suzy and he'd want me later, in a few years, or he'd want me much later, he'd come find me when I was sixty-eight and he was seventy, but by then, who cared? I wanted him while we were still the people we were now. Besides, he'd violated the terms of what I'd seen as our unspoken agreement.

I decided to move to Albuquerque because I didn't know anyone there, because it was far from Chicago and Boston and Philadelphia, and if the terrain was different, dry and mountainous and spiked by strange plants, I imagined maybe I could be different, too. Escape, like unrequited love, is an old story. Less than a month after Henry had told me Suzy was pregnant, I was ensconced in the second bedroom in Lisa's house here on Coal Street. I spent the summer working as a hostess at a French restaurant, and in August I was hired for my current position as an assistant teacher at Praither Exceptional School. I knew little about special ed when I started – my only real exposure to anyone with developmental issues had been my cousin Rory – but I felt ready for change. My salary now is not high, but luckily, neither is the cost of living in New Mexico. I am especially pleased to report that as of February, I have paid off my student loans.

Last week we took the boys out for recess – the other teachers in my classroom are named Beverly and Anita, and the head teacher is Graciela, though she stayed inside to prepare ingredients for the English-muffin pizzas we were teaching the boys to make that afternoon – and a few of the students were shooting baskets while the others climbed on the jungle gym. I was standing by the slide as a boy named Ivan described to me his wish to buy a tractor, when I heard a wail. It was Jason – he's the temperamental one who carries the cat brush and other items in his pockets – and I turned and saw that he was sitting on the platform that connects the two sections of the jungle gym and that his fingers were stuck in one of the platform's drainage holes. I should point out here that the jungle gym is designed for children smaller and younger than my students. I climbed onto the platform and knelt next to Jason, thinking that if he held still, I'd be able to pull his fingers out. He was shrieking and weeping, and, as gently as possible, I tugged at his hand, but his fingers – it was his middle and ring fingers – stayed where they were. Anita and Beverly came over, and the rest of the boys were watching us by then.

'Can one of you go get some Vaseline?' I asked the teachers. 'Or maybe soap and water?'

'We'll take the kids inside,' Anita said.

After the playground emptied out except for us, Jason was still howling. 'Jason, what's on your shirt?' I said. 'That's a fish, right? A fish from Texas?' He was wearing a turquoise T-shirt that said SOUTH PADRE ISLAND. 'What kind of fish is that?' I asked.

His wailing slowed and dropped in volume.

'I wonder if it likes to eat candy,' I said. 'Do fish eat candy? Not in real life, but maybe if it's a movie fish or a pretend fish.' The candy reference was cheap on my part – to help students work on math (I assume you know it is far from true that all autistic people are mathematical geniuses) as well as to practice making purchases, the classrooms hold sales on alternating days. Our classroom, Classroom D4, sells popcorn for thirty cents a bag; it is Classroom D7, the oldest kids, who sell candy, and many of our boys, including Jason, are fixated on it.

Jason had stopped crying. I pulled a tissue from my pocket and held it out to him. 'Blow,' I said, and he scowled and turned his head in the other direction.

'What about a lollipop?' I said. 'Would a fish ever eat a lollipop?'

His head swiveled back around. In my peripheral vision, I could see Graciela and the school nurse emerge from the building and walk toward us. Jason was staring at me. 'Are you fourteen?' he asked.

I shook my head. 'You're fourteen,' I said. 'Right? You're fourteen years old. But I'm a grown-up. I'm twenty-eight.'

He regarded me impassively.

'Twenty-eight is twice as old as fourteen,' I said. Jason still didn't respond, and I asked, 'Why are you staring at me like that?'

'I'm looking for social cues,' he said.

I had to bite my lip. 'That's great!' I said. 'Jason, that's wonderful. That's just exactly what you should be doing. You know what, though? When you're looking for social cues, you usually don't tell the other person. You don't need to.'

He was quiet. Sensing that I'd discouraged him, I added, 'But I'll tell you a secret. I'm looking for social cues, too. It's not easy, is it?'

Graciela and the nurse had reached the jungle gym. They'd brought Vaseline and soap, and Beverly soon followed with dental floss and ice chips. Nothing worked. Graciela and the nurse stood under the platform pressing ice against Jason's fingers, slathering them with Vaseline, turning and prodding them, and they stayed stuck. The nurse called the paramedics. I kept talking to Jason as they hunched under the platform – I could tell when they were really pushing at his fingers because he'd yelp and then, as if preparing to ride the wave of a new set of tears, glance at me. I'd shake my head. 'You're fine,' I'd say. Or, 'They want to help you feel better.'

The paramedics showed up twenty minutes later. The police came, too – they have to by law – and it turned out to be my roommate, Lisa, and her partner, which has happened before. 'What have we here?' she said. She offered to let Jason put on her hat, but he didn't want to. I could feel his capacity for hysteria growing again with the arrival of the new cars and people, and he teared up a little but stayed composed. Even when the paramedics jammed his fingers out – I suspect all they did was use more force than Graciela or the nurse could bring themselves to – Jason stayed composed. When his fingers finally were free and he could stand, I hugged him. We try as much as possible to treat the boys as we'd treat other fourteen-year-olds, to impose the same boundaries of physical contact – Mickey in particular has difficulty with this and will wedge his head beneath my armpit and croon, 'I love you, Ms Gaahv' – but in this instance, I could not help myself. I sensed that Graciela simultaneously disapproved and understood.

I was wearing a gray button-down shirt, and as

Jason headed inside with the nurse, I noticed that Vaseline was smeared on it in several places, and I felt in that moment – you can see the Sandia Mountains from the school playground – that I was meant to live in the desert of New Mexico, meant to be a teacher with Vaseline on my blouse. I do not want to idealize the boys or pretend they're angels; on a regular basis, Pedro picks his nose until it bleeds, and all of them stick their hands in their pants and fiddle with their penises so often that we have pasted paper hands on their desks where they're meant to place their palms. 'Public hands!' we remind them. 'Public hands!' And yet I feel somehow that my students contain the world. This is difficult for me to express. Like all of us, they are greedy and cranky and sometimes disgusting. But they are never cagey; they are entirely sincere.

My students' lives will be hard in ways they don't understand, and I wish I could protect them – I can't – but at least as long as I'm trying to show them how to protect themselves, I don't think that I am wasting my time. Perhaps this is how you know you're doing the thing you're intended to: No matter how slow or slight your progress, you never feel that it's a waste of time.

I am glad, honestly, that I didn't get what I thought I wanted back in Chicago. If I'd gotten what I wanted, I'd never have learned to physically restrain a teenager trying to attack me, I'd never have pinned a dashiki to a bulletin board while decorating for Kwanzaa, I'd never have stood before a classroom of boys, making a presentation on puberty and hygiene. And sincerely I feel that I am *lucky* to have stood there simulating the application of deodorant. What would Henry and I have been like if we'd married? I picture us spending Saturday afternoons at upscale houseware stores, purchasing throw pillows or porcelain platters meant for serving deviled eggs.

Sometimes in the afternoon, after I've used the bathroom and am approaching the sink to wash my hands, my reflection in the mirror is that of a person whom I know that I know but cannot immediately place. This, too, is because of the boys: because of how they require all my attention, how they consume me and make me forget myself. Or if, while washing my hands, I notice that a piece of food is stuck in my teeth and I can infer that it's been there for several hours and during those hours I've talked to other teachers, including male teachers, I would not say I don't care at all, but I don't care very much. In my life before, both in Chicago and in Boston, how embarrassed I'd have felt to know I'd been talking to people with food in my teeth. But that never would have happened, because I cared enormously about such things.

Out here, I do sometimes miss my family, but they seem to be getting along well. Allison is pregnant again, and Fig is pregnant, too – the world is a very fertile place these days – and relishes discussing with anyone who cares to listen that the anonymous sperm donor she and Zoe used has an IQ of 143. Darrach and Elizabeth and Rory visited me in the winter, and we did lots of touristy things – they all three bought turquoise necklaces in Old Town – and Elizabeth kept saying, 'It's so stinking cool that you live here. I've wanted to come to New Mexico for my whole life.' I'm not sure if you'd remember my friend Jenny from Tufts, but she lives in Denver, which is a short plane flight away, so we keep talking about trying to see each other; she's in her second semester of nursing school. (I hope in providing updates about other people I am not assuming in you an excessive degree of interest in my life now that I am no longer paying $105 an hour. Please know also I am not trying to mock the fee, as I'm aware that other clients paid up to $70 more. I guess part of the reason I haven't written to you before is that when you said to let you know how I was doing, I just didn't know if you meant once or regularly.)

But back to Henry: I suppose the easiest explanation is that he didn't find me that attractive. But my attraction to him was flattering, and he genuinely enjoyed my friendship. What did he have to lose by keeping me near? I don't resent him for suggesting that I move to Chicago, because the fact is, I didn't require much persuasion – I heard in that conversation at Fig's wedding what

I wanted to hear. Or maybe he was sufficiently attracted to me but didn't want the person he told everything to also to be his girlfriend. I can see this, how one might prefer a little distance. I can see, too, how because he denied me, I had the luxury of being sure of him, but because I never denied him, he was burdened by uncertainty. And then I think, no, no, it was none of that. It was me – all along, I was the one who resisted. I wanted to hold happiness in reserve, like a bottle of champagne. I postponed it because I was afraid, because I overvalued it, and because I didn't want to use it up, because what do you wish for then? That possibility, that I was intimidated by getting what I wanted, is the hardest one for me to consider, which might mean it is the likeliest. On three or four occasions Henry would, I think, have kissed me, and on all these occasions, I turned away. Sometimes only an inch, or only with my eyes. It was never purposely; I'd always done it already, before I'd decided to. One of the times was when he was lying in my lap in front of the TV, and he looked up at me, he *gazed* at me, and I should have gazed back, but instead I wondered if he could see my nose hair, and I tilted my head so we were no longer making eye contact. I never felt ready in those moments, I felt like first I needed to go take a shower or prepare some notes, and so, I guess, it was my fault; I choreographed my own devastation. A part of me thinks, *But why couldn't he have accounted for my nervousness, why couldn't he just have set his palms against my ears and held me still?* And then another part of me thinks, *He was never single anyway.* Maybe it all did turn out for the best.

I sometimes remember driving back from the Brewers game, how I believed I would never love anyone more than I loved Henry. In a sense, I may have been right: I can't imagine ever again feeling that infatuated and free of doubt. I think Henry may have been the first and last person about whom I believed, *If I can get him to love me, then everything else will be all right.* That I am no longer that naïve is both a loss and a gain. I have dated a bit since moving to New Mexico – I even once really did meet a guy at the supermarket, which was something I thought happened only in movies – but I am not in love. I am writing you now anyway, not in love. If I had to guess, I'd guess I will get married eventually, but I am far from sure of it. When I think of Henry and Oliver and Mike, I feel as if they are three different models – templates, almost – and I wonder if they are the only three in the world: the man who is with you completely, the man who is with you but not with you, the man who will get as close to you as he can without ever becoming yours. It would be arrogant to claim no other dynamics exist just because I haven't experienced them, but I have to say that I can't imagine what they are. I hope that I am wrong.

Mike is the only one of the three I look back

on with much nostalgia. I do think it might be different if we met now, when I have enough of a frame of comparison to recognize how rare his goodness to me was, but then I think how I grew sick of kissing him. How can you spend your life with a person you're sick of kissing? Regardless, I have heard through the grapevine that he is married. Oliver is still in Boston, and we exchange occasional e-mails. I don't harbor ill will – I really did get a kick out of him – but I'm glad we didn't stay together any longer than we did.

As for Henry, we haven't been in touch since I left Chicago. I assume that he and Suzy are still together; when I picture him, I picture her in the background, cradling an infant. The day I left Chicago, Henry and I had breakfast together at a diner, at his suggestion, and as we hugged goodbye, he said, 'I feel like I made some mistakes with you,' and I said, 'I feel like you did, too.' Yet again he looked like he might cry, so I shook my head, almost irritably, and said, 'It's not that big a deal.'

Incidentally, I described Henry to my room-mate, Lisa, once, soon after I'd moved to Albuquerque. Though I'd been speaking for about fifteen minutes, I'd barely, in my own view, gotten going, and she glanced over we were in her car, and she was driving – and said, 'He sounds like a pussy.'

That day last week on the playground, after Jason had gone inside, Lisa called into headquarters on her walkie-talkie, then paused as her partner headed back to the police car. She said, 'Hannah, what did I tell you about sticking your students' fingers in drainage holes?' She grinned. 'So you want to grill out tonight?'

'Do we have stuff?'

'I'll stop at Smith's on the way home.' Lisa climbed into the car, then unrolled the window, poked her head out, and said, 'I can't believe you're wearing clogs. You're such a teacher.'

Dr Lewin, I am telling you all of this so you'll know I moved on; I progressed. During the time we met, I must have seemed so stuck – in my ideas of myself, of men, of everything – and it must have seemed as if I were hearing and absorbing nothing, but all along, I was listening to you; I *was* learning. And I'm learning still: Even after I moved out here, I felt that I ought to send a present to Henry and Suzy to wish them well, plus, because I was bitter, I believed it was a way to show how not bitter I was. So I bought a grill one day, at a sporting-goods store, and I brought it home and started to address the box, and then I thought, *What the fuck am I doing?* This is the grill Lisa and I use in our backyard. The grass in the yard is long dead, but there's a deck to sit on. It is spring now; in the evening, the light over the mountains is beautiful, and the hamburgers we make on Henry's grill are, I must say, exceptionally delicious. If you should ever find yourself in Albuquerque, I hope that you will look me up and let me fix one for you. I send this letter with the greatest affection and appreciation for the many ways in which you helped me.

All my best,
Hannah Gavener